AND…WHO IS THE REAL MOTHER?

CONTACT ME

I love hearing from readers, so feel free to drop me an email telling me your thoughts about the book or series.

Email: roberta@robertakagan.com

Check out my website http://www.robertakagan.com.

Come and like my Facebook page!

https://www.facebook.com/roberta.kagan.9

Join my book club

https://www.facebook.com/groups/1494285400798292/?ref=br_rs

Follow me on Bookbub to receive automatic emails whenever I am offering a special price, a freebie, a giveaway, or a new release. Just click the link below, then click follow button to the right of my name. Thank you so much for your interest in my work.

https://www.bookbub.com/authors/roberta-kagan.

DISCLAIMER

TABLE OF CONTENTS

PROLOGUE

Warsaw, Poland

Zofia Weiss' fingers reached up to her neck to caress the Star of David that she wore. Her newborn baby girl was asleep in her arms. This was the first time Zofia had ever held her little girl. She had carried this child inside of her body for nine months. And for nine months she'd wondered what this moment would feel like. Would her baby be a boy or girl? What would the child look like? But now, the baby was here, right here with her soft head resting on Zofia's breast. Her daughter, Eidel.

When my precious child is older, I will give this necklace to her, Zofia thought. *It was my father's last gift to me before he died. And someday, it will be my gift to her. Then, God willing, she will pass it down to her own child.*

"My baby, my own little girl," Zofia said, kissing the child's cheek. Then carefully, Zofia removed the blanket that the baby was wrapped in and counted the child's fingers and toes.

"Look at her. She is so perfect," Zofia said to Fruma and Gitel, the two kind, older women who had taken her in when her mother threw her out for getting pregnant out of wedlock. Fruma was an expert seamstress; she'd been kind enough to give Zofia an apprenticeship when the rest of the town had turned its back on her. Gitel was Fruma's long-time lesbian lover.

"Yes, she is absolutely perfect, isn't she?" Fruma smiled.

"It's hard to believe but I don't even care about her father breaking my heart anymore. I am just so happy to have her," Zofia said.

"What will you name her?"

"Eidel," Zofia whispered, looking into the face of the tiny infant. "Eidel for my father. His name was Eli."

"It's a beautiful name. It means gentle," Fruma said.

"Can I hold her?' Gitel asked.

"Of course you can. This is such a happy day, but I wish my mother were here to see it," Zofia said. "She wanted no part of her granddaughter. She hated me so much she killed herself because of the shame I caused her. I will always feel guilty about my mother."

"Don't think like that," Fruma said. "She didn't kill herself because of you. She missed your father. You knew she miserable after his death. Don't blame yourself."

"It's hard not to. Both of my parents are gone. I am an orphan and my Eidel has no family."

Gitel held the baby carefully in her arms.

"She has two grandmothers. Fruma and I."

"Yes, and I am blessed for that, for sure," Zofia smiled, but tears were in her eyes.

Eidel, Zofia's daughter, was born in 1938 to her single mother. A scandal. People were outraged in the small Jewish community on the outskirts of Warsaw. But Fruma and Gitel didn't care. Because they were lesbians, these two women had endured living on the edge of society since they'd moved in together. They were the only people who had been warm and understanding when they found out about Zofia's predicament. And so it was that Eidel, the precious little girl, was not only loved by her mother but was worshiped by two kind and adoring grandmothers, Gitel and Fruma.

Despite the joy the child brought, life was not easy. Hitler had promised not to attack Poland, but by 1939 Germany rained bombs upon Warsaw. The once beautiful and peaceful capital city was now in ruins. It was the first step towards a Nazi conquest of Poland, as planned together with the Soviet leadership. The Führer was determined to destroy anything that reflected Polish culture. The Nazis were hell-bent on creating a Jew-free Europe. And so the little world of Zofia and Eidel, Fruma and Gitel was turned upside down.

The more they heard about what was happening in the heart of Warsaw, the more anxious the women became. Everyday brought news of disturbing developments. The ghetto, officially the Jewish Residential District in Warsaw, was established in the Muranów neighborhood of the city at the end of 1940, within the new General Government territory of German-occupied Poland. A year earlier, the Jewish Council, the Judenrat, was formed when the Nazis appointed twenty-four prominent Jews who would be responsible for carrying out German orders.

The persecution began soon thereafter. The imposition of Jewish forced labour began, first to clear the rubble from bomb damage and then to perform similar tasks. Bank accounts of Polish Jews with balances of more than two thousand złoty were blocked. Before 1940 rolled around, all Jewish establishments had been ordered to display a Star of David on their doors and windows. By year's end 1939, all Jews were forbidden from using the buses and trams of public transport.

The ghetto-wall construction started in the spring of 1940, circling the area of Warsaw already inhabited predominantly by Jews. The work was supervised by the Judenrat, who helped the Nazi authorities with the expulsion of 113,000 ethnic Poles from the neighborhood and the relocation of 138,000 Warsaw Jews from the suburbs into the city centre. The Germans closed the Warsaw Ghetto to the outside world in November of 1940. The wall around it was almost ten feet high and was topped with barbed wire. Zofia, Fruma and Gitel had heard that escapees were shot on sight.

One evening as the three women were feeding Eidel her dinner, there was a knock on the door. Three Gestapo agents with long leather coats and harsh frightening voices were rounding up all of the Jews in the sector where Zofia and her two friends lived.

"Mach schnell, you have five minutes to be ready to go. Pack what you will need."

Gitel tried to protest. "We are not going anywhere. This is our home. You have no right."

One of the Gestapo agents hit her across the face with the butt of his gun. Her nose spurted blood. Fruma picked up a rag and gave it to Gitel.

"Mach schnell, I said!" The man raised his gun to hit Gitel again.

"We will hurry." Fruma took Gitel's hand. "Come on. Let's all do as he says. You too, Zofia."

The baby had started to wail.

"Shut her up, or I'll shoot her," the Nazi said.

Zofia grabbed Eidel and ran into the bedroom to pack. Fruma, who had always had a way with the child, turned to Gitel. "Keep packing, I have to help Zofia to quiet Eidel. I am afraid that the Nazi will shoot the baby. Are you all right to pack by yourself?"

"Yes, I will be fine. Go and help Zofia, Fruma."

Fruma ran into Zofia's room and took Eidel from her mother's arms. "Pack, Zofia. I will take care of her."

Zofia nodded, then began tossing things into a suitcase. The tension in the house caused the child to let out a piercing scream. The sound was unnerving. For an instant, it felt as if the scream had caused the world to stand still. Fruma and Zofia's eyes met in fear. They knew that the Nazi would think nothing of shooting the baby. "Shhh," Fruma whispered in Eidel's ear, still looking at Zofia. "Shhh, please God, help us to keep her quiet," she whispered as she pulled Eidel close to her chest and began rocking the baby. Fruma sang softly in Yiddish, her voice cracking with every word. Eidel was red faced and the small strands of her baby hair stuck to her head with sweat, but Fruma was finally able to quiet the child.

The three women and the baby were herded into the back of a truck. Zofia saw the fresh blood seeping into Gitel's shirt and felt as if she might faint.

As in all Nazi ghettos across occupied Poland, the Germans assigned the internal administration to a Judenrat headed by an Ältester, an Elder. The Council of Elders was supported by the Jewish Ghetto Police, the Jüdischer Ordnungsdienst, formed at the end of 1940 and comprising three thousand men charged with enforcing law and order as well as carrying out German ad-hoc regulations.

The imprisoned Jews did their best to make a terrible situation better. Many of the inhabitants of the ghetto were musicians, actors, comedians and artists. They tried to keep the culture alive by offering performances. But the truth was that the conditions were horrendous. In an area of 1.3 square miles, an average of over seven persons occupied a single room, barely subsisting on meager food rations. In a small, overcrowded area they were faced with disease, starvation, and filth. Time passed and death became a regular and frequent visitor to the little area known as the Warsaw ghetto.

"The chances of Eidel surviving here in this place are slim," Fruma said to Gitel and Zofia one night after Eidel had fallen asleep.

"We have all been trying to give her some of our rations so she will have enough to eat," Gitel said. And they did. Each of the women adored the child and they gave up parts of their preciously small food rations in order for Eidel to survive.

"Eat, yes, we can help with that. We can give her our food and I am happy to do it. But TB is running rampant here. She is young. Her body is not strong enough to fight all of this disease and dirt. I am afraid for her."

"So what can we do?" Zofia asked

Fruma shook her head. "The only way we can hope to really help her is to get her out of this terrible place."

"You mean to get her out of the ghetto?" Gitel asked. "But how?"

"I will have to arrange it. I will contact Helen."

"Helen? You mean my friend Helen?" Zofia asked Fruma. "The one whose wedding dress you and I made together?"

"Yes, Helen, the girl who married Nikodem Dobinski."

"How can you contact her?"

"I have ways. I will take care of it. If Helen will take Eidel we can find that man who sells things from the black market and pay him to take Eidel to Helen."

Up to eighty percent of food consumed in the ghetto was brought in illegally. Private workshops were set up to manufacture goods to be sold secretly on the Aryan side of the city.

"Why would he do that for us? It's a big risk for him," Zofia said.

"Because I will pay him well. I will make sure it is worth his while," Fruma said.

"You have money?" Gitel asked.

"I have a large diamond. It was a gift from my mother. It is all I have left of any value."

"I couldn't let you do that," Zofia said.

"I am not asking you to let me do it," Fruma said. "I am offering to do it. I am insisting, in fact."

"But she will be so far away from us," Gitel said.

Fruma nodded. "Yes, far from us, but also far from this hell where we are imprisoned. And that will be good for her. Our feelings are not important. Her life is at stake."

"I couldn't let her go without me, Fruma. I wouldn't know if she was safe." Zofia's hands were shaking. "Please, a child should be with her mother," Zofia said, choking on the words.

"Yes, in normal circumstances, you're right. But here and now, if we want her to live, we must get her out of here. She must live her life as a gentile. It is the only way she will have a chance. And we must give her that chance, Zofia. We must."

Zofia began to weep softly. Gitel put her hand on Zofia's shoulder.

"I am sorry, Zofia. I love her too. Gitel loves her. I know how hard this is for you," Fruma said

"I don't know," Zofia said shaking her head and wringing her hands.

"You are her mother. You have the final say so. Why don't you take the night to think it over. I won't try to make any arrangements until you tell me your decision."

Zofia did not sleep that night. Her mind raced. She remembered the story of King Solomon. Two women came to the wise king, each claiming the child to be hers. King Solomon said that he would cut the child in two and give each woman a half. The true mother was the one who was willing to give her child up to the other woman rather than have it cut in two. The real mother was the one who was willing to give the child away in order to save its life.

And so I must sacrifice my own happiness and give Eidel away because it is what is best for her. I must do this for Eidel, Zofia thought.

The three women slept crowded together on a small cot. Zofia wept soundlessly so as not to disturb the others. But she'd made her decision.

In the morning when Fruma awakened, Zofia took her hand.

"Get Eidel out of here any way that you can," Zofia said.

Fruma began to search for help and to make a plan for Eidel's escape. She took risks to find out if Helen was willing to raise Zofia's daughter. Once she knew that Helen would take Zofia's child, she met with a-man who worked in the black market, bringing goods in and out of the ghetto to sell to the inhabitants. His name was Karl Abendstern, and many of the people within the ghetto knew that he slipped out of the ghetto during the night and returned with much-needed food to sell in the morning. Fruma approached him. She offered him the diamond. The man held it up to the light. Fruma knew that it was a stone of fine quality. It was a large and beautiful blue-white, almost flawless, diamond. There was no doubt that the stone could be used in exchange for many things on the other side of the wall. At first, Karl was reluctant. Even though the diamond was of great value, he was taking a great risk. However, Fruma was strong and insistent. She finally convinced him to help her.

It was a dangerous mission to try and smuggle such a young child out of the ghetto. Anything could happen. If the baby awakened she would cry, alerting the guards and that would get them both killed. But Karl was used to danger and he felt sorry for the baby. So together, he and Fruma put together a plan to smuggle Eidel out of the ghetto.

This is the beginning of Eidel's story…

CHAPTER ONE

Karl Abendstern carefully tucked the warm bundle that was Zofia's young daughter, Eidel, under his arm like a sack of potatoes. He had insisted that Fruma bring the child so that he could see how big she was before he agreed to their plan.

"She's not an infant, so it's going to be difficult for me carrying her this way. I will only have the use of one arm," Karl said.

"Don't worry. I have some fabric. I will make a pouch for you to carry her on your back that will make it easier," Fruma answered.

Karl nodded.

Although Eidel was three years old, she was very small and light.

Poor child, she's been starving in the ghetto, Karl thought as he looked down into the sleeping, innocent face. The baby was breathing softly. They had probably given her something so that she would sleep through the meeting. As Karl looked at the tiny face, he remembered the story his father had told him when he was just a child. It was the story of Moses, who was fetched from the Nile by the Pharaoh's sister. How odd it was that looking at this sleeping toddler brought back the biblical tale he'd loved when he was a boy, so long ago. Well, there was no time for sentiment. He had work to do. Once he was done making the arrangements for his plan with Fruma, he still had to do his nightly work. Every night, Karl navigated his way in and out of the Warsaw ghetto to bring back goods to sell on the black market. It was a daunting task, but people depended on him, and not only that, he and his girl friend, Ada, needed the food as well. Two days prior when Fruma, the old lady who was living with Zofia, had come to him, he had immediately refused. But she had been so persistent that he finally agreed to see the child. Then tonight, as he looked at the little girl, Fruma found his soft spot again. She was a wizened old woman and she had dug through his tough exterior until she found the soft heart that beat inside of him. Fruma grabbed onto his sleeve and with her eyes pleading she'd said to him, "If you don't take her, the child will die. Her name is Eidel, look at her."

"Are you her grandmother?" Karl asked.

"I am a dear friend of her mother's," Fruma answered.

"You are her mother?" Karl asked, turning to Zofia.

Zofia nodded.

"You are willing to let your child go without you?" Karl asked.

Before Zofia could answer Fruma said, "What choice does her mother have? Eidel has a chance to survive, if you can deliver her to our friend Helen Dobinski. If not, I am quite sure Eidel will be dead within a year. Do you want the blood of this little girl on your hands?"

Karl had no doubt the old witch was right. Between the disease, starvation, filth, and overcrowding, a child so young had a slim chance of making it through this Nazi-made hell.

"Are you sure that this woman, Helen, will take her?" Karl stared into Fruma's eyes.

"Yes. I am sure. Everything has been arranged. Helen is expecting you," Fruma said.

"How? How did you arrange it?" he asked.

"That's none of your business. All you need to know is that Helen will take the child."

"It is my business." Karl looked into Fruma's eyes and growled. "I'm the one who will be hiding from the Nazis while making my way through Warsaw with a drugged up little girl on my hands. I'm putting my life on the line for you. I don't want to get to Helen's house only to find out that she doesn't want any part of this. You either tell me the details or you can find someone else to help you."

"All right, so you are demanding to know how I put this whole thing together?" Fruma glared at him. "If you must know, I'll tell you. Zofia and I do embroidery work for the Nazis. I have become friends with the woman who brings us the fabric and threads. I had to find a way to help Eidel so I took a risk and asked her to take a message to Helen for me. She was afraid, but she did it for the child. I asked her to ask Helen if she would take Zofia's daughter in to live with her. Helen answered just as I knew she would. She promised to care for Eidel as if she were her own. I've known Helen a long time and I trust her."

"You have to understand my point of view. It's not going to be easy to carry out this plan for you. I just wanted to make sure that there won't be any problems when I arrive at your friend's home."

"You will get paid well. That diamond is worth plenty."

"To hell with your diamond. If I am dead what good will it be to me then?"

"You are taking a risk, yes. But you needn't be worried about Helen. I have a promise that she is expecting you. All you have to do is make sure you deliver Eidel to her safely."

Karl didn't want to get involved in this. But he couldn't say no. His conscience haunted him. So he agreed.

"Meet me right here after sundown in two days. Make sure that the child is ready to go. Give her some strong Šljivovica to make sure she sleeps. I can't have her waking up and crying. Is that understood?"

Fruma nodded.

Two days passed and then Karl, Fruma, Gitel, and little Eidel met in the alleyway. Karl felt sure that the past two days that Zofia had spent with her daughter had flown by far too quickly for the mother. But there was little time for him to think about Zofia's feelings. He had a mission, and he had his daily work. The night was only so long and if he were to be back before sunrise he had to leave now with Eidel.

Zofia wept softly. It touched Karl's heart. She was so young; probably still a teenager. In many ways. she reminded him of his sister Leah, whom he hadn't seen since the night he'd escaped Berlin after he'd killed a boy in the Hitler Youth. For a moment, he allowed himself to think of Leah. He quickly said a silent Hebrew prayer for his sister and the rest of his family, asking God to keep them safe.

"I did as you asked; I gave her something to make sure she would sleep," Fruma said, pulling Karl back to the present. Then she took a thick fabric blanket out from under her dress.

"I made this thing for you like I promised. It's sort of like a kangaroo pouch, but backward. You'll slip it over your shoulders then I'll put Eidel inside, there are holes for her legs. She'll ride on your back. You will have both of your hands free. I've tested the pouch; it is strong enough to hold her. This will make it easier for you to carry her."

Karl slipped the contraption over each of his arms. Then the old hag took Eidel and gently placed her in the sack. The child still slept as Fruma placed a kiss on the top of her blond curls. Gitel kissed Eidel, and then Zofia kissed her child's cheek, her lips, her eyes, and gently touched her hand.

"I am sorry, but I have to go now," Karl said.

"God be with you," Fruma whispered to Eidel. Then she turned to Karl. "And God be with you, too."

Karl wished he could reassure the mother that her child would be all right, but all he could promise was that he would try his best to get her to Helen safely. He gave Zofia a sad smile and rubbed her shoulder.

"I'll do everything I can to make this work," he said to Zofia.

Then with the lithe ease of a panther, Karl climbed up the broken bricks in the alleyway and scaled the wall of the ghetto. Karl navigated through the darkness until he found the opening where he escaped into the city every night. He'd been dealing with a group of Poles from the underground for a while now, Armia Krajowa, the Home Army. They sold him food, which he brought back into the ghetto, some of it to sell on the black market and some for himself and Ada, the woman whom he loved. He would meet with his Polish connection in a little while, but first he had to hurry and fulfil his promise and deliver the child to Helen.

Karl hugged the building as he manoeuvred cat-like through the streets. He tucked into a dark alleyway when he saw a group of German soldiers walking by. They'd missed him by seconds, just seconds. His heart beat wildly. Karl turned his head and looked behind him into Eidel's sleeping face.

Just stay asleep, he thought. He hadn't gone this far into the city since his confinement in the ghetto. The men from the black market were willing to meet him closer to the ghetto walls. But now he was in a lower-middle-class residential neighbourhood, searching for Helen's address.

Before he'd been arrested and sent to the ghetto, he had lived in Warsaw so he had some idea of where he was. From what he remembered, he was fairly sure the apartment building he was seeking was on the next street to the left. Moving quickly while staying hidden in the shadows, he made his way through the dark city.

Again, he checked on Eidel. Thank God, she was still asleep. She was sleeping so soundly that he hoped she was alive. For a moment, he wondered what the old witch had given her. But there was no time to check the baby or to speculate on what kind of drugs she'd been given. Right now, seconds counted. He found the building.

Get rid of the child as quickly as possible, he thought.

The doorbell read "Nikodem and Helen Dobinski."

Karl rang the bell.

Three flights up. Karl took the stairs two at a time.

Helen opened the door quickly and pulled him inside. The apartment was sparsely furnished. There was a slight odour of cooked cabbage.

“You must be Karl Abendstern?” Helen asked.

“This is Eidel.” Karl handed the baby to Helen. He’d done his job. He turned to go, but Helen stopped him by grabbing his sleeve.

“How is her mother? How is Zofia?”

“As good as can be expected. She is depending on you to take care of her baby.”

“Please tell her that Eidel will be safe here and that she will be waiting for her when she returns. Tell her not to worry … please.”

Karl nodded. Too much time spent already on this project. He had to meet with his contacts then get back to the ghetto with supplies before sunrise.

“I have to go,” he said.

Helen nodded and opened the door. She was holding the baby in her arms.

Karl peeked out the door of Helen’s apartment. No one in the hallway. Without a goodbye, he climbed down the stairs and out of the apartment building. Helen closed the door behind him. Karl began to race quickly towards his meeting with the underground but then something told him to stop for just a moment. Karl felt a shiver run up his spine; he felt as if he were touched by the hand of God. He looked up at the stars and said a prayer in Hebrew, asking God to watch over the helpless little girl he’d just left in a stranger's arms.

Then Karl Abdenstern faded into the darkness.

CHAPTER TWO

Nikodem Dobinski walked out of the bathroom. He carried a rag that he was using to blot his face dry. He'd just returned home following twelve hours of work at a tedious job packaging razor blades in the back of the Polonus razor factory. His work always left him feeling grimy so he spent his first fifteen minutes at home washing his face and hands with cool water to rejuvenate before his evening meal. Every morning, he left the house before the sun peeked through the clouds in order to arrive on time for his shift. Then it was already growing dark outside by the time he walked through the factory gates and headed back home. Except for Sunday, when he was off work, Nikodem never saw daylight.

He entered the living room to see his wife, Helen, holding a youngster in her arms. At first he thought it was their son, Lars, then he realized that the child was wrapped in a pink blanket and was much smaller than Lars. He had a bad feeling in his gut.

"Helen?" Nik walked over to his wife and removed the cover over the baby's face. "Who is this?" he asked, but he already knew what Helen had done. Nik shook his head, then throwing his hands up in the air asked, "What did you agree to?"

Helen had been talking to him about taking the Jewish child of a friend of hers into their home, and he'd been adamantly against it.

"It's Eidel. Zofia's daughter. Zofia Weiss. Remember?"

"Of course I remember, Helen. How could I forget? You have been talking about doing this for a week and I told you that I was not going to allow you to do it. I would think you would remember that. The

Nazis hate Poles. You think they will take pity on you if they find out that you've taken in a Jewish child? I said you were not to do this when you asked me about it a week ago. Try to remember, Helen, that I said no. No! Do you know what that means? NO? You've defied me. Why?"

"Because, Nik. I'm sorry, but I had to. I couldn't leave an innocent baby to suffer and starve in that terrible ghetto. It's a horrible thing that they are doing to the Jews, Nik."

"Yes, I agree with you, but you are forgetting something. You are not a German. You're a Pole and that means that you are one step away from being right there in the ghetto with them. Or worse, you could be dead. The Nazis would kill you and not think twice, they would kill us both. In fact, if you don't care about yourself or me, just know that they wouldn't hesitate to kill your son. Do you care about Lars, Helen? The Nazis are heartless people. You know that if Poles are caught harboring Jews they are immediately sentenced to death. There will be no discussion, Helen. You won't be able to sway them the way you do to me. I am telling you … death. Do you understand what this means to us? You realize what you're asking of me, of us, of our family? The best thing you can do is to get rid of that child. Get rid of her now. Throw her outside. I don't care what you do, but get her out of here."

"Look at her, Nik. She's a beautiful little girl. I am going to tell everyone that my sister died and she left her baby to my care."

"You don't have a sister, Helen. Are you crazy? All of our friends know you are an only child. You're doing a real dance with danger here and I can't believe you're so headstrong. I have been getting you out of trouble since we met but this time I won't be able to save you. If the Nazis find out we are doomed."

"Yes, I know, Nik. I know. I have to think of another story to tell people. I can't put her outside. She is so small and helpless. I couldn't just turn my back on a little girl. What if it was Lars? What if someone turned his back on him?"

"But your lies are absurd. The further you venture from the truth, the less convincing the lie. Your sister left you a child? For God's sake, Helen." He shook his head then folded his arms across his chest. "You are digging a grave for us. For all of us, you, me, and Lars," he said.

"All right, all right," she stammered. She looked at him and held the baby tighter. "Then how does this sound? I will say a woman friend of my family who lived on a farm died and left the baby with no one to care for her. I will tell them that the woman was Polish. Please, Nik, we can't be as cold-blooded as the Nazis. We can't throw this innocent little one out to be eaten by the wolves."

"Helen, my God." His eyes locked with hers. "What am I going to do with you?" He sunk into a chair looking at her, his eyes filled with worry and defeat.

"You and Lars have such a wonderful relationship and I am happy that you do. I love Lars with all my heart. But, as you know, I have always wanted a daughter."

"We can try to have another child. Don't be crazy, Helen. Please. Get rid of this girl. She is a Jew. This can only mean trouble for us," he tried again to convince her, but he knew he'd lost.

"I know you. I have known you most of my life. You are a hard man, Nik, but underneath that hard shell you wear to protect yourself is a heart, a warm heart. That is why I love you and why I married you."

He shook his head. She was a stubborn woman, but she was right. He did have a heart, and he couldn't throw that little girl out to be found and murdered by Nazis, not in good conscience.

"Damn it, Helen. I hope this doesn't cost us our lives, and even worse…our son's…our Lars."

"But what if this child was Lars, Nik? What if Lars was alone and helpless and we had to send him to live with strangers so he wouldn't starve or die of disease? Wouldn't you hope that those strangers would be willing to take a risk in order to save our son?"

He nodded and turned away in frustration. "I can't talk about this now. I'm tired and I'm hungry."

"I know. I have your dinner ready. It's on the stove."

He sat down at the table. Helen laid Eidel on a blanket on the floor. Above their heads, a picture of Helen hung on the wall. It was a beautiful oil painting that Nik had spent hours working on when he and Helen were first married.

"She's so tired and limp. I have never seen Lars sleep like that," Nik said looking down at Eidel. "Are you sure she's alive?"

"Yes. I checked her. She is breathing, just sleeping very soundly. They doped her up so she wouldn't cry when the man from the black market took her out of the ghetto," Helen answered.

"I hope whatever they gave her didn't affect her brain." Nik took the fork and began eating. "All we need is a half-wit on top of everything else."

Helen frowned at him.

I hate when he says things like that but at least he has stopped telling me that I have to get rid of her. Ultimately, he is my husband and he is the man of the house so he will have the final say so.

Helen placed her own food in front of her. Even though the Poles got more rations than the Jews, they were still starving. But Helen was slender and young, she didn't require a lot of food to be satisfied so she always gave part of her portion to her husband. Nik was gripping the fork as he chewed quietly. She glanced back over at Eidel, who was sleeping with her thumb in her mouth.

"Nik?" She had to ask him. Before things went any further, she had to get his verbal agreement.

He looked up at Helen. His eyes were narrowed and he looked angry. But Helen knew him well enough to know that once again, he was going to give in to her.

"Can she stay? Please?" Helen asked in a small voice.

He nodded, resigned.

"Thank you for being the kind wonderful man I always knew you were."

"You can't call her Eidel. You will have to change her name."

"Ela. I'll call her Ela."

"Yes, Ela is fine. I don't care what you call her as long as it's not a Jewish name. Now, since I have agreed to this madness you must listen to me. After tonight we will never discuss Zofia Weiss or the Jewish heritage of this child again. Do you understand?"

"Nik, don't you think it's only fair that we should tell her the truth as soon as she is old enough to understand?"

"No. She must never know that she has Jewish blood."

"But when the war is over?"

"The war may never be over, Helen. But if it is, we will worry about telling her when the time comes. For now, we are at great risk taking her in like this. I've agreed to let her stay. However, from this day forward we will never again discuss where she came from again. When she is older, all she need know is that you are her mother and I am her father."

"But if people tell her the story we have made up about the farm woman? And what if she wants to know more about her birth mother…then what?"

"Then we deny that the story about the farmer is true. We tell her that she is ours and we don't know what people are talking about."

"Oh Nik, so much lying."

"Poland is in danger. We are occupied by a terrible regime. You and I must do what is necessary for our family to survive. I have given you what you want. You can keep the child. But these are my terms."

"Very well. I will do as you say," Helen said.

CHAPTER THREE

Both Lars and Ela were almost the same age when Ela arrived at the Dobinski's home. At first, Ela cried all the time. She was looking in all directions, searching for her mother and for Fruma and Gitel. Everything was different. Ela was surrounded by unfamiliar faces, smells, and noises. Because Lars had grown up with his father, the little boy was used to hearing Nik sing as he dressed for work in the morning, his strong baritone voice filling the house in the wee hours of the morning. But for Ela, the sounds were strange and frightening. However, after a week passed and because Ela was so young, she slowly began to forget her past and assimilated to her new family. She and Lars fought over toys. They played together. Then they fell asleep on a blanket on the floor, rolled up like two kittens. Helen was relieved to see that Lars and Ela were getting along so well.

One afternoon in early September, Helen dressed both children in light jackets and took them into town to the bakery to buy bread with her ration cards. She could see the walls of the Jewish ghetto from her side of the street. Somewhere behind those walls, Zofia was trapped in the Warsaw Ghetto.

I am sure that right now, Zofia is probably thinking of Eidel, Helen thought. Because she knew that if she were in Zofia's position she would be thinking constantly of Lars. If only she could speak to Zofia and reassure her that Eidel was safe. But she couldn't. It was too great a risk for her to try to find a way to get into the ghetto.

I must put Zofia out of my mind. There is nothing I can do for her. The only thing I can do is to take good care of her child. And right now I must hurry and get to the bakery before they are all sold out of bread, she thought as she carefully navigated her way through the rubble of broken buildings caused by the bombings. Helen had been born and raised in Poland. It broke her heart to see what had become of Warsaw during the terrible two weeks when the Nazis bombed it relentlessly before they invaded. She held on to the children's hands. It was not easy for her to handle two, but she would never consider sending Ela away. She had already become attached to the little girl, and so she would find a way to manage somehow. Ela tripped on a piece of broken rock and fell, scraping her knee. She began to cry as Lars looked on. Helen lifted the little Ela and held her to her breast to comfort her. Ela rested her head on Helen's shoulder. As Ela lie breathing softly against Helen's chest, feelings slowly began to develop in Helen. She started to feel as if Ela were her biological child.

Helen stood in line outside the bakery, holding tightly to both children as she waited her turn. The line for bread was long, stretching around the corner. Lars and Ela were fidgeting. It was hard to keep them still for such an extended period of time. They wanted to run, to play and explore, but she dared not let them loose. Lars began pulling away from his mother. Helen reached down to lift him up and take him into her arms in order to quiet him. As she bent over, two young, handsome Nazi officers walked by. One of them reached out as he passed and grabbed her buttocks. Helen's mouth dropped open in shock and her face turned red with embarrassment. She was so stunned that she put Lars back down on the ground. He tried to get up and start running, but because she was so taken aback by what just happened, instead of picking him up and hugging him she spanked his backside. Helen almost never struck the children. She saw the look of astonishment on Lars' face and was immediately sorry. Lars didn't move. He stopped fidgeting and stared at her wide-eyed for a moment, and then he let out a wail.

"My, my, gnädige Frau. But you are having a difficult time with the little ones today," the Nazi officer said in fluent Polish. "Allow me to help you," he said, leaning down and patting Lars on the head. Lars looked up at the Nazi. The child was stunned and a little frightened by the attention of a stranger. Lars grew quiet and leaned into his mother's leg. The Nazi added, "By the way, I'm Hauptsturmführer Rolf Boltz."

Anger rose like a volcano inside of her.

How dare you put your hands on me without my permission?

A few of the other women saw what happened, but no one said a word.

"I'm not having a difficult time with the children. I'm having a difficult time with you. You have no right to touch me that way," she growled.

"Oh?" He tilted his head and smiled as if she'd said something amusing. "I see. I was just trying to help."

I'll be damned if I'll let him see that I am afraid of him, she thought, straightening her back. "I am not talking about your helping me with the child. I am talking about you putting your hands on my backside."

"My apologies," he said in a condescending tone. "I would never want to offend you, gnädige Frau."

"Well, I am offended."

"Apologies, again," he said but she saw the threat in his face and knew that she must not push him too far. He was a Nazi and she was a Pole. At any time he could get angry and punish her, and worse, punish the children.

"So, gnädige Frau …who are you? What is your name?"

"Dobinski. Helen Dobinski."

"Helen Dobinski ..." He hesitated. Then he ran his finger over his chiseled chin and looked into her eyes. Something in his stare made her shiver as the hair on the back of her neck stood up. "I've seen you around here before. I am quite sure of it actually. I mean, after all, who could forget such a pretty face?" He took a cigarette out of his breast pocket and lit it.

"Would you like one?"

She shook her head. "No, thank you."

"You don't smoke?"

Again, she shook her head.

"I don't blame you. Smoking is a filthy habit. You know the Führer says that all Germans should quit smoking. I believe he is right. I will have to do just that," he said, taking a puff of his cigarette. Then he studied her for a minute and added, "And, if I remember correctly … and I must admit I am usually correct. You only have one child. A son. So, my question to you is … who is this little girl?"

Helen's heart was beating so hard that she thought it was going to come right through her chest and continue its rapid thumping right on the pavement. "This is Ela," she said trying to sound casual.

"Your daughter?"

Do I dare change the story now?

Suddenly the lie about Ela being a child of a family friend who died sounded foolish.

I am so afraid. This Nazi is toying with me, and I don't know what to do. My God, what have I done to my family? To Lars? Maybe Nik was right. I have to answer. I have no choice. I will tell him the lie. God help us.

"Oh, you mean Ela? She is the daughter …"

"Never mind." He cut her off mid-sentence and smiled a knowing smile. "The little girl is not important. There are things I can overlook when a situation is resolved to my satisfaction. If you know what I mean." He winked and she saw wickedness, triumph, and power in his eyes. "Do you understand me?" he asked, his voice soft but menacing.

At that moment Helen was sure he knew the truth about where Eidel came from. She was more afraid then she'd ever been in her entire life.

"Yes. I understand," she said.

"Tonight, then, you will come to see me. I'll be expecting you to arrive at my flat. Let's say around eight o'clock? You look like a smart girl. I'm sure you won't make the mistake of disappointing me." He took a pen and a small pad of paper out of the inside pocket of his jacket and wrote down his address. Then he handed the paper to her and walked away.

CHAPTER FOUR

For the rest of the day, Helen agonized over having taken Eidel into her home. Not only was she frightened by what had happened, but she was trapped and she knew that she had no choice; she must go to the Nazi and do whatever he asked of her. Whatever he asked, even though she was repulsed. And then what about Nik? She'd never cheated on him before. The very idea of being with another man was repugnant to her. Yet there was no doubt in her mind that this was what that Nazi bastard expected. Her mind was whirling so fast it felt like there was a tornado in her brain. In all the years Helen had known Nik she had never lied to him. But now she was faced with a terrible choice, either she kept her virtue and paid with the demise of her family or she did as the Nazi asked and betrayed her husband.

Dear God, what a web I have found myself caught in. I don't even know how I am going to get out of the house alone this evening. What can I possibly tell Nik? I can't tell him the truth. But I must make sure the lie is believable. And I know that once I've broken the trust between Nik and I there will be a wedge between us forever.

The very idea made her stomach feel sick.

But what choice do I have?

The evening began as it always did. Nik arrived home from work and washed while Helen put his food on the table. She sat beside him with a small plate of food but was unable to eat. After Nik finished his dinner, he played with Lars for fifteen minutes. Then Helen put both children to bed. There were sharp pains in her chest as she dressed quickly. Once she was ready she went into the living room where she found Nik sitting on the sofa. He'd been reading the paper and fallen asleep. When she entered the room he stirred awake. She had put on her worn, rust-colored fall coat.

"Is everything all right? Where are you going?"

"I have to go to the pharmacy and pick up some medicine. I have a terrible headache. I've had it all day. You can go on to bed if you'd like. I know how tired you are. I'll be home in a little while."

When she and Nik were first married he would have insisted on going for her. But he was working harder, longer hours these days and Helen knew Nik was too tired to offer to run the errand. In fact, in the last few months he'd started falling asleep on the sofa as soon as she put Lars to bed.

"Are you all right?" he asked.

She heard the genuine concern in his voice and she felt sick with guilt for what she was about to do.

"It's just a headache," she said.

"Be careful. There is a lot of madness going on out there on the streets. It is not safe. Even though there are still a few hours before curfew, it's already getting dark. Things are not the same anymore in Poland. You are going to have to face that, Helen, and be more cautious. For God's sake, Artur has been bothering me every day at work about joining some sort of Polish group that is trying to fight against the Nazis. There are all kinds of things happening in our world now. What if you were outside and a fight broke out? There could be gunshots. Who knows what these groups are planning to do? They can't fight Germany. They are crazy and I don't want any part of it. But most importantly, I don't want you to get caught up in the middle of any crossfire. All I want, Helen, is just for our little family to stay safe and survive. So, please, stay out of trouble, and hurry up and get back home," he said.

She could hear the exhaustion in his voice. She felt sorry for him when she saw the deep purple circles around his eyes. Nik, who was once a tall slender man, now slumped with the effort of trying to protect his family.

Over the years they had been together, he'd slowly grown comfortable in their marriage. Part of it was his job and she knew that but somehow, it often felt as if he took her for granted. He had stopped trying to do little things to please her. It hurt her. She missed the silly romantic things he had done in the beginning of their marriage, like leaving a flower and a note that said "I love you" on her pillow in the morning.

In order to stay somewhat happy with her husband, Helen made excuses for Nik. She constantly reminded herself that his job was exhausting. But that wasn't enough to satisfy her. Deep inside, she had begun to see him as lazy and uncaring. And tonight, if she'd actually been ill, she would be angry with him for not forcing himself to get up and take care of her the way she always took care of him, no matter how tired she was. It wouldn't be the first time she would be cursing him for what she often called his lazy selfish ways. However, because of the situation, that night for the first time she was glad he wasn't offering to go to the pharmacy for her.

Earlier that day, Helen had looked at the address the Nazi had given her and, because she knew the city, knew exactly where she was going. She walked as quickly as she could. It was going to take her at least fifteen minutes to arrive at her destination. As she raced through the streets, she kept her head down. The last thing she wanted was to see someone she knew who might ask questions. Then she would have to explain things and she was beginning to feel like she was drowning in lies.

Rolf's flat was on the second floor of a well-maintained red brick building. Helen knocked on the door. She waited outside for several minutes. Perhaps he forgot.

I am going to leave. If I see him on the street again, I will tell him I came but he wasn't home. I can get away if I go now ...

Helen turned to run down the stairs. But just as she did, the door opened.

"Come in." Rolf smiled. "Please, sit down. Would you like a coffee or tea? I have both, you know. Real coffee, not that garbage you get. So, Helen. It was Helen?"

She nodded. He looked like a wolf to her.

"Which do you prefer? Coffee or tea? I can also offer some ham on a slice of real wonderfully aromatic rye bread? Yes?"

The apartment was tastefully decorated with beautiful expensive things. Lovely and expensive artwork hung on the walls. It was not that the paintings were done by more talented artists than Nik, but that the frames were made of far better wood with more intricate carvings. Helen had never seen such finery. There was a foyer with a large Persian rug that almost completely covered the polished hardwood floor.

"Thank you. That won't be necessary, I am not hungry or thirsty," she said. Her knees were buckling. Her voice was unsteady. Helen had never had sexual relations with anyone but Nick. Her mind was racing. Her throat was parched. She was deeply searching for something to say that would make him take pity on her.

I need a way to convince him to let me be. Does he know the truth about Eidel or am I just imagining it? If he does know, how can I keep him from touching me, but still keep my secret about Eidel. Is this possible?

"Come on … let's go into the living room. It's silly for us to stand here in the doorway," he said, gesturing her forward with his left hand. She followed him.

"You're looking radiant tonight, Helen."

"How did you know my name was Helen? I don't remember telling you my name. Did I?" Helen was shaken even more by the idea that he'd known her name.

Has he been watching me? For how long? And why? Oh God, no … this man has set his sights on me. There is no way out. No safe way out.

"You did tell me your name, my dear, but you didn't have to. I already knew that your name is Helen Dobinski. In fact, I know everyone in this area including all the Jews in the ghetto," he smiled. "Well, that's not exactly true. I don't know all the Jews by name. But I do know that the little girl who was with you at the bakery earlier … she is the child of a Jew. I don't know how you smuggled her out but I am quite certain she isn't yours."

Did she dare lie? Did she dare tell him the story about the farm woman?

Don't be foolish. He knows. He knows everything. He probably knows Zofia's name. A lie would only make things worse.

"Oh please sit down," he said, frustrated with her. "You are standing there looking like a colt who stood up for the first time. You are trembling so badly you look as if you might fall over."

"Is this amusing you?" she asked more boldly than she dared.

"Yes and no." He glared at her. "But I am rapidly getting bored. So do as I tell you. I said sit."

She sat down on the sofa, holding her handbag tightly in her lap, her knuckles turning white as she squeezed the handle.

"I don't need to tell you what happens to Poles who hide Jews …"

She swallowed hard and shook her head. "Have mercy on me, please." Her voice was barely a whisper.

Rolf patted her hand. Helen felt a shiver run through her as if a tarantula had crawled across her skin

"Now," Rolf began. "I am a reasonable man, and I like you. So I have decided to treat you with kindness. We both know that this is more than you deserve for having broken the law by taking a Jewish child into your home. However, I have no doubt you will be filled with gratitude for my unexpected generosity."

He hesitated for a moment and stared into her eyes. Helen had never been so frightened.

"So, lovely Helen, I won't waste your time or mine … here is my offer. I find myself attracted to you. Don't make the mistake of thinking you're a great beauty. You are not Helen of Troy. I mean, you aren't bad looking, but I have seen better. However," he stopped speaking for a moment and bit his lower lip as he studied her. Then he began to speak again. "There is something about you that appeals to me. Perhaps it's your shy and quiet ways. I like that in a woman." He brushed his hand over her hair then added, "Or it could be that you remind me of someone I once knew long ago. Either way, it doesn't matter. Here is what I've decided. In order to keep your family safe, you will come here to my flat twice a week. And we will, shall we say, get to know each other better."

"I can't."

"You can't?" his eyebrows flew up. At first, he looked angry then he burst out laughing. "You can't?" he repeated, as if he couldn't believe the words he was hearing.

"I am married. What will I tell my husband? Please don't make me do this."

"Ahhh, so the husband is the problem. You needn't worry about him. He is insignificant. Nothing to worry about, really." He smiled reassuringly.

She looked away.

"You will listen to me. Here is what you will do …" his voice was commanding. He gently turned her face towards his, as his voice grew softer, almost loving.

"Helen," he said. "You will tell your husband that you have taken a job caring for an old woman two nights a week while her daughter is working. I will provide the name of a woman you can use as your cover. Of course, if you are working you must be paid, so you can show your husband that you have earned some money. No need to worry, I will provide the earnings. I will give you a personal note that you can present to the police in case you are on your way here or back home after curfew."

Helen nodded. He wasn't bad looking. In fact, he was handsome. But the very idea of such an arrangement made her feel cheap and sick to her stomach. But what could she do? If she refused him, he would arrest her and probably do something terrible to Nik and Lars.

Oh God, not Lars. And Eidel? He would probably kill her instantly.

Helen could feel her hands shaking. Nik had warned her when she took Eidel in to live with her that something horrific could happen, and he was right. But if she had it to do over again, she still could not leave a precious little girl to die in the ghetto. Rolf walked to the window and sat down on a large comfortable chair. He lit a cigarette.

"Would you like one?"

"No," she said.

"Are you sure? I know you said that you don't smoke. But I find that smoking sometimes calms the nerves."

She shook her head. Helen felt like a small animal that was caught in the talons of a hawk.

"How about a drink? A little alcohol is also quite relaxing."

"I don't think so."

"I insist."

Rolf stood up and stretched his legs. He walked over to a finely crafted wooden liquor cabinet and took out a bottle, poured two drinks, and walked towards her. After placing the glasses on the coffee table, he sat beside her on the sofa and pulled her close to him. He moved so fast, like a centipede. It felt as if he had a thousand disgusting slimy feelers. His hands were all over her, on her breasts, on her thighs, and his lips were pressed against hers. Helen gagged but he didn't notice. He was breathing heavily. Bile rose in her throat as he entered her, but she didn't vomit. She dared not vomit. She closed her eyes and let the tears run down her cheeks as he did what he wanted with her.

CHAPTER FIVE

The chill of the autumn wind sent a shiver through Helen as she walked home after the terrible night with Rolf. Pulling her coat tighter around her did nothing to alleviate the chill inside of her. Her body was no longer her own. She'd been violated. Something sacred was taken from her that night. It was an innocence that she knew she would never know again. The thought of facing Nik after the shameful experience with Rolf made her feel even worse. She would have to look into her husband's eyes and all the while in the back of her mind she would know that she had broken her wedding vows. She would have loved to fall on the floor and tell Nik what had happened. If only he would understand why she'd done what she did. But she knew she could never tell him. If she did, he would never look at her in the same way. Besides that, he would be adamant about her sending Eidel back to Zofia, and she couldn't do that, not in good conscience, and not with the way she'd come to care for the little girl. Ela, not Eidel, Helen reminded herself. That name must be buried with the truth if the child is to survive.

Helen straightened her disheveled hair. She could still smell Rolf's cologne emanating from her skin. Would Nik smell that? When she arrived at her front door, Helen wanted to say a prayer before she entered. But she dared not.

I cannot turn to God for help after what I did tonight. I have broken one of God's sacred commandments. I believe he would forgive me but I am too ashamed.

Her hand trembled as she turned her key in the lock and opened the door. Then purposely facing away from Nick, she took off her coat.

"You were gone a long time, Helen. I was worried. Are you all right?" Nik was starring at Helen as she hung her coat up on the rack.

"Yes. I'm sorry. I saw an old friend, and we started talking. I guess I lost track of time." She tried to sound as casual as possible, but when she heard herself speak her voice was just slightly higher in pitch than normal. Something only she would notice.

"An old friend, Helen? Who? I almost left the children alone in the apartment to go out and look for you. I was very concerned. I thought something happened to you. Look at the time; it's after curfew. I couldn't go to sleep, and I have to work in the morning. I need my rest. You are out talking to old friends? Are you crazy? You go around as if things in Poland are the way they were before the Nazis," he said, his tone of voice sounding borderline hysterical.

"I didn't realize the time. I am so sorry. It was just that I saw this girl who I knew from church many years ago. I never meant to cause you to worry."

"Helen, how can I not worry? You take such foolish chances for no reason. I don't know how to get it through your head that we are in grave danger in our country."

She swallowed hard. "I really am sorry …"

"Well," he said, shaking his head and getting up from the chair where he was sitting. "Now that I know you're home safe, I am going to bed. I have to be up early for work." He walked into the bedroom and slammed the door.

Alone in the living room, Helen sunk down into the lumpy old sofa. She glanced at her purse where she'd left it on the table. She knew that inside was a note for the police to use the next time she went to see Rolf. The note was rolled around several reichsmarks.

What have I gotten myself into? Rolf is expecting me to return in three days. The very thought of him touching me again makes me cringe. But I have to go to him. And worse, I have to explain this crazy story about working for an old woman to Nik. I hope he believes me. He was like a madman tonight.

Once Helen heard Nik snoring, she went to the bathroom and scrubbed herself clean. She scoured her skin so hard that it turned red. Then she lay down in bed beside her husband, felling cold and alone. Although she was exhausted, it was impossible to sleep. She stared at the ceiling until it was time to get up and prepare Nik's breakfast.

Before Helen married Nik, he'd shown interest in everything she did. They shared long talks and romantic sex. But things began to change after Lars was born. Nik's hours increased at work and Lars had colic which kept him up during the night. It seemed to Helen that Nik grew distant. Their lovemaking slowed down considerably. He even seemed to lose interest in painting, which was his beloved hobby for years. All he seemed to want to do was come home to eat and rest. Nik rarely noticed any changes she made in herself or in the apartment. For a long time, Helen was becoming increasingly disappointed in her husband's lack of attention. But, after last night with Rolf, she was glad that Nik was oblivious to everything. It made the horrible act of lying to him much easier. Although she was trying to hide her anxiety, she was sure she was behaving differently. But, from what she could see, Nik perceived nothing. He ate his breakfast, got dressed, took his lunch pail, and left for work.

When Nik got home that night, Helen told him that she'd taken a job caring for an old woman two nights a week.

"The old woman I will be working for got me a pass from a Nazi officer who is somehow related to her. So if I am stopped after curfew on my way home from her house it will be all right. And besides, I will be earning some extra cash for us. I will be able to help you pay the bills," she said.

He didn't question her. And even though she was relieved that he didn't, she resented him, too. All he did was sigh, and say, "The money will help. I get sick and tired of trying to make ends meet. Maybe this is a blessing."

Nik didn't know what she was going through. How could he? Helen knew she should not direct her anger at him. But it had surprised her that he didn't even warn her about the dangers again. It was as if he'd given up caring at all. And then when he seemed so pleased about the money, Helen wanted to spit in his face.

CHAPTER SIX

The meetings with Rolf continued. He was not rough with her, but the sex was forced and therefore it was terrible for Helen. However, he did his best to be charming. Helen told herself that she should be happy to have such a good setup. She got extra money. And truth be told, Rolf was a handsome man who was always trying to do things that would make her desire him. He insisted on giving her gifts of food, buying her trinkets, and raising the salary he was paying her from time to time. He was as kind to her as an owner could be to a slave.

But she resented him.

She'd heard how cruel the Nazi guards were to the Jews in the ghetto. There were rumors of guards shooting and killing innocent people, children even. Helen often studied Rolf and wondered if he was vicious to the Jews when he went into the ghetto. Had he ever murdered anyone? Had he ever killed a child? She didn't know, because Rolf had never shown her any side of him that was cruel. It was true that he was dominating and demanding, but she had yet to see him as the kind of man who could commit murder. And yet, when she looked closely, there was something in his demeanor, a slight tilt of his head, a wink of his eye, the way that he combed his hair. Nothing definite, nothing that she could put her finger on. But something ... something told her to fear him. A little voice said that he was capable of executing horrendous crimes.

One night in late December, after Rolf was finished with her, Helen was getting dressed. She'd known him for a while now and for some odd reason, that night she felt daring.

"Rolf …"

"Hmm?"

"Do you ever go into the ghetto?"

"Yes. I have duties that I must fulfil there."

"Do you feel bad for the Jews?"

"Not at all. They are filthy scum, Helen. You should see how they live. They are like animals. If it were up to me, I'd have them all done away with quickly, like garbage. They spread disease like rats. That ghetto is full of disease and I would hate to see it spread beyond the walls. When I leave there, I wash myself but good, and even then I don't feel clean. The smell lingers for hours."

"They're human beings. You must have some sympathy …"

"I have more for a dog. Jews are manipulative liars. Given the opportunity, they will cheat you out of everything you own."

She shook her head. "I feel bad for them," she said, her voice barely a whisper.

"Your girl child is a Jew. One day you will regret having taken her in. This I can promise you. She will grow up to be what she is genetically programmed to be. She will turn on you, you'll see. Do you understand?"

"No."

"It's like this. If you get a poisonous snake as a baby but you raise it to think it's a pet dog, what do you think will happen?"

"I don't know." Helen shrugged. She was tired of listening to his insane logic. She was sorry she'd started this conversation. It was bringing out a side of him that made her hate him even more than she already did. And it was terrifying her that he was talking about Ela.

"One day when your pet snake grows up she will bite you and kill you."

"You will not turn my Ela into the authorities? Promise me, please

Rolf, promise me."

"As long as you do as I ask I will not turn her in. But you are a fool, Helen."

"Perhaps I am Rolf, but it is my choice. I will do as you ask."

"Fair enough." He smiled.

"You have a cold heart."

"Not towards you. Have I ever been anything less than kind or gracious to you?"

She was sitting on the bed fixing her stockings. Rolf sat up and gently caressed her shoulder.

"You have always treated me well. But you do realize that I am not here with you of my own free will?"

"Can you honestly say you don't have any tender feelings for me? None at all?" he asked, raising one eyebrow.

Helen was afraid to tell him how she felt. If he turned on her all would be lost. She whipped her head around to look into his eyes. It was obvious to her that he cared for her. But even so, she didn't trust him. "I do care for you," she lied.

CHAPTER SEVEN

The children were growing fast and little Ela brought Helen as much joy as her own son. She was an affectionate child. While Lars was busy trying to figure out how to take everything apart and then put it back together again, Ela was laying quietly in Helen's lap listening closely as Helen told her stories.

But in June 1941, the Polish territories previously occupied by the Soviets were taken over by the Germans and the atmosphere in Warsaw became even more depressing. It seemed to Helen that she hardly saw Nik anymore, and it had been months since they'd made love. She didn't want to acknowledge that he'd gotten even more distant towards her since she'd taken Ela in to live with them. Perhaps it was because she had defied him; perhaps it was fear. She had no way of knowing, but the changes that had begun after Lars was born had gotten even worse after she took Ela in. Nik never felt like talking to her. If she asked him a question he gave her short answers, if he answered at all. When he got home from work and she asked him how his day was his answer was always the same, "I'm tired." To make matters worse, lately he'd begun drinking heavily.

Perhaps he is sensing something? Perhaps somewhere deep in the recesses of his heart, he knows I am no longer his alone.

The thought disturbed her deeply. She was filled with confusion; part of her wished that things between her and Nik could be the way they were in the beginning of their marriage. But due to the circumstances between her and Rolf, in a strange way she was glad that Nik hadn't made any romantic advances towards her. She felt that if they made love, he might somehow feel a change in her body. After

Rolf had been inside of her she felt soiled and ruined. Intellectually, she knew that she was being ridiculous; there was no way that Nik could feel a difference, but emotionally she could not deny that she was changed. The woman who'd stood at the altar and married Nik was an innocent virgin. Helen was not that woman anymore. And she was trying desperately not to hate the woman she had become

The meetings with Rolf never became pleasurable for Helen, but they became easier to tolerate. She was having sex with him routinely, and since it had been so long since she had intercourse with Nik, Rolf became almost like a normal partner to her. She couldn't honestly say that she loved him, but she had stopped hating him. With a lot of denial, Helen found ways of ignoring the fact that Rolf was a Nazi. She had somehow convinced herself to disregard the fact that he was a Nazi and her conqueror. She forced herself to look for good qualities in him, to see him as a man like all other men. Thinking this way made it easier for her to endure the sex. She tried to pay no attention to the fact that his apartment and all of its beautiful furnishings had probably been stolen from arrested Jews. She was careful never to ask him any questions because she didn't want to hear his answers. Helen didn't want to accept the truth. The more reasons she had to dislike him, the harder this unwanted affair would be on her.

One evening Helen arrived at Rolf's apartment. He was standing at the kitchen sink cursing. His hand was bleeding from a deep gash.

"What happened?" Helen asked, looking at the bright red blood that had begun to pool in the bowl of the sink.

"I got bitten by a dog. I was trying to train him and the bastard bit me."

"It looks bad. Here let me help you," she said, washing his wound gently.

She caught him looking at her and Helen saw the affection in Rolf's eyes. "You are such a good woman. You remind me so much of an old and dear friend of mine."

She smiled. Taking a rag from his kitchen drawer she said, "May I use this to bandage your hand?"

He nodded. Then he watched her silently for a moment before he spoke.

"I know you hate everything I stand for. Yet you are kind to me. Why? Is it because of Zofia, your child's mother?" he asked, his voice soft and gentle.

Helen trembled. This was the first time he'd revealed that he knew Zofia's name. "You know my friend Zofia?"

"Yes, Zofia Weiss. I made it a point to know who she is. I went to the ghetto and found out everything I could about her. She is a young Jewess known to have given birth to a child. The little girl that you call Ela is really Eidel. Eidel Weiss. Zofia was never married. Your little girl was born out of wedlock."

Helen felt a shiver run up her spine. He knew so much, so very much. "Is Zofia all right? You didn't let them hurt her?"

"Of course I did not let them hurt her. And that is because of you. I enjoy doing nice things for you, Helen. I can tell you this much; one of the despicable Kapos in the ghetto is romantically interested in her. I don't think she likes him much. But because of me, she is safe."

"Oh!" Helen gasped. "Thank you. But what is a Kapo?"

"Jews I have to deal with on an almost daily basis. The lowest of the low," he said, handing her a roll of tape. "You can use this to tape the towel," he said. She took the roll and began to tape the makeshift bandage.

The Kapo, he explained, was a method of prisoner self-administration, minimizing costs by allowing ghettos and camps to function with fewer SS personnel. Helen was horrified to learn of the Jüdischer Ordnungsdienstt—the Jewish Ghetto Police—auxiliaries who were recruited from among pre-War Jewish organized crime groups. The local Judenrat, the Jewish Council, preferred to recruit from organized criminals rather than from the more numerous political, religious, or racial prisoners. The Kapo were known for their lack of scruples and for their brutality toward other prisoners and towards other Jews.

"There are already over two thousand seeing to law and order in our ghetto here. They are terrible vermin. I know, for in my liaison capacity, I work with them every day. I see how filthy and untrustworthy they are. These are Jews who work with us, the Nazis, against their own people."

Helen gasped.

My God, Zofia must be terrified of this man.

"May I ask you a question?" he said as she finished taping the bandage she'd wrapped around his hand

She nodded. "Yes."

"I realize that the Reich is persecuting Catholic priests, and you probably don't want to answer this … but you are a Catholic, aren't you Helen?"

How did he know everything? He was like an omnipresent demon.

"Yes. I was raised Catholic."

"That's all right. I knew it. You have that good Christian attitude. Do you want to know a secret? I like that in you. Your kindness and virtue, of sorts, is attractive to me. And of course, I can see that you are a devout Christian by the way you are always ready to forgive. But, you should know this … the best thing for you to do is just stay away from the church. In case you are not aware, the Nazi Party has been executing priests, and I wouldn't want you somehow to be caught as a practicing Catholic. It could be very bad for you."

"Executing priests?" Her mouth fell open. She knew that this was happening but hearing the words spoken aloud sent shock waves through her.

"Yes, Helen. Yes. Stay away from the church," Rolf said, smoothing her hair with his good hand.

Helen couldn't let Rolf know how much she longed to go to church. He would never understand. And although he had always been kind to her, she instinctively felt that lurking just below the surface of Rolf's gentlemanly conduct lay an angry and dangerous animal that could be pushed to attack by the smallest incident. However, Helen was raised to believe in the teachings of Jesus. It was because of her upbringing that she always treated Rolf kindly even though she often found his way of thinking to be vile. To Helen, every living creature should be cared for with compassion. But she knew she dared not ever tell him that. Each night, before she fell asleep, she wished that she could go into a confessional booth and rid her soul of the burden she carried because of her physical relationship with him. If he only knew that every time she lay with him, her stomach turned because she knew that she was breaking one of God's sacred commandments.

Helen couldn't bear to discuss the fate of the doomed priests any longer. She tried to change the subject. "You'll have to be more careful when you are training that dog tomorrow. It seems like he is a bit vicious."

"I won't be training that lousy dog ever again. I shot him." He looked at her and smiled nonchalantly.

Helen cringed.

CHAPTER EIGHT

Nik sat at the breakfast table eating two hard-boiled eggs and two slices of toasted rye bread with real butter. He never questioned Helen about where she got the extra rations or how she'd gotten a slab of butter or real rye bread when both were so hard to come by. He was just happy to have the additional food and the extra money she brought in from her job.

When she got home late in the evening he wasn't even waiting up for her. He should have been worried that she was out alone in the dark after curfew, but he wasn't anymore. Helen came home to find him snoring comfortably in his bed. She knew he worked in the morning, and she also knew she should be understanding. But she wasn't. She was bitter. Sometimes she actually wished he cared enough to question her, to ask her if she had taken a lover. She would have liked to tell him what she was putting up with so that he could enjoy his bread, bacon, and butter.

Where is the man I married? The man who swore to love and protect me?

She looked at Nik and wanted to cry. If only he would do something that showed he cared, showed that he wanted to rescue her, then he would prove to be the man she had fallen in love with. But, on the other hand, she knew that if he found out about Rolf, Nik wouldn't be her savior. Instead, his rage would be directed at Helen for bringing Eidel into their lives, not at Rolf. He would blame Helen for everything. No, Nik was not her prince. He had certainly not turned out to be the man she'd once believed him to be, Helen mused.

How funny, Helen thought. *When we first met I thought Nik was everything*

I wanted in a man. He was tall and handsome. And he was an artist. I was so taken in by his beautiful paintings. But that was only his outside. Inside, I have learned he is weak and he is a coward.

Even worse, he could look right into her eyes and not see her pain. And, even though she knew it was best that he didn't ask any questions, she seethed with anger that he just seemed oblivious to everything. How could he not see her how miserable she was when he looked at her? He just sat there in his chair, eating his food, and never realizing the horrors she was putting up with in order to bring him the good fortune he believed had just fallen into his lap.

Nik had always enjoyed alcohol. She didn't mind until he became over-indulgent. She mentioned his excessive drinking several times, but he always seemed able to evade discussing it. If his wasting money on drink bothered Helen, he didn't seem to notice. It was easy for Nik to overlook everything going on around him as long as he could spend an hour or two with his work buddies having a few shots. He had begun to work on his art again and could easily lose himself in his painting. His talent impressed Marci and Artur Labecki and many of their other friends. But Helen was no longer impressed with Nik's artwork. In fact, it was becoming difficult for her to look at him, let alone admire anything he did. Sometimes she even found herself hating him.

How have I ever come to this? I am sharing my life with two men, neither of whom I love.

CHAPTER NINE

January 1942

In Wannsee, part of the Berlin borough of Steglitz-Zehlendorf and the westernmost locality of Berlin, a group of senior Nazi officials gathered at one of its many elegant villas to attend a private and secret meeting. The agenda was to examine how they could ensure a better life for the generations of Germans to follow. In order to create a perfect environment for their future Aryan race, they decided that they had to wipe the slate clean and rid the world of Jews and other undesirables.

As these family men, with wives and children safe at home, gathered around a table and sipped their coffee and ate their dinners, they laughed, talked, and discussed trivial matters like vacations to Munich. As they relaxed, SS-Obergruppenführer Reinhard Heydrich outlined how European Jews would be rounded up and sent to extermination camps in the occupied part of Poland where they would be killed. The fate of millions was decided. Without any human compassion, all of the Jews in Europe—men, women, children, even tiny infants—were to be systematically murdered.

"We will leave behind a better place for our children and grandchildren. This will be an enormous feat. But someday, the Third Reich will be recognized for our great accomplishments. We will leave behind a world that is completely Judenfrei," Heydrich schemed.

They all agreed.

"Yes, the world will thank us one day!"

CHAPTER TEN

January 1942

On a frigid January morning, Helen woke up feeling too ill to get out of bed. Her head pounded as if there was a bomb that might explode in her brain, and her eyes watered and burned. She was so weak she could hardly lift her limbs. Since the day that she and Nik were married, even during her entire pregnancy with Lars, Helen had always prepared his breakfast and packed his lunch pail. Every morning she'd climb out of bed quietly and once she had everything ready for Nik she went back to their room to wake him. Today, however, although she woke up at her usual time, she was unable to move. Her voice was barely a whisper when she called his name.

"Nik. I don't feel well at all. I can't prepare your food this morning. I am sorry. Please, you must get up. You'll be late for work."

He stirred and saw that she was still in bed. "What is it? What's wrong? Did you say that you are feeling sick?"

"Yes."

"Talk to me, please? What is bothering you?" He turned over on his elbow to look at her.

"I just don't feel well." She was exhausted, too ill to explain her symptoms. All she wanted was to be left alone so she could go back to sleep. "I can't prepare your breakfast. I'm sorry."

He got up, shivering from the cold as he left the bed and stepped on the chilly wood floor. "Don't worry about me. I'll manage. I will go and see Mrs. Klien from upstairs and tell her you are not well. I'll see if she can help with the children today."

"Thank you." Helen's eyelids felt like lead. It was impossible to keep them open.

The children? Mrs. Klien, yes ask her. That's a good idea. Someone must care for the children. I am so cold. This blanket is too thin.

Even though her body was trembling and her teeth chattered, she fell into a deep sleep, and slept the entire day.

Nik came into the bedroom quietly when he got home from work. He gently awakened her. He brought her a plate of food but it was hard for her to sit up. All she wanted to do was close her eyes and go back to sleep.

"You must eat," he said. She tried, but the food stuck in her dry mouth. It tasted strange, like sulfur. Every mouthful made her feel like she might vomit.

"I'm sorry. I can't," she said, sinking back into her pillow. Within minutes she was fast asleep again.

Helen missed her meeting with Rolf that night. She awakened for a few minutes and realized he was waiting for her. A pang of fear shot through her but she was too ill to get out of bed.

Two days passed and it was time for her to go to Rolf, but she was still in bed and wasn't feeling any better. She couldn't go to him, and Helen was afraid of the consequences.

What will he do when I don't show up again tonight? Will he arrest us? Will he kill Ela? Oh dear God, I have to try to get out of this bed.

Her temples pounded, and she was nauseated. She tried to stand up but when she did she vomited bile from her empty stomach onto the floor.

I don't even have the strength to clean this up.

She lay back down as tears welled in her eyes. Never had she done anything so humiliating in her life, but there was nothing she could do. She was weak and helpless. The vomit lay in a pool on the floor as sleep overtook her again. In the morning, however, the vomit was gone; Nik cleaned up the mess sometime during the night.

She opened her eyes and saw Rolf sitting on a chair at her bedside. A chill ran through her.

Rolf?

Helen thought she was dreaming until he spoke.

"You're ill?" He got up from the chair and knelt beside her, and he put his hand gently on her head. "You're burning up with fever."

She looked at him, dazed. Her eyes were so glassy, she still wasn't sure if she was dreaming or not.

"Rolf? Is that you? What are you doing here?"

"Yes, Helen. It's me. It's Rolf." His voice was kind, soft. "You missed two of our standard appointments. I didn't know why. So I came here to your house to see what had happened to you. Your husband told me that you are ill."

"My husband? My husband, Nik?" She was still very disoriented.

Nik must be wondering why a Nazi officer had come to our home looking for me.

"Why did you tell him you were here?"

"Don't worry, Helen. I took care of everything. I told him my aunt was the old lady you have been working for. You have nothing to fear. He knows nothing about what is going on between you and I. But more importantly, right now I must send for a doctor."

"A doctor? For me?"

"You are very ill, Helen."

"Doctors are expensive. I don't need a doctor."

"Never mind about the expense. You do need a doctor and soon. I will take care of everything. You just rest. The doctor will be here before the day is out and I will come back tomorrow to check in on you and see how you are doing."

He left. Helen lay in her bed staring at a crack in the wall for a few seconds.

Am I dreaming? she wondered, as she drifted back to sleep.

Rolf didn't lie. She woke to find herself being examined by a local doctor. He was an older man with a head of thick gray hair, and gentle blue eyes.

"How do you feel?" the doctor asked.

She shook her head. "Not very good."

"I'm going to give you something that will help. You will start to feel better soon," he said reassuringly.

Helen looked at him. His face was blurry and distorted. Then she fell asleep again.

CHAPTER ELEVEN

Helen had no idea how long she'd been laying in her bed. The days passed, fading from light to dark and then back again as she drifted in and out of consciousness. She recalled a few fuzzy moments but for the most part, she was very confused. She thought she recollected Nik awakening her to ask her how she was feeling. She thought she recalled awakening twice to find Rolf at her bedside. But she hadn't seen the children in what seemed like a long time.

Are my children all right? Was Rolf really here or was I dreaming? He had to be here, he sent the doctor. Or was the doctor a dream too? Oh, I am so lost. I pray that Rolf hasn't taken Ela away. If Rolf demanded to take her Nik would not resist. Please ... please God, watch over the children."

The sun shone brightly through her window one afternoon. Or was it morning? Helen wasn't sure, but when her eyes slowly opened she saw the snow melting on Rolf's black boots. She let her eyes follow his body up to his face.

"How are you feeling?" Rolf asked. "You've given me quite a scare but the doctor says you will be all right."

"Lars? Ela? Where are they? Are they all right?"

"Yes, you needn't concern yourself with anything except getting well. I've taken care of everything. I hired a woman to look after them. At first, she was coming in while Nik was at work but to be quite honest with you he isn't much help even when he is at home. So she is staying overnight until you are feeling better."

"Ela is still here? You haven't done anything to her, have you?"

"No, my dear. Ela is fine. I promised you. And a promise is a promise. You didn't defy me. You were ill. I can forgive that." Rolf smiled.

"What's wrong with me?"

"I'm not sure. Don't worry yourself about it. The doctor has everything under control."

"Rolf, please tell me."

"It's your heart, Helen. The doctor says it is your heart but no need for concern. You are going to be just fine."

Rolf was so kind and helpful; it was hard to believe that a man with such compassion could be so cruel to others. It was easy to forget that there was another side to him.

Slowly, Helen began to recover. Nik told her that Rolf had taken care of everything they needed. He'd sent food to the Dobinski home twice a week. If Nik suspected that Helen was sleeping with Rolf, he never said a word. In fact, he seemed glad to have all of the benefits of Helen's friendship with a Nazi officer. She couldn't believe how excited he was about having things taken care of for him. Helen had been losing respect for Nik for a long time but now Nik looked so greedy to her that she couldn't help but wonder what she'd ever seen in him. He had no character, no inner strength. In her eyes, he was less than a man and the thought of his touch made her cringe.

CHAPTER TWELVE

As Rolf promised, Helen did recover. However, the illness left her weak, so weak that even the slightest exertion would have her gasping and out of breath. Rolf insisted that the woman he hired stay on longer to help Helen. Even though Helen assured Rolf that she was fine, he paid the housekeeper for an additional week just to be sure that Helen was able to handle her chores again. But once a week passed, Helen was on her own and back to her old work schedule. Nik treated her as if she'd never been sick. He expected his meals prepared and served to him. And in order to purchase the food, Helen had to take both of the children into town with her to the market. She bathed the children nightly. Even though she was exhausted, every week she scrubbed the floors, washed the windows, and cleaned the linens and the clothes.

One afternoon when Nik was at work, Rolf came to Helen's home to speak with her. He looked at her and decided that she was healthy enough to return to their old schedule of coming to his flat twice a week and so their meetings resumed. Helen found that even though she couldn't say she loved him, she didn't hate him anymore. He'd treated her so well when she was ill that she had come to appreciate him.

She slowly began to give herself permission to enjoy the small gifts he gave her, and she even found that she was genuinely touched when he brought her toys for the children. Lars and Ela had so little to play with. All they had were the things Helen made for them out of old ribbons, fabric, or string. Nik was barely able to afford food so toys were out of the question. It touched Helen's heart to be able to see the smiles on Lars' and Ela's faces when she gave them the playthings. Rolf offered to take Helen out to restaurants and beer halls, but Helen begged off. She didn't want to be seen with him by her neighbors. They would surely ask questions and she would have to explain.

"You would enjoy going out for a nice dinner, and because of who I am I have the power to do that for you, Helen. We could share a beer, perhaps some music?"

"Yes, Rolf that would be nice. But it would cause me difficulty. People would talk. I'm sure Nik would find out. I would have to find a way to explain. It would be so much trouble. Why tempt things? Aren't you happy with the way things are?"

"I'm happy with you, Helen. I think, in fact, that I might be starting to really care for you."

Helen smiled and touched his face.

CHAPTER THIRTEEN

As the snow and ice began to melt, little tender blades of grass began to peek through the ground. Tiny buds formed on the bushes. There was hopefulness, a sort of freshness to the spring air that seemed oblivious to the horrors of the Nazi regime. Helen lay in bed beside Rolf. They had been lovers for a long time already and although she hadn't developed deep feelings for him, she had begun to feel at ease. She looked up into his face. There was something she'd wanted to ask him for a long time. She'd avoided it, and now she finally felt comfortable enough to say the words she'd kept in her heart but had not yet spoken.

"Rolf? I have something to ask you." Helen's voice was barely a whisper as she lay with her head on his hairless chest.

"Of course," he said softly as he twisted the curls of her hair around his finger.

"Remember Zofia?"

"The Jewess? The one who is the mother of your little girl Ela?"

"Yes. That's Zofia." She cleared her throat and added, "Have you seen her? I mean we haven't talked about her for a long time. Is she still all right?"

"Yes, she's fine."

"Is she still being pursued by that Kapo you told me about?"

"I don't know. I don't have time to follow Jews around to see what they are doing. She is alive. That's all I know. What difference does it make to you anyway? She is gone. That is all you need to know."

"She's a friend of mine, Rolf."

"She's a Jew, Helen. An enemy of the state."

"I know … but I am asking … as a friend … as your lover … can you help her?"

"I've helped her as much as I can."

"What have you done?"

"How dare you question me? Who do you think you are to ask me what I've done? I've done what I can."

"Is it possible that maybe you can arrange for me to see her?"

"Don't push this." His face hardened like a mask made of concrete.

"But she is all alone. And you told me yourself that the ghetto is a terrible place."

"You don't need to remind me of what I said about the ghetto, Helen."

"Then you know. If I could only talk to her, reassure her that her daughter is all right."

Rolf shot up to a sitting position. Helen slid off of his chest.

"You think because I care for you that you have an advantage over me, don't you?" He turned and glared at her. "What you are asking of me could cost me my position. Even my life."

Helen sat up and held the sheet over her naked breasts. She suddenly felt exposed and dirty. It had been a while since she was reminded of just who Rolf really was. "I can't help it, I feel sorry for her. I keep thinking of how I would feel if I were locked in a ghetto and couldn't see Lars. I know you, Rolf. You're not that heartless. You want to be like the rest of them. But you're not …"

He turned to her. His eyes were dark and as hard as glass marbles.

Then without warning, he struck her with the back of his hand. Blood trickled down her nose and lips. "Don't tell me who or what I am. I am a strong German. I am an SS Officer. I serve the Fuhrer. And I am a proud Aryan man. You had better take heed, Helen. You will find that I am not softened by silly sentiment. Or Jewish lies." His voice sounded like an icicle that had fallen from a roof and shattered on the frozen ground.

"Rolf. I don't believe you …"

"Get out of my house, Helen. Get out now. Get up, get dressed, and go home."

CHAPTER FOURTEEN

Still naked, Rolf paced around his apartment. His body was lean, not muscle-bound, but certainly not fat like some of the SS men he knew. Hitler's elite had access to good food and drink. He'd watched as others had eaten until their bodies were a sloppy mess but not Rolf. He was too self-disciplined for that. Over-indulgent people who had no control of their appetites were disgusting to him, and he refused to be one of them. Every morning he got up an hour early to do the exercises he'd begun when he was just a boy in the Hitler youth. Rolf had always taken pride in his ability to exercise self-control in every way.

That was why he was so shocked to realize what he'd become when he was with Helen.

I must be out of my mind. This silly Polish woman could cost me everything for which I have worked so hard

Stupid. I've been stupid. I really should turn her into the Gestapo for keeping that Jewish child. That would be the honourable thing to do. It would be a fine demonstration of my absolute loyalty to the Party.

Helen!

Who does she think she is? Even more importantly, who does she think she is toying with when she dares to confront me?

The bitch thinks I am weak. She must be deluding herself to believe that I am in love with her. How could she possibly believe that I, an Aryan a member of the master race, would ever be in love with a Pole?

This insignificant woman has dared to play me for a fool.

I am not weak.

A true German man is never weak.

He was ashamed of his behavior towards Helen. He had allowed her to poke at his soft underbelly. Their relationship was supposed to be nothing but a mindless diversion. He was all right with things as long as she was nothing but a whore who he used to satisfy his needs two or three times a week. But he had started to treat her like she was a real person, a real woman, and maybe even begun to care for her (if he dared admit it to himself) and that was when she thought she had him. She tried to take advantage of his kindness, just like a Pole.

Damn her!

How could I ever allow myself to forget that she's an inferior and should be treated like one? Even if I did love her, which I don't, I could never, would never, marry her. Never bring her back to Germany as my wife. Never! She is nothing but a plaything. She is a part of an inferior race. It seems I have let this thing with her go much too far.

CHAPTER FIFTEEN

Helen was terrified as she closed the door to Rolf's flat. The click of her heels on the pavement sent chills up her spine. The night was so quiet. She was out after curfew, and even though she had the letter of permission that Rolf had given her months ago, she knew if she were arrested right now he would not stand behind her. She was so distressed that she had to stop twice on the way home from Rolf's apartment, just to catch her breath. Tonight she'd seen a side of him that she'd never seen before. The Nazi. Tonight she didn't see Rolf, she saw Hauptsurmfuhrer Boltz, and she trembled in fear at the true man who lay behind the mask he'd worn since they'd begun sleeping together.

She wiped the blood that dripped down her face with the back of her hand. What if she'd made Rolf so angry that he decided to turn her and her family into the Gestapo? Or he might decide to have Ela taken away and sent to the ghetto. With the snap of a finger, Boltz could destroy everything and everyone she loved. Rolf might decide to go to the ghetto and take his rage out on poor Zofia.

What was I thinking? What had compelled me to push him so hard? I wanted to believe that he was different than the rest of them.

Helen had convinced herself that under that black starched uniform was a human being. He'd been so kind when she was ill that she'd almost started to believe she could learn to care for him. But now it was evident that it was only wishful thinking. Her nose hurt. Helen reached up and touched the dried blood on her face. He'd struck her. He'd struck her hard, meaning to hurt her. She had been stupid. Helen had believed she was capable of appealing to his human side. Now she realized that the human side that she wanted to believe was there was nothing but a façade. He was a Nazi; she'd dared to challenge him and for that, he lashed out.

Helen just hoped he wasn't going to do anything more to hurt her.

CHAPTER SIXTEEN

Two days passed. It was time to go to Rolf's apartment again. She was expected on Thursday nights but Helen didn't know what to do. She dared not avoid him but she was afraid to go, worried that he would still be angry with her. All day she was anxious. She was short with the children and annoyed with Nik. As she watched her husband sitting at the table eating his dinner, she wanted to spit in his face. He was so oblivious.

I saw Nik as the man I wanted him to be, not as the man he is.

His eyes were a little glassy and she knew he'd had a few beers. If she could have afforded to leave him, she would have taken both children and moved out of the apartment so she didn't have to see him and be constantly reminded of the mistake she'd made in marrying him.

"Are you working tonight?" he asked, dunking a thick slice of bread in his soup. A bit of the broth ran down his chin.

"Yes," she said, thinking that the only good thing that came out of their marriage was Lars.

He just nodded. Was he truly that stupid? Didn't he see her pain at all? Or did he just look the other way when things made him uncomfortable?

After the children were in bed Helen left the apartment.

The spring is so beautiful, Helen thought, as she felt tears well up in her eyes. She was walking down a cobblestone street on her way to his flat and her heart ached with longing for the innocent life she'd led before

Rolf. How optimistic she'd been on the day of her wedding, on the morning Lars was born. Sadness overcame her and she had to stop for a minute and sit down on a bench.

It was there, in the soft glow from a street light, that she noticed a tiny yellow flower that had poked its head through the rubble of the bombed out buildings. It was that blue-gray time of day when the sun and the moon traded places. The beauty of the evening sky was a tender contrast against the remains of the broken city.

Even when she was just a child, Helen had loved the spring. The Polish winters were brutal but now that the terrible chill had broken she was able to walk through the streets with a light jacket. It was wonderful not to have to endure trying to sleep while she felt like she was freezing, or to walk without fear of falling on the slippery ice. If only she could feel the complete joy of spring the way she did as a young girl but knowing that she must see Rolf again was not only distasteful, it was horrifying. Anything could happen tonight.

Anything at all.

He could be kind or he could be cruel. Rolf had absolute power over her and over the future of everyone she loved. He could wield that sword for good or he could strike them down. The decision was his, and Helen felt powerless. It was hard to believe that she had almost started to see good in him.

I so much wanted to believe that he was not the monster that I always feared he was. Helen shook her head.

I am always trying to see the good in people. It has to be my religious background. Even when I am lost in the darkness God is always guiding me like a beacon of light. He is always helping me to find the good in people. It has been this way since I was a child. That's because my mother always told me, "God created all of us, Helen. If you look hard enough, you will find that there is goodness in all living creatures." Mama, Mama, thank God you never lived to see the Nazis.

He'd never been violent with her before the previous night. She wondered if they had somehow crossed a barrier in their relationship, and she was uncertain as to whether there was any way of going back to the way it was before. It wasn't the slap or the bloody nose that bothered her but the threat behind it that consumed her every thought. She'd made a terrible mistake treating him as if he were her real boyfriend.

For a minute, she'd forgotten the truth. She was his slave, he her master. All day long as she went through her chores, she considered not going to see Rolf that night, but she was too afraid of what he might do if she tried to avoid him. Every so often she would sit down for a few minutes and look at Ela. Anyone else would probably think that taking the child had been a mistake.

And yet, if I had it to do over again, I would not change a thing, she thought.

She was caught like a poor tiny white mouse in a trap. Her chest ached and she found it difficult to breathe deeply.

I am afraid to go, but I am also afraid not to go.

Evening came and Helen decided she must face Rolf.

When she arrived at his building her heart began to race and sharp pains ran down her left arm. Breathing heavily, she leaned against the side of the building. It took her several minutes to catch her breath, then she knocked on Rolf's door and waited. From where she stood she could see there was a light on in the small living room window so she knew that he was at home. He never left the lights on when he went out. Helen's entire body trembled as she waited. Her head ached. If only she could lie down and relax. Then she knocked again. Still he did not come to the door. Her heartbeat was racing and she felt as if she might vomit. It was becoming so hard to breathe. If he'd lost interest in her then what? Would he just leave her and her children alone? Or would he exercise that terrible power he and his Nazi Party held over the Polish and destroy her world? The idea that she had laid with him, that he had been inside of her body made her feel disgusted with herself. However, she knew she must stay at the door until he opened it.

I must face him. I have to look into his eyes. I will force myself to touch his face and then, somehow, no matter what I must do, I will find a way to win his affections back.

Only then could she even hope to ensure that her loved ones would stay safe. Again she knocked, harder this time. Still no answer.

Tears welled in her eyes. She wanted to turn and run, run until she couldn't run anymore. Run until her weak heart stopped beating. But her feet would not move.

Five long minutes passed. Panic rose in her belly. Her bowels twisted and turned. From where she stood outside the door, Helen could hear noises coming from inside the flat. She cleared her throat and said his name loud enough for him to hear.

"Rolf?"

Her body was trembling so hard she feared she might fall over. The uncertainty of what he might do next was all consuming. Sweat seeped from her brow.

"Rolf?"

Her voice cracked as she said his name even louder. Still, he did not answer

Finally, shaken and unnerved, Helen left. Terrified and alone, she walked back home. She didn't sleep at all that night.

CHAPTER SEVENTEEN

For the next several days, Helen's nerves were on edge. Every time she heard the sound of an automobile she was sure that the police were coming to arrest her. When she saw Nazi officers or Gestapo agents near the market she could hardly contain her feelings of dread. The most difficult part of it all was that she had no one to talk to about her fears. Certainly not Nik.

Nik is good for nothing. If I tell him, he won't be a comfort to me. Instead, he will make me feel worse. I know he will blame me for everything. He'll want to throw Ela out. And if God forbid something happens and Rolf turns on us, he'll accuse me. Not that I don't already blame myself.

Helen was friendly with many of the other ladies who lived in the neighborhood. They talked, shared recipes and ways to stretch their pathetic rations. But she couldn't really call them friends; they were friendly acquaintances, nothing more. And with the Nazis always hovering, Helen felt that it was best not to put her trust in anyone. So she did not share her feelings; instead, she swallowed her worries, watched, waited, and prayed.

Two weeks passed and she heard nothing from Rolf. She began to feel a glimmer of hope that maybe by some miracle her nightmare with Rolf was over. Could it really be possible that Rolf had been kind enough to let her go without any further punishment?

Oh, how grateful I am, she sighed in relief.

Every day she thanked God that Rolf was gone and finally, Helen began to relax. Then one afternoon as Helen was taking the children into town, she saw Rolf walking across the street. Their eyes met. She felt her neck burning; it was like a rash had sprung up. Her skin began to itch. He stared at her, and his eyes seemed to shoot beams of fire. Her eyes were frozen on him; she could not turn away. He was still staring at her as he crossed the street. She felt dizzy. Her vision blurred. He was coming towards her.

A sharp pain shot through her chest. There was nothing she could do but stand where she was and wait to see what he had to say.

God, please help me. Please don't let him do anything cruel. I beg you to use your power to make him free me.

"What's wrong Mommy?" Ela asked, looking up at Helen. The child seemed to sense her feelings. Not Lars. He was busy playing with something he'd found on the ground.

"Nothing sweetheart," Helen said, trying to manage a smile. "What is it you're playing with?" she asked Lars.

Lars held up a dirty piece of wood. Helen shrugged her shoulders and nodded. In normal circumstances, she would have insisted that Lars put it down before he got a splinter. But at that moment she was distracted and petrified.

"Helen," Rolf said.

She couldn't smile.

"How are you?" he inquired.

"I'm all right, Rolf. "

"You've been on my mind. Actually, I must admit that I've been checking here at the market for you every day. I've wanted to talk to you. And here you are." He smiled. His teeth reminded her of a wolf.

"And looking lovely, I might add. I would like you to come to me tonight."

Dear God, why did I ever come into town today? Because we needed food. I don't know what to do. I can't get away from him.

"Rolf, I don't think …" She looked away.

"You're absolutely right! You don't think. You don't have the brains to think. You will do as I say. Tonight. Eight o'clock. Be there." His tone of voice was soft with a threatening undertone.

CHAPTER EIGHTEEN

Helen went through the motions for the rest of her day. She gave the children their baths. Watched them play on the floor. Prepared and served Nik his dinner. Robotically, she put on her clothes. Then she went into the living room and told Nik she was going to work. The old lady had sent for her again. He just nodded and went back to reading the paper. She glared at him with laser beams of hatred coming out of her eyes.

Why don't you ask me where the old lady has been for the last weeks? Why do you just sit there and not see that I am suffering?

As she walked toward Rolf's flat, for the first time Helen considered suicide.

I wish I were dead. It would be so much easier to just end my life. I can't take this anymore.

But what about Lars and Ela? If I were gone would Nik be able to care for the children? He is like a child who can hardly care for himself. And as much as I wish that Nik cared enough to notice how unhappy I am, would his knowing about Rolf change anything?

No.

He is powerless. He can't help me. It would take a miracle to save me now. And Nik is hardly a man. He doesn't deserve my respect and he's not worthy of being a husband.

I hate him.

I have never felt so much anger towards anyone. Not even Rolf. I never expected Rolf to be anything but an animal. But Nik was supposed to be my hero, my prince, my true love.

He is not.

I do wish I could find peace in death, but if I were dead would Rolf punish Ela and take her to the ghetto? Would he punish Lars too?

Helen was conflicted in every way. The feminine part of her, who'd grown up to believe that men always protected the women they loved, longed for a husband that would be like a prince in a fairy tale. But the reality was that if Nik found out about Rolf—and by some miracle took her side—things would be even worse. If Nik ever even made an attempt to stand up and defend her against Rolf, the result was sure to be disastrous. Rolf would never take such an offense and challenge of his power lightly. She had no doubt that Rolf would see to it that Nik was imprisoned or even murdered Not only had Rolf destroyed her self-respect, but he had also destroyed her marriage and any illusions she'd ever had of her husband as the perfect man.

CHAPTER NINETEEN

With a heavy heart and feelings of defeat, Helen knocked at the door to Rolf's apartment.

Rolf opened the door immediately, as if he had been waiting. His hair, the color of brushed gold, was usually styled perfectly but not that night. Tonight his hair was uncombed. There were dark sweat stains under the arms of his white shirt. She'd never seen him so unkempt. It was frightening to see him that way. He didn't speak. Instead, he just nodded his head and motioned for her to come inside. She felt like she was entering the bowels of hell. Rolf closed the door behind her. The click of the lock made her jump. Helen bit her lip and tried to look deep into his eyes. She had to try and make out what he was thinking but his eyes looked like marbles, cold glass, non-human things, emotionless. Fear shot through her but she dared not say a word. For several uncomfortable seconds, Rolf stared into her eyes. Helen looked back at him, her face begging for mercy but she could read nothing in his expression; he was like a blank board.

Then Rolf pushed Helen against the wall with a force strong enough for her to hit her head. She winced in pain. Helen felt her knees buckle and her body shake. He was unmoved by her pain or her terror. Rolf lifted her dress, tore off her panties, and took her without even allowing her to remove her jacket. His movements were hard, rushed, violent, and painful. Pushing into her, forcing his body inside of her resistant one. Sweat was dripping from his brow. With a loud grunt, he finally finished.

When he stepped away from her, Helen breathed a sigh of relief but she was still trembling. This time he did not offer her beer or food. He just walked away and went into the bathroom leaving her standing by the front door with his semen dripping down her legs, a ripping ache in her vagina, and tears rolling down her cheeks.

When Rolf came out of the bathroom, Helen still stood by the front door. He couldn't look at her. Instead, he shoved a roll of the money in her hand.

"Here give this to your husband. Tell him you have started back to work with the old woman. Come again in three days. Now get out of here. I don't want to look at you."

She stuffed the roll of bills into her pocket then left. Once she was a block away, Helen leaned against a building and wept.

CHAPTER TWENTY

After Helen left Rolf locked the door behind her, then he went to his knees. He'd hurt her and he knew it. At the time, he'd wanted to hurt her for making him feel pathetic and weak. Weakness was his biggest fear. While he was pounding himself into her it had made him feel powerful again. But now he was sorry. If she were still there with him he might even beg for her forgiveness. It was best that she was gone. A weak man is a worthless man.

I am not a Pole. I am a future leader. A part of the magnificent Third Reich and a member of the Germanic race. I am an Aryan, a superior man. It is certainly time that I behaved like one.

Rolf went into the kitchen and poured himself a shot of vodka. He downed it, then another. Then he went into the bathroom and washed until his skin was raw. Once he was finished he went to bed.

CHAPTER TWENTY-ONE

The three days separating Helen's visits to Rolf went by quickly and before she knew it the time had come to return to Rolf's apartment. This time he was drunk. His shirt hung out of his pants and again he appeared disheveled, but in his sloppy, drunken way he was apologetic for his rough behavior the last time they'd been together. However, his regret didn't last long. Before the night was over Rolf turned violent again, slapping her face so hard that she twisted her neck. Something had happened to him that night she'd challenged him by asking about Zofia. He was not the same towards her. His moods changed within minutes and Helen was never sure how to answer his questions. She realized that she had pushed him too far that night when she dared to question him and now he was determined to prove to her and himself that he was a true Nazi.

There was nothing Helen could do but endure. She was helpless. She made every effort to tell Rolf how strong and important he was. However, he detected that she was lying and it only made him angrier. And now, every time Helen left Rolf's apartment she couldn't help herself; she thought about dying.

Caring for a home, two children under five, and a husband left Helen exhausted. But she couldn't ever seem to sleep all the way through the night. Sometimes she would wake up and weep, and other times she would find herself weeping in her dreams. Whenever she combed her hair, she found clumps of hair in the comb and on the bathroom floor. And lately, she'd noticed that she'd begun forming a small circular bald spot on the side of her head. Her nerves were always on edge, and she felt like a wounded, hunted animal, always wishing she could find an escape. Once, when things were so bad and Helen could hardly stand it anymore, she even considered sending Eidel back to Zofia. Then she looked at Eidel on the floor playing with Lars and begged God for forgiveness. She began to create elaborate fantasies in her mind of shooting Rolf. But she knew she didn't have the courage to kill another human being, even if he was a demon. And, although she knew it was wrong, her thoughts of suicide became more frequent. She even considered methods, but Helen's belief in God and the Bible were very strong. Suicide would not only leave her children vulnerable, but she knew that she dared not commit such a terrible sin. It would be so wonderful to escape the pain she felt but the consequences of dying would be horrific, even more horrific than what she must endure every day, if that was even possible.

On a hot, still night in mid-July, Helen laid in bed beside Nik watching him sleep. The graying white bed sheets stuck to her body with sweat. As she listened to Nik breathing softly, she was suddenly overcome with a sad and strange feeling of tenderness for him. He was pathetic, a man stripped of his manhood. For a long time, Helen had blamed Nik for not defending her against Rolf's assaults. She looked over at him. He'd aged since the Nazis had conquered Poland. Helen never noticed the toll it had taken on him. All she had thought about was the fairytale hero she wanted. But Helen had to accept that she didn't live in a fantasy world. She lived in a dangerous world where anyone could be arrested at any time, or worse.

I have to keep reminding myself that it is better that Nik never noticed that something has been going on with Rolf. It is his ignorance that saved him and our family.

Nik wasn't perfect by any means, but at least she knew she could trust him. He wasn't the great love of her life, but he was her friend and by law, he was her husband, an imperfect person. But she too was imperfect.

Wasn't everyone?

However, most importantly, he was alive. He was paying the bills and doing the best he could to help her raise the children. He never complained about Ela. He could have walked out on her for taking a Jewish child and causing them so much worry, but he didn't. That was something to be admired.

And let's face it. If Nik wasn't around, I would be completely dependent upon Rolf for everything. Rolf is a bastard and not someone I could ever truly trust.

And then still, every three days, regardless of what Helen had going on at home … it didn't matter if the children were ill or if she was worn out or if Nik had problems at work. No matter what happened … with misery in her heart and her body trembling with anxiety, she walked through the streets of Warsaw to go to Rolf's flat.

CHAPTER TWENTY-TWO

1942, late July.

Since they were young boys, Nikodem Dobinski and Artur Labecki had been best friends. They lived just a few blocks away from each other. The two boys went to the same school, and their families attended the same church. When they got old enough to marry, they both married their wives within six months of each other. But as similar as they were, they were also very different. Nik was a quiet man who'd always kept to himself. He was born with a slight limp that was hardly noticeable to anyone but him. However, he saw it as a great handicap and was very self-conscious of it. When the other boys played sports, he would look for reasons not to play, afraid the others would laugh at him when he hobbled as he ran. Sadly, he never found any enjoyment in sports. He hated his job but accepted the responsibility that he must arrive on time and do as he was told. However, Nik did have a hobby that he loved. Nik was an artist. He painted faces with such depth that if one stared at them long enough they could inspire one to feel as if they were walking inside the subject's soul. Nik was not able to express what was buried in his own heart, but he could capture the essence of every emotion on canvas. All that he could not express in words came alive in each brush stroke. Artur, on the other hand, was an excellent speaker. Before the Nazis invaded he'd considered studying to be a lawyer. He loved to read, to write, and to engage for hours in intellectual arguments with friends. And whereas Helen was an average, somewhat pretty, but certainly understated girl, Artur's wife Maci was a true beauty. She spoke her mind like a man and was an outrageous flirt. Marci smiled at every fellow she met, winked her eyes, made jokes, and charmed even the most difficult of men. She even flirted with Nik, and although he knew she had no real interest in him, her silly flirtation would often make Nik feel uncomfortable. Her outrageous behavior never seemed to bother Artur. If it did have any effect on him, he certainly hid it well. The two couples met at least twice a month at one of their apartments where they had a simple dinner and an evening of card games. However, that week Artur had proposed that instead of their regular couples date, he would like to invite Nik and Helen to attend a very secretive meeting. Artur quietly explained to Nik that he had been involved with a special organization that was fighting against the Nazis for a long time and, since Nik was his best friend, he wanted to introduce him to the others.

"You must not ever mention this group or this meeting to anyone," Artur said. Nik had tried to beg off, but Artur was insistent until finally Nik shrugged his shoulders and accepted the invitation. When Artur wanted something he could be terribly convincing.

Helen told her friend who lived upstairs that she and Nik were going out for dinner with another couple. Helen asked her neighbor if she would watch the children for a few hours and since Helen often watched the neighbor's daughter, the neighbor readily agreed to return the favor.

The Dobinskis walked two blocks to the home of Marci and Artur Labecki then both couples went to the meeting. As they were walking, Nik whispered to Artur, "What is this all about? You are involved with a group fighting against the Nazis?"

Nik had heard of the bravery of the underground fighters from the ŻOB, the Żydowska Organizacja Bojowa or Jewish Combat Organization, and the ŻZW, the Żydowski Związek Wojskowy or Jewish Military Union that had infiltrated the ghetto. The Armia Krajowa, or Home Army, was growing in strength and audacity, as non-Jewish Poles did whatever they could to make life difficult for the occupying Germans. It was said that the resistance members who worked in the factories had built faults into 92,000 artillery missiles.

"Let's not discuss these matters out here on the street," Artur said, putting his arm on Nik's shoulder. "I'll just tell you this …I wouldn't have asked you to come if I didn't trust you implicitly."

"Artur, I am not sure I want to get involved in all of this."

"You can come to the meeting and listen and then you can decide what you want to do," Artur said. He was so strong and persuasive. Nic had always yielded to Artur's will in the past and so tonight was no different.

The two couples arrived at a tall, red brick building. They walked up three long flights of stairs and then knocked. The man who answered recognized Artur immediately. He opened the door and they walked into a stuffy apartment that had a strong smell of sweat. It was June and not yet exceptionally hot, but the flat was warm and clammy. Groups of people were scattered about the room speaking in low tones. Helen was a little intimidated. After all, she had Ela to think of and that terrible secret affair she was carrying on with Rolf. And besides all of that, everyone knew it was not safe to discuss anything that pertained to the Nazi government. She felt her skin tingling as if she were breaking out with a heat rash. Coming there had probably been a mistake. Nik had told her a little about what to expect, and from the little that Artur had explained to Nik, both Nik and Helen devised that this was going to be a meeting of people who wanted to oust the Nazi occupiers. Helen looked around and wished she could leave. The last thing she needed right now was trouble. If anything, she wanted to cover herself with a cloak of invisibility and stay quiet, unnoticed.

"Artur!" A man walked over and patted Artur's shoulder.

"You're looking radiant," the man said to Marci, who smiled widely. Then turning back to Artur the man said, "Introduce me to your friends."

"Vincent Bolinski, this is my oldest friend Nikodem Dobinski and his wife Helen." Artur smiled

"My pleasure."

Nik nodded and so did Helen but she felt her lower lip trembling.

"Sit down, make yourself comfortable. The meeting is about to start," Bolinski said.

The Dobinskis and their friends sat in the back on wooden crates. As she sat down, Helen felt a splinter go into her leg. Pain shot up her thigh, but she didn't make a sound. The room grew quiet. Then a heavy-set man who looked like a bear with thick, wavy black hair and a heavy beard began to speak

"I would like to extend a warm welcome to those of you who are new to our group. You would not be here unless you were a very trusted friend of one of our members. We are a group of Polish citizens who love our country. This meeting is about our country. This meeting is about Poland and those of us who want to see the miserable German invaders go back to where they came from."

There was a quiet cheer of approval from the crowd, just loud enough to show support but not loud enough to be heard outside of the apartment walls.

"We can't help but see the evidence everywhere of the disaster that these terrible Nazis have made of our beloved Poland. The streets are filled with rubble from their bombs. Our homes have been destroyed or confiscated. The rations they give us are hardly enough to keep us alive. Hitler, the bastard, had promised to stay out of Poland, but now we know that the word of a German is worthless. It means nothing. They humiliate our women. They've taken all the Jews who were our neighbors and friends and locked them up in that ghetto that they built and surrounded with barbed wire in the middle of our beautiful city. Then they moved Nazis into the homes that they have stolen from our citizens, Jews and Poles alike. How much will you put up with, my friends?"

"I don't give a shit about the Jews," Artur said, his voice raised just a smidgen too loud for the clandestine meeting. "My concern is for us, the Polish nationals who were born and raised here. This is our home. It is for our sake that we must get the Kraut bastards the hell out of our country."

A male voice came from the back of the room. The voice was soft, deep and somehow demanded to be heard. "We are all Poland, you, me, and the Polish Jews. I will gladly fight the Nazis and if fate has it, I will die for this land. But I will die not only for those of us who are here tonight but for everyone born on this soil for all of Poland. And that means the Polish Jews too."

"Who are you? Are you a Jew?" the man leading the meeting asked.

"My name is Eryk Jaworski. I am not a Jew but what does it matter? The Nazis are persecuting all of us. They have stolen our homeland and demoralized our culture."

"Who brought you here, Jaworski? I have not seen you before."

"I heard about this meeting from a friend of mine. His name is Rutkowski. We work together."

"I know him. You work in the sewers?"

"Yes."

"Rutkowski." The man looked out into the audience. "Rutkowski if you are here tonight please stand up."

"I am here." A burly man with a thick head of curly red hair stood up. "This fellow, Eryk Jaworski, is a good person. I will vouch for him. You can trust him."

"Good. Then welcome Jaworski. Now let's get down to business."

The group broke off into small segments. Helen wasn't sure, but she thought that each segment was being given their orders for some kind of mission against the Nazis. Since she and Nik had not yet agreed to join the group they were asked to leave. Again, Artur asked Nik to seriously consider becoming a part of the movement. When Artur spoke about defeating the Nazis, Helen saw the conviction in his eyes. She couldn't help but admire him. Nik had no real passion about anything. His only desire was to slip by unnoticed and stay alive.

The Labeckis left the meeting with their friends the Dobinskis. The couples had just enough time to walk back to their apartments before the curfew went into effect.

"So what do you think, Nikodem? You want to join us?" Artur put his arm around Nik's shoulder.

"I don't know. It's very dangerous, Artur."

"So is living under the Nazis' thumb."

"Yes, that's true. But I can't give you a quick answer to such a question. This is a very serious issue. I have to think it over."

CHAPTER TWENTY-THREE

Nik never asked Helen what she thought about joining the underground. In fact, when she mentioned the meeting he told her that he didn't want to discuss the issue. Helen just looked at him. Her eyes glared as she thought, *Good old Nik. He's always trying to avoid facing anything head on. He can't help it. He is weak. And sadly to Poland, he is worthless.*

Finally, Helen told Nik that she believed that they should join their fellow Polish citizens and do what they could to rid their country of the Nazi invaders. Nik was eating his dinner when she told them. He dropped the fork and turned to face her. His face was crimson as he glared into her eyes, "You expect me to join a group that will put our family in even more danger? Haven't you put us at risk enough already by taking your Jewish friend's child into our home? Our neighbors don't ask questions because they like us. But believe me, Helen, for some reason you are blind. You refuse to see that we are walking a tightrope every day. Look around you; people are getting arrested constantly. They disappear and never return. I wish you would realize that we can't trust anyone. You are such a stubborn woman. You had to have that child. No matter what I said, you wouldn't listen to reason. And so the little girl is here with us. But every day that she is in our house our very lives are in jeopardy. I will not add more fuel to the fire you started. I will not make the foolish mistake of thinking we are strong enough to fight against something as monstrous as the Nazi Party. Let's lay low. Stay out of trouble. If not for our sake, then for Lars," Nik said.

Anger rose in her, but again she vacillated between pity and resentment. She stared at him but said nothing. How could she not pity him? He was a man stripped of his manhood by a regime that had reduced him to a whimpering, frightened weakling. But she resented him for exactly the same reasons. She asked herself many times what was it that she expected him to do? He was doing what he believed was best. Helen had to face facts. Nik was not a fighter, but at least he paid the bills. Why was it that with all the misery surrounding her, the thing that bothered her most and was most often on her mind was her anger towards her husband? She'd had to look the other way and hurry the children along when she saw people being arrested or beaten on the streets. She'd had to face limited rations and sometimes if the children were exceptionally hungry she'd gone to bed without eating. She'd lost her morals and her peace of mind. Yet the thing that hurt her the most was the loss of respect for her husband.

CHAPTER TWENTY- FOUR

Rolf had his own demons to conquer. He vacillated between obsession with Helen and hatred for the power his desire for her held over him. He was confused and unable to control his own emotions. And so he had personality changes that would occur within the blink of an eye. One night, when he was feeling kind and generous, he gave Helen an intricate hand-carved wooden horse for Lars.

"I walked by a toymaker's shop and saw it," Rolf smiled as he gave the sculpture to Helen. "I thought perhaps your son might like it."

When he did things like that she he found it easy to smile at him. Sometimes he could be almost endearing. There was kindness inside of him; she'd seen the evidence. Not often, but on occasion, she glimpsed the man he might have been had he never known Hitler. But, sadly, he'd buried any trace of humanity under all of the hatred he'd developed trying to be a good Nazi. Even though he never gave her any gifts for Ela, Helen still appreciated him going out of his way for her son. However, later that same week, Rolf proudly presented her with a set of children's books for Lars. She opened one to find that it was filled with frightening pictures of old Jewish men with long hook noses and evil eyes threatening to kidnap and kill Aryan children and drink their blood.

"Read these to Lars," Rolf said with conviction. "He's not Aryan, of course, but it is important that he knows that he must be very careful not to trust Jews."

Rolf laid the rest of the books in her lap.

"Take a few minutes and look at them. These are wonderful books for Lars."

She leafed through the picture books and felt a sick churning in the pit of her stomach. The illustrations in the books were grotesque and terrifying to her as an adult. She could only imagine the nightmares such images would give a child.

Rolf never mentioned Ela. It seemed that he purposely did not acknowledge her existence. They both knew the little girl's mother was Jewish, but it was an unspoken agreement that neither of them would ever bring Zofia or Ela up in their conversations again. After all, if he was angered, Rolf could change his mind at any time about looking the other way with Ela and he could have Ela returned to her mother in the ghetto.

"Thank you for the gift, Rolf," Helen stammered. "I'll read these books to Lars."

Helen nodded, forcing a smile.

He knows that I don't agree with his hatred of Jews.

But she dared not say anything derogatory about the content of the books. Since that fateful night when she'd mentioned Zofia she had learned to keep her eyes cast down and never challenge his actions or ideas again. Helen would never again ask him for anything. And the subject of the ghetto and the Jews was off limits. If he brought it up, she would just agree with whatever he said.

Rolf smiled, patting her hand. Helen could see that he was satisfied with her answer about the books.

Rolf laid her down on the sofa that night and took her the way a man eats a meal or picks a bunch of flowers, with no thought for the food or foliage, only the temporary pleasure it gives him. Helen knew she was little more than a plaything for his amusement and as long as she kept him amused, he would keep her and her loved ones safe. So she allowed him to do as he wanted with her again. Never once did she equate his touch with lovemaking. But since she did nothing to aggravate him and she'd learned to keep her mouth shut and never question him, he'd become a little easier on her and he'd started to give her gifts of food again.

For this, I must be grateful. A can of meat or a couple of oranges will keep the children healthy. If Nik doesn't get to it first. I can see how Nik resents it when I give the oranges to Ela. I can't blame him, there is so little. But I am happy to give Ela what would be considered my share.

The following week Rolf sent a gift to Helen's home. When Helen opened the box to find an electric refrigerator her eyes flew open wide. She'd heard that such things were available for wealthy people to buy but would never have dreamed she might own one. It was a small round box that could be plugged into a wall socket. The note from Rolf said that the refrigerator could keep food from spoiling for up to three days. Helen ran her hand over the smooth door.

Such a gift? How can I hate him when he does things like this? And yet ... I do.

CHAPTER TWENTY-FIVE

1942 Late September

Autumn crept in slowly, each day growing just a degree or two cooler. Although Helen was born in the fall, she knew that there would be no celebration of her birthday. Gifts and cakes cost lots of money, money Nik wouldn't spend on her. On liquor, yes; but not on her.

Yet even though life had dealt her a rough hand, the season still brought back fond memories. In fact, one of her earliest recollections was of a time when her mother took her out to collect the leaves that had fallen. They had put together a pile of them. She glanced at the ground, which was now blanketed in a dazzling array of their beautiful jewel colors, and she smiled thinking of how much her mother had loved her.

One lovely brisk afternoon, she dressed Ela and Lars to take them into town to purchase the potato starch she needed to mix with sawdust in order to bake the dark heavy bread that had become a staple; that bread was keeping them alive. Lars was irritable and difficult. He didn't want to get dressed. He wanted to play in the homemade cave that he'd built. Helen had given him and Ela an old piece of fabric that they draped over two chairs, creating a private little enclosure in the kitchen. Lars would go inside but then not allow Ela to come in. He would ask Ela questions and she had to give him the answers he wanted before he would allow her entrance. Helen had tried to intervene, telling Lars to be nice to his sister, but Ela didn't seem to mind the game. So Helen just let them play.

Helen had made a doll for Ela out of an old dishrag, and sometimes Lars would be exceptionally mean and hide the doll inside his cave. Ela would cry for her dolly. At those times, Helen thought he went too far and she would punish him.

Today, Lars was being exceptionally nasty to his sister. He was crabby and Helen hoped he wasn't coming down with some illness.

"All right, you two. Enough fighting. Let's get dressed. There is no time for this nonsense today. We have to get going. If we don't hurry, I won't be able to get the bread in the oven in time for dinner. So come on, let's get ready and leave," Helen said. Lars was still hiding under the sheet taunting Ela about something. Ela wasn't crying; she was trying to please Lars. "That's enough Lars, come out of there or I am going to take the fabric away and there will be no more cave."

Lars didn't answer her. "Ela, you go and get dressed."

"Yes, Mama," Ela said.

"Come out now, Lars." Helen was getting angry. She was in too much of a hurry to coddle him. She removed the sheet and Lars let out a piercing cry. Ignoring his protest, Helen felt Lars' forehead to see if his body temperature was hot. He felt fine.

"Be nice to your sister, Lars." Helen frowned at him. Ela was trying to dress herself, but she wasn't capable. So Helen finally got both children dressed.

The little scuffs between Lars and Ela never lasted very long. Helen smiled at them as the two children held hands walking to the market. Helen thought back to her own childhood, shaking her head. Her only sister had died of a mysterious ailment when she was eight years old and because of that, Helen had always considered herself an only child.

My sister and I used to fight all the time. Then we'd make up. Just like these two. Oh, how I wish she had lived. I would love to be able to talk to my sister now.

"Park?" Lars asked. "Me go?"

"I'm sorry, Lars. We can't stop now. We don't have the time."

"Can us go tomorrow?" Ela asked in her broken baby talk.

"Perhaps," Helen said. Although Lars and Ela were the same age, Ela's vocabulary and ability to communicate was so much better.

Maybe it's the difference between boys and girls. I've heard that girls develop faster.

Holding hands with both children, Helen went to the end of the long line in front of the general store.

CHAPTER TWENTY-SIX

She'd been waiting two hours. Her legs ached. Helen wanted to get home to put a soup on the stove for dinner. It would need time to simmer but without the potato starch there would be no bread. So she had to wait. Nik would be angry if his dinner wasn't ready when he came home from work. The women in line chatted with each other about ways to make do with less and ways to reuse old fabric. Helen didn't take part in their conversations; she just smiled at them sweetly. The people in the neighborhood liked her because she was quiet and never talked badly about anyone. They all thought she was shy, but it was more than that. In truth, she had no interest in all their trivial conversations, which were often nothing but malicious gossip. Helen had too much to hide to talk freely with strangers. Casual conversations could easily become a doorway to her secrets. Best to stay quiet.

Several children, including hers, were fascinated with the heaps of leaves on the ground. They sat surrounded by the leaves, sorting them into piles by color; arranging the gold with the gold and the amber with the amber. Helen smiled at Ela. She was so careful and meticulous, organizing each group of leaves with its like. Lars was already fighting with one of the other boys. He had grabbed a bunch of leaves that the other child was playing with and now the boy was crying.

"Lars!" Helen scolded.

"Mine!" Lars said, holding the leaves.

"I'm sorry," Helen said to the other child's mother.

The woman shrugged. "Boys. That's just the way they are. They are always fighting."

Then Ela handed the little boy who'd been fighting with Lars a bunch of her leaves. The child smiled through his tears. Then he glared at Lars, got up, and sat down next to Ela.

What a sweet child she is, Helen thought. *What a good little girl.*

When Helen finally made it to the front of the line, she looked next door in the window of the butcher shop. The butcher's glass case was almost empty. There was a chicken, but she didn't have enough rations to buy such a luxury. Meat of any kind was far too expensive for the Dobinskis.

"Do you have any potato starch?" she asked the general store owner.

"Let me look. I think I sold the last of it," he said. He was a heavy-set man with dark wavy hair and a handlebar mustache.

"I have a little left. You want it?"

"Oh yes. Thank you."

She gave the clerk a cloth bag that he filled. Then Helen took out her wallet only to find that she'd forgotten her ration cards. A chill shot through her.

"It seems that I have forgotten my ration cards. Please, can I take the potato starch and bring you the cards tomorrow?"

Helen noticed that there was a build-up of sweat on the man's brow and he looked tired from working all morning.

"I can't do that," he said. "As you can see by the line of people, I have plenty of buyers for this. I can't trust that you will come back."

"Oh please. I have been waiting in line for a very long time. I promise you I will bring the cards tomorrow."

"Promises don't count for anything. I'm sorry," he said, then turned to the line. "Who's next?"

Helen felt tears forming behind her eyes, a single one slid down her cheek. She must have squeezed Ela's hand without realizing it because

Ela looked up. "Mommy, are you crying?"

"No." Helen tried to smile at the children. Lars stopped what he was doing and looked at his mother with a worried expression. "No, please don't worry, children. I'm just fine."

But she wasn't fine. If he didn't give her the potato starch there would be nothing to eat for dinner.

"Please …" She begged the grocer again, her voice cracking. "Please. I have known you for years. You can trust me. I have been shopping here for as long as I can remember. I promise you I will bring the cards."

The other women surrounding her stood with their mouths agape. They knew what Helen must be feeling because the situation could easily happen to any of them.

"Please move along now, Pani Dobinski. I have other customers to take care of before I can close for the day," the store owner said in a firm voice. But then he added sympathetically, "If I start to extend credit to one customer, everyone will be asking me. I can't do that. I wish I could help you. But I have a business to run and a family of my own to think of."

Helen nodded. What could she do? Her shoulders slumped in defeat. There would be nothing to eat tonight. Nik had finished everything that Rolf had given her. Oh dear God, what am I going to do?

"Come on, children," Helen said, taking their hands and turning towards the door.

"Helen Dobinski?" A man stopped her by touching her arm.

"Yes, I am Helen Dobinski." She recognized his face but could not place him. "Do I know you?"

"We met once. You probably forgot."

She looked at him. Then it dawned on her. He was the handsome man she that she'd seen when she and Nik had attended the underground meeting with Artur and Marci. How did this man know her name? She'd never been introduced to him. She was sure she'd never spoken to him before.

"I'm Eryk. Eryk Jaworski. You might not remember me but I remember you," he smiled.

"Where? Where did we meet?" She did remember him, but she wanted to see what he said.

"I can't recall right now …"

"I see," she said.

Of course, he is not going to mention the secret meeting. How stupid of me to think he would discuss something like that here in the middle of the shop with all these people around.

"Who that man?" Ela asked.

"An old friend." Helen smiled down at Ela.

"Are you having problems here with the shop owner?" Eryk asked Helen.

Helen nodded. "Yes, but it's not his fault. It's mine. I forgot my ration cards."

"Let me talk to him. Let me see if I can help. You go on outside," Eryk said. His voice was kind but strong and commanding.

"I would appreciate anything you could do," she said.

Helen took the children's hands and went through the door to wait out on the sidewalk.

A few minutes later, Eryk came out carrying the sack of potato starch. "I believe this is what you wanted." He handed it to Helen.

"Oh thank you so much, Pan Jaworski. I can't tell you how much this means to me. I will bring my ration cards to the store owner tomorrow."

"No need. I took care of it. I had a few extra cards."

No one has extra rations, Helen thought.

"And please," he smiled. "Call me Eryk.

His hair was dark brown, but in the sunlight there was a deep auburn cast to it that reminded Helen of a beautiful horse she'd once seen in a photograph. Eryk's eyes were the color of amber—deep, rich, and mysterious, like an old gemstone that had survived many lifetimes.

"Thank you again," she stammered. "I don't know what to say."

"You thanked me. That's enough."

Helen smiled at Eryk. He smiled back, waved at the children then turned and walked away.

CHAPTER TWENTY-SEVEN

November 1942

Helen thought it strange that with all the girls in Poland, Rolf still had not grown tired of their twice-weekly meetings. She wished he would find a new girl that struck his fancy, a new challenge to conquer. Her mother had always warned her that almost all men had a roving eye. "It's your job as a wife to keep your husband's interest. You must watch him closely, Helen. Men can't help themselves. They are just made that way," her mother had said to her on the night of her wedding. That motherly advice had seemed so important then, but now it was worthless to her. All she could hope for was that Rolf was like the men her mother had told her about.

If only he was always looking for someone else. If only his eyes strayed to another woman and he lost interest in her, but so far she couldn't get rid of him. And the more invested he became in the relationship, the more difficult he was. It had gotten so bad that she had to watch every word she said to him, lest she spark his anger.

In September, Rolf said that his father had called to tell him that his mother had fallen ill. As the time passed, his mother did not improve. In fact, she was getting worse. Several months went by and it was now late February. One night, Rolf told Helen that his father had sent him a telegram to tell him that he was afraid that his mother might not recover. "My mother might die," Rolf said, his voice filled with disbelief.

Helen didn't know how to answer, so she just rubbed his shoulders in response. He looked as if he might cry.

"I immediately sought a pretext for a series of meetings which would require my presence in Berlin. I am going home to be with her," he said.

She was careful to hide her enthusiasm at having him go away. He said he hoped to return in a week, but it might be longer.

And she thought *let it be a year or, God willing, forever.*

"Don't come back here to my apartment until I contact you. When I return from Germany I will send you a message," Rolf said as Helen was getting ready to leave his apartment. "Here, take these cans of sardines," he added.

She nodded. "Thank you." Then she patted his hand. "I wish your mother well."

He nodded then turned away from her. Helen was sure he was crying. He did not look back at her. Instead, he walked to the window while she let herself out of his flat.

Helen's steps were as light as a feather as she walked home. She hated to think that her happiness was derived from the suffering of another person, as Helen would never wish anyone ill. But she couldn't help but feel blessed that Rolf was going away. She would not have to put up with him for a while and the very thought made her giddy.

In fact, Helen felt so good that she decided to bake a cake. Several months earlier, Rolf had given her a bag of sugar and a bag of flour, which she had saved for a special occasion. Real sugar and real flour were so hard to come by; she felt so blessed to have them.

Both children had turned five that year and she had not been able to do anything for them. Perhaps she would tell them that the cake was a way of celebrating both of their birthdays. Helen couldn't help but think of Zofia. Poor Zofia, she'd missed so many of Ela's first moments. Helen had the joy of watching Lars and Ela grow up together. Both children babbled in the beginning, but it was rather strange that Lars' first word was 'Dada' but Ela's was 'Mama.' That fact had torn at Helen's heart. When Ela said "I love you, Mama" she was reaching for Helen, but Helen was thinking of Zofia, who had never even heard her daughter speak in complete sentences. She had probably heard Ela babble, but the child had been so young when she'd been separated from Zofia. Helen's heart hurt for Zofia. She imaged how much it would have touched Zofia's heart to hear her daughter say I love you and to feel her child's little arms around her. .

CHAPTER TWENTY-EIGHT

Rolf caught a ride from Warsaw to Berlin with a group of soldiers. Once there, he caught a local train that would take him back home to the little town where he had grown from a small boy, with dreams of being someone important, to the often confused and sometimes tortured man he was today.

The train rumbled along the tracks as it headed southeast, out of the congested Berlin streets and into the lush green countryside. Rolf was on his way to Werder an der Havel, adjacent to Potsdam, where his family owned apple orchards. The lavish rolling hills were covered with emerald grasses and wildflowers. It had been several years since Rolf had returned to his home. In fact, his last visit to Werder on the Havel River had been before the Party had sent him to work in Poland. He looked out the window and felt a sort of peace come over him. It had been so long since he'd felt so calm. Sweet memories of his childhood began drifting back to him. He was an only child, adored by both of his parents. His father, a decorated veteran of the Great War, had been so proud when his son—his pride and joy—had joined the Nazi Party. His father was a strong advocate of the Third Reich and a patriotic German who wanted what was best for the land he loved. He had told everyone that would listen how much he believed in Hitler. "Hitler will elevate Germany to her rightful status," his father always said. Rolf wondered what his parents would think if they knew what he was doing now in the ghetto in Warsaw.

In the beginning, Rolf's career had shown so much promise, but now it seemed he'd been reduced to policing Poles, imprisoning Jews and then, of course, there was Helen. "Shameful," is what his father would say.

"Rolf, we didn't raise you to be a man with no morals. You weren't taught to behave like a common brute. We always gave you the best of everything. We taught you to be a gentleman, to be refined. How could you turn out to be such a man as this?" That's what his father would say if he knew the truth. Of course, Rolf could always answer that, in order to preserve the greatness of the fatherland, the inferiors must be dealt with. It was a necessary part of the rebuilding of Germany. Rolf could make a strong argument that he was doing important work. The Party would agree with him, but he knew his father would not. So rather than explain, he would simply not discuss his job with his parents. Instead, he would walk into the house in his starched black uniform, looking impressive with his shiny black boots, and speak of how successful the Party was in bringing the fatherland back to the greatness it deserved. The last thing Rolf ever wanted was to lose his father's respect.

When he thought about his mother being very sick, maybe even dying, he was frightened. He couldn't admit such a weakness to anyone, but he was like a terrified child. She had always been his biggest supporter. When he brought home his school work, she'd always been the one to encourage him in every way. She told him how smart he was, how much she believed in him. She'd laugh at his jokes and listen to his problems. Even if he didn't see her as often as he wanted to after moving to Warsaw, he needed to know that she was still there somewhere in the background supporting his every effort. The very idea that one day she might not be there left him feeling lost.

As a child, Rolf was a good student but far from a genius. He needed to study hard in order to make his grades. Yet no matter how busy she was, his mother always made time to help him as much as she could with his school work. She was not an educated woman, but she would always stop whatever she was doing and sit down and listen as he read over his homework. Once he'd finished, she would tell him how wonderful he was and encourage him in all of his ambitions. Although he had to work hard to achieve any success in academics,

Rolf had always been athletic. He was not a great athlete, but a good athlete. Good enough to be chosen for teams in the Hitler Jugend. However, even in the sports arena, he fell just a little short. He was never quite a star. But he was outgoing and friendly, making him popular with the other boys.

Then the time came and he joined the army and was faced with several opportunities to prove his bravery. Finally, he had found his niche. Finally, he had found a way to shine. It was in the SS that Rolf came into manhood. Rolf grew tall and lean; he had blond hair, a strong chin, and his superior officers liked him. They recognized his Aryan good looks and his fearless devotion to the Party. More importantly, Rolf excelled during his training and showed an aptitude for future leadership. His superiors were impressed, and so he'd been offered a position of authority in Poland. He'd taken the promotion because it gave him power over others, and power felt good. It made Rolf feel important. At the time when he accepted the work, he had no idea how brutal the job would be.

Rolf watched as they passed a field of orchards, and in his mind's eye he saw his mother and remembered how beautiful she'd been when she was young. Many spring and summer days, she would pack a lunch for the two of them then take him by the hand and they would walk together out amongst the apple trees. He could see her hair blowing in the wind, her eyes smiling as they spread out the blanket where they would sit. How was it possible that although he'd only been six or seven years old, he could remember so many details? Even now, if he closed his eyes, he could hear her laughter. He could still taste the sweet doughy bread she'd baked and savor the tart apple juice that made his lips pucker as it ran down his chin. As a child, he had thought his mother was the most beautiful woman in the world.

The train jerked to a stop, jolting Rolf back into the present moment. Rolf pulled his suitcase down from the overhead rack and climbed the stairs out of the train car.

His legs were stiff from sitting for such a long time. He set his valise on the ground and stretched his arms and his back and then he picked his suitcase back up and headed across the bridge into the peaceful, picturesque little village where he had lived as an idealistic little boy.

It was as if time had stood still in Werder an der Havel. Except for the airfield in the north of the city and the Nazi flags hung around the town, there was little evidence that Germany was at war. Yes, it was true that several of Rolf's friends and classmates had been lost at the front but, unlike Berlin, the buildings had not been bombed and the little shops still operated as they had when Rolf was a child. Of course, all of the Jews were gone. They'd been rounded up and taken away, their homes and property distributed. But this was a subject best avoided and so no one ever really addressed it.

It was a mile from the train station to the Boltz home. As he walked down the dirt road, he saw the villagers turning to look at him. The young girls stared at him with admiration in their eyes. Rolf looked around.

Is she here?

He felt his heart skip a beat.

"Anne-Marie Hofmann," he whispered to himself. It had been a long time since he'd said her name aloud.

I know why I was attracted to Helen from the first time I saw her. She has that same helpless, lost look about her as my Annie. The same shy blue eyes and slim build. Maybe they are both a little too skinny. My mother used to say that a strong wind would knock Anne-Marie across the street. Mama never liked her but oh Anne-Marie! When she looked at me with those eyes I felt like I wanted to be the strongest man in the world. I wanted to hold her in my arms and protect her from anyone or anything that might harm her.

He was a teenage boy when they first met. She turned his head the first time he saw her. Her bone structure was so delicate and when she walked into the room his heart fluttered. How he'd wanted her to be his girlfriend and then later his wife and the mother of his children, but it hadn't worked out that way at all. She had not been attracted to him. Anne-Marie had fallen for a Jew, a studious intellect with a thick mane of black hair and the athletic abilities of a turtle. But it didn't matter to her. She'd gotten herself all wrapped up with that Jew and they had run away and gotten married. Then to make matters worse, she'd left Germany with him. Anne-Marie … Rolf knew that his love for her had weakened him. His longing for her had broken his heart and made him less of a man in his own eyes. His relationship with Anne-Marie had hurt him so deeply that when she left Germany with the Jew he swore to himself that he would never let any woman under his skin like that again. Never. Then, damn fate, along came Helen.

A few months earlier he'd had to go to the Łódź ghetto, the second largest in Poland, for a meeting. It was there that he ran into an old friend he'd known who had also grown up in Werder an der Havel. They went out for a few beers. When Rolf was drunk he asked his friend if he'd heard anything about Anne-Marie. "Yes," the old friend said. "I heard that Anne-Marie returned to her father's farm … alone … without that Jew of a husband."

"Really?" Rolf said, hardly able to contain his excitement.

"So I hear. But what decent man would have her now that she's laid with a Jew? She's dirty, damaged, spoiled."

Rolf lost control of himself, perhaps it was the alcohol, but he started punching his old friend and didn't stop until a local policeman pulled him off and sent him home to sober up.

Had Anne-Marie really returned to the little town where they both grew up? Was it possible that she was divorced, single, and available again?

Will I see her by accident while I am here?" he thought as he looked around at the people walking in the streets for her lovely familiar face.

I wonder if she is sometimes sorry for what she did to me? For how she ruined things that might have been between us? Well, the truth is that I am too good for her now.

But still, every time I got another promotion I wanted her to know about it. I wanted her to regret what she did, what she lost, what she could have had if she had chosen me rather than that subhuman thing she married.

I do hope I run into her. I would love to see the look on her face when she sees me. My uniform is quite impressive. I don't know how I am going to arrange it, but I do hope that somehow I can find a way to see her so I can show her how far I have come from the boy I was when I left this village.

I love my father. I love the orchards, but I am not just the son of a farmer anymore. I have risen to a new station in life.

I am Hauptsurmfuhrer Boltz, and I am a man of power.

The very lives of many people depend on my mood. It is me that the Jews must answer to in the Warsaw Ghetto. It is I who decide if they live and how they live. I can give food or take it away. Anne-Marie must already have heard that the Führer declared that we must put Poland in order. This is an important aspect of building our thousand year Reich.

Yes, I must see her. I must!!!

Maybe if I can make it clear to her that she has made a terrible error, I will be at peace. It's time she felt my pain. I would love to let her know that she could have been at my side in the upper echelons of the Nazi Party had she not been such a damn fool.

CHAPTER TWENTY-NINE

There it stood. Rolf felt a slight pain in his heart as he looked across the road at the solid low farmhouse with its red, shingled roof. The building appeared so much smaller than he remembered. It was there, within those rooms, that he'd enjoyed his idyllic childhood, sheltered by parents who believed he could be anything he wanted to be when he grew up. Rolf smiled a wry smile. From his appearance, anyone would think he was accomplished. His parents would see how proud he looked in his uniform and they would think so, too. But of course, they could only see what was on the outside.

For as long as Rolf could remember, his father had whitewashed the window shutters every spring. But as he got closer, he could see that the paint was now peeling.

It must be difficult for Father to get up on a ladder and paint. After all, he is getting up in years. Perhaps, if the weather holds, I will do it for him while I am here. Time permitting, of course.

As he got to the door, Rolf shivered. He was nervous. He couldn't be sure what awaited him inside. He was afraid to see his mother suffering and, until now, he'd tried to deny what was happening. Even as he stood there in the doorway, something in Rolf's mind would not allow him to accept that this might be the last time he would ever see his mother alive. The flower garden in the window box under the large picture window in the front of the house was empty. If his mother had been healthy it would have been ablaze with color when the spring came. And it made him sad to know that she would not be planting flowers this year. How his mother had loved that little garden. As far back as Rolf could remember, she'd nursed it every day of her life; the memory made him sad. His heart was heavy as he turned his old rusty key in the lock. The maple wood door creaked open.

"Herr Boltz." The housekeeper met him at the door and took him into her embrace. Her large flabby arms comforted him the same way that they had when he was a child.

"Your Mutti is in her room."

"Thank you, Ida," Rolf said. He'd known Ida for his entire life, and the memories of her caring for his family made him feel melancholy. She had aged. Her hair was gray. The years had etched lines into her full, kind face. He had never realized that Ida, too, would age. Because he'd known her all of his life he expected her to be the same as she was when he left.

How silly of me. Of course, she is older; we are all older. The years are passing so quickly.

He was a man now, wasn't he? Why did he feel like a child as soon as he walked through the door to his home? What was it about this place that filled him with such shame for the man he'd become? Ida smiled at him and took his hat. The wrinkles around Ida's eyes were a frightening reminder of the mortality of everyone that he loved. But Ida's smile hadn't changed; it was still warm and kind. Her once-rounded figure was now very fat, but when Rolf looked at her he still saw her like she was when he was a young boy. He'd had a secret crush on her then. No one ever knew. The thought brought a heart-rending smile to his face.

Rolf walked into his mother's room.

"Mama …"

His voice was soft as Rolf sat beside his mother's bed. She didn't look good. Her face was drained of color and her skin was shiny and waxy. Thin, stringy hair stuck to her head with sweat.

"Rolf" she managed to smile as she reached for his hand.

"You came home."

"Yes, I am here …" His heart ached. He wanted more than anything to believe that by some miracle she would recover. But once he actually saw her, he knew deep in his soul that she was dying. It could be a matter of days or hours, but his greatest fears were being realized. His mother was leaving him. The love that he'd had for her as a little boy now encompassed his entire mind and body. He was, in essence, that child again. Rolf raised his mother's cold hand to his lips and tears ran down his face.

"Don't cry," she whispered. He could see that it took effort for her, but she reached up and cupped his cheek.

Her labored breathing assured him that it was hard for her to find the strength to speak. Rolf wanted to scream and cry out in desperation. His heart yearned to pray to a God he'd abandoned long ago.

Why is there nothing I can do? Nothing to stop this … I can't lose my mother … I can't…

"Rolf." His mother's voice sounded otherworldly as she spoke his name.

"Yes."

"I am dying. I want you to promise me something. Will you?"

"You're not going to die … you can't die."

"Promise me …"

"Yes, anything, Mama, anything."

"I have given this matter a lot of thought, Rolf, and I don't have the energy to speak a lot of words. So I will get right to the point. I want you to marry Ivonne Bauer. I am sure that you must remember her?"

"I do remember her."

"You need a wife, Rolf. You are all alone in Poland with no family. I worry about you. A man shouldn't be alone like that, it will get you into trouble."

"I'm all right, Mama."

"Of course you are, but you must remember that a mother knows her own child. I know you. You grew inside my body. We will always be attached because of that. I was the one, Rolf, who dried your tears. You may not tell me everything, but I can hear your thoughts … I can feel your pain. No matter how old you are, you will always be my child. And … I know the truth. I realize that you don't want to admit it, but you still love Anne-Marie."

He looked away. Unable to deny the reality of her assertion, he stayed silent. She squeezed his hand and he turned back to look at her.

"I heard Anne has returned back home to her father's house. Is she here in Germany alone or is her husband here with her?" he asked.

"Her husband was a Jew. I don't know what happened to him. No one knows. But from what I've heard, she is living with her parents without her husband. She is here alone."

Rolf's eyes lit up, he felt a flock of wild butterflies take flight in his stomach.

So it is true. Anne-Marie IS here and she is not with her husband. Perhaps they are divorced. Maybe he's dead. Maybe I have a chance ...

"Rolf," his mother squeezed his hand again in order to get his attention. "Anne-Marie would not make you a good wife. She doesn't share our love of our fatherland. Even as a child, Anne-Marie was rebellious. She was trouble then and I would bet she is still trouble now. Besides all of that, she is tainted; she married a Jew. She is soiled. If your superiors ever found out it would ruin your chances of rising in the Party. Rolf, you deserve to be a success in your career."

She stopped for a minute to catch her breath, then she continued speaking. He could see how important it all was to her by the conviction in her eyes.

"You are a good boy, you should have a good wife. One who will take care of you at home and help you to be promoted in your career. You only want Anne because she spurned you. But if you had her you would find that she is not for you. I don't want her for you. Mark my words, Rolf. If you were married to her you would never be happy."

He sighed and shook his head. "Oh Mama, if this is what you want …"

She nodded her head. "It is what I want."

"Only, please don't die …" Rolf choked on the tears that were closing his throat.

"Ivonne is a nice German girl. She is the right girl for you. I trust her. She will take my place in caring for you when I am gone. You do know that she has always loved you?"

"Yes, I know." He hung his head.

"But you don't love her. I know that. But you must forget Anne-Marie, Rolf. She is no good. Let her go. Promise me you'll marry Ivonne. Once you and Ivonne are married and you are happy, you won't even give Anne another thought." His mother's voice was desperate.

Ivonne. She is second best. Not my first choice at all.

Poor Ivonne. He'd always considered her a good friend but had never had any romantic interest in her.

"Yes, Mama. If it's what you want me to do, then I'll do it. Anything you want. I promise you, I will propose to Ivonne …"

"You've always been such a wonderful child." She smiled, but her eyes were growing even more glassy and her breath even more shallow. "I'm tired now, let me get some rest."

"Yes, you rest Mama."

The funeral for Rolf's mother took place on a gloomy morning in early March. His mother was laid to rest in the family plot on the north side of the orchard. She would spend eternity beside her parents and once spring arrived, her coffin would lie beneath a luxuriant emerald grassy field strewn with wildflowers.

Rolf stood at the grave site looking regal in his black SS uniform. The neighbors gathered around the family and offered their condolences but Rolf was too distraught to talk to anyone. Ivonne walked over to him, followed by her family. They extended their sympathy but Rolf just nodded. He couldn't bear to carry on a conversation with anyone. His throat was raw with held-back tears. Once the funeral ended he longed to be away from people. He wanted to go to his childhood bedroom and lie down so he could be alone in his grief and weep without worrying about shaming his uniform.

How can the apple trees still stand? How can the birds still sing? How can all of this be when I have lost my greatest supporter, my best friend, my Mama?

Rolf watched as the black coffin was lowered into the ground.

CHAPTER THIRTY

The sun rose and set three times, and still Rolf didn't want to see anyone. He was hiding in his room, refusing food and companionship. He wouldn't even speak to his father or Ida. But even as he lay there alone in the dark, Rolf knew that he must keep his promise to his mother. Every time he fell asleep, he saw his mother's face in his dreams. She would speak to him in a gentle voice and remind him of his vow.

Finally, on the fourth day after the funeral, Rolf got out of bed and without bathing or even washing his face, he put on his uniform.

Ivonne Bauer lived two farms to the west of their orchards. When Rolf was growing up, he'd been to many parties at the Bauer farm. Now he was on his way there to see Ivonne and fulfill his mother's deathbed wish. If only things had worked out differently with Anne-Marie.

I wish she had been the one who loved me and not Ivonne. How much better I would feel if it were Anne my dear mother had chosen! If only ... if only ... by some miracle ... Anne and I were going to be married. But that is no longer possible, not even if Anne were willing. My mother wanted me to marry Ivonne. I promised and so if Ivonne will have me I will marry her.

When he arrived at the Bauer farm, Ivonne's younger sister Heddy answered the door. She was in her early teens and it was obvious to him that she was in awe of the way he looked in his uniform. In fact, the poor girl was so taken with him that she tripped on the rug as she was running towards the stairs to call her sister.

"Sit down, please," Heddy said, turning on the top stair to look down at him. Then she giggled and disappeared quickly into one of the bedrooms.

He smiled and was flattered. After taking a deep breath, Rolf took a seat on the sofa and waited. He was not expected. So he knew Ivonne would be surprised to hear that he was at her home. He wondered how long it would take her to get ready to see him. Rolf hoped she would hurry. And much to his delight, she was quick. Ivonne came down the stairs within a few minutes, still straightening the braids she'd plaited into her brown hair.

"Rolf, what a nice surprise! I am so glad you came over to see me." She sat down on the other side of the sofa. "I am sorry about your mother," Ivonne said, her eyes warm and sincere.

He nodded, "Yes, I am too."

"You were close to her, I know."

"I was, yes."

"Can I get you something to eat or drink?" she asked, getting up to walk towards the kitchen.

"No, nothing, thank you," he smiled. "But if you have a few free minutes I would like to speak to you."

"Yes, of course." She sat down on a chair facing him. Ivonne smiled but her lips were quivering and she was twisting the material of her dress between her fingers.

"We've known each other for many years," he said, then cleared his throat.

Ivonne leaned forward. "Yes, we have. We have been friends since we were young children."

"You have always been a good friend to me …"

She smiled and with the back of her hand she wiped a bead of sweat that had formed at her temple.

"I'm not really sure how to ask you this …" He looked down at his boots. There was a pregnant silence. Then he began. "I am serving the Reich in Poland … and well … sometimes I get lonely."

"Go on …" she stammered.

He could see the hope light up in her eyes and for a moment, he felt sorry for her. Rolf knew that in his heart Ivonne would never be the prize Anne-Marie would have been. Every wife should be her husband's first choice, the queen of her husband's heart.

"I have come here to ask you if you would like to marry me?"

"Oh," she said. Then a joyous laugh sprung from her throat. "Oh, Rolf … really? Really? Yes, my answer is yes."

He got up and walked over to where she was sitting. She stood. He could see that her knees were shaking and her body was trembling. Tears rolled from her eyes and her face glowed. There was no doubt in his mind that he'd made her very happy but Rolf felt awkward. This was his mother's wish. Not his. Still, he took her in his arms. She sighed. He felt a little sick knowing that he would probably never love her the way she loved him. But his mother always had his best interest at heart. She'd always known what was best for him. And so he gently pulled Ivonne to him, close enough to where her breast was against his chest. Then trying to obliterate all doubt from his mind, he kissed her.

"We are officially engaged then?" he asked, clearing his throat. His voice was emotionless, his movements awkward. When he heard himself speak, he cringed inside. It sounded more like a business deal than a proposal.

Perhaps I am speaking a little too abruptly.

"Yes …" She nodded. "Yes, we are engaged." She was laughing and crying and hugging him. If only he felt the same way.

"I don't have time for you to make arrangements for a big wedding. I was thinking of a civil ceremony within the next two weeks. You see, I must return to Poland. I have a very important job. You can take a few weeks to put your affairs in order. Then you will join me in Warsaw?"

"Of course, I will. I will be your wife. I'll go anywhere you want me to go."

Perhaps my mother was right. Ivonne is a good girl. She is not the type to cause me trouble. And she will do whatever is necessary to further my career. It is more than obvious to me that Ivonne loves me. I can see it in her eyes. Maybe this is what I need after all.

CHAPTER THIRTY-ONE

The next two weeks flew by at an alarming rate of speed. Even though the ceremony was to be small, Rolf and Ivonne were busy with wedding plans. And although Rolf had never thought of Ivonne as a beautiful woman, the excitement of their wedding brought a glow to her face that gave him a glimpse of a certain sort loveliness in her that he'd never noticed before. The Bauers were very pleased about the match that Ivonne had made, and they overspent in order to make the wedding as memorable as they possibly could. They had invited all of their friends and relatives to the farm for a celebration dinner. Mrs. Bauer told all of her friends how proud she and her husband were of their daughter's betrothed.

"He is not only handsome, but he is very patriotic and holds an important job serving his country. What else could a family ask for?" Mrs. Bauer said to anyone who would listen.

It made Rolf feel good and important to be discussed in such a manner. Everyone in his hometown treated him with the utmost respect.

"You are such a rising star," Ivonne's mother told Rolf as she cupped her future son-in-law's cheek. "We are so fortunate that Ivonne has made such a good match."

Rolf just smiled.

"We are proud and honored to have you as a part of our family, son," Herr Bauer said. "I've known you all of your life and I must say, you are the perfect man for my daughter."

Again, Rolf just smiled. He would have been the happiest man in the world if all of this had been happening just as it was, but with Anne-Marie as his future wife, instead of Ivonne.

Ivonne's mother cleaned and pressed the dress she'd worn for her own wedding for her daughter to wear. It was a traditional German folk dress, white with a full dirndl skirt. Her father brought his own dark blue Sunday suit out of the back of his closet to wear for the occasion. Heddy and Frau Bauer planned to wear the best dresses they owned. Frau Bauer, Heddy and all of Ivonne's aunts were busy racing about the kitchen preparing a feast for the guests. Everyone in town was talking about the wedding. However, although Anne-Marie, Rolf, and Ivonne had been friends since they were children, neither Anne-Marie nor anyone in her family was to be invited. Although the subject of Anne-Marie was never discussed, Ivonne knew Rolf's feelings for Anne and she wanted to be sure that he did not see her, lest he change his mind about the marriage. If anyone asked why Anne-Marie and her family were not invited, Ivonne would simply tell them that it was because Anne-Marie had been married to a Jew. That would be enough of a reason. It was against the Nuremberg laws. Anne-Marie had made herself an outcast. Everyone would accept that. No one need know the real threat that Anne posed to Ivonne's future happiness.

Over the weeks of planning the wedding, Rolf and Ivonne grew closer. Rolf had to admit that his feelings for Ivonne still lacked the wild passionate romantic desire that he had felt when he looked at Anne, but at least his friendship with his future wife was growing stronger. Rolf and Ivonne took long walks through the apple orchards where they talked about everything, from their affection for dogs to their love for Germany. The snow crunched under their feet and their breath came out white against the cold air. Rolf held Ivonne's hand. When she looked into his eyes and she smiled up at him he could clearly see how much she loved him. They both agreed that they were optimistic about Hitler's leadership in Germany and his promise for a thousand year Reich. On a couple of the nights during Rolf's visit, he and Ivonne went to the local pub where they shared the enjoyment of a good dark beer and some good bratwurst. Ivonne sat close to her true love and they talked in whispers. They laughed about funny stories of things they'd shared in the past, always careful not to mention Anne-Marie. On one such evening, after they'd both had several beers, Ivonne turned to Rolf.

"Do you want to have children?" she asked, already knowing that he must. It was what the party required of him.

"Of course, as soon as possible. Don't you?"

"Yes, I want to be the mother of your children more than anything in the world, Rolf. I always have."

He smiled at her and patted her hand. Sometimes the love in her eyes made him uncomfortable.

"Well then ... it certainly is a good thing that we are creating a better world for our children. They won't have to worry about being conned by Jews or Roma. And once we weed out the homosexuals, and the physically and mentally ill, then there will be less of a chance of the race ever becoming mottled with filth again."

"What is it like in Poland?"

"The Poles want their freedom, they are trying to fight the Reich. They don't have a chance. But once this is over and they are fully conquered, they will know their place and serve their Aryan masters."

"They are fighting? Are you in danger?" She squeezed his hand.

"No. Please don't worry. The Poles just cause mischief, nothing to concern yourself about."

"Hitler is building a good world for us, Rolf, and I am so proud that you are going to be my husband and you are a part of the creation of the new Germany."

"Yes, our Fuhrer is good to us. We will live to see a world where Germany has taken her rightful place as the most powerful nation."

A few evenings later, Ivonne went to the cellar to see if she could find a jar of apple preserves to share with Rolf. It was very cold as she walked down the stairs to the cellar. She pulled her shawl tighter around her body. In her hand she carried a candle. Ivonne thought she heard a noise as she got to the bottom of the stairs. She looked around her and saw a young boy. He couldn't have been more than ten.

"Who are you? What are you doing here?"

His clothing was torn and he was filthy. His dark hair hung long almost to his shoulders. Shaking from fear and the cold, he watched her.

"You're a Jew aren't you, hiding in my cellar, eating our food?" Ivonne asked.

The boy hugged the wall. His breath came white from the cold against the darkness.

"Please, let me go," the child said.

"Where are your parents?"

"Dead. Murdered. I saw it all. They were killed by Nazis."

"Why?"

"Because they were Jews. Just like I will be killed if you turn me in. Please, I am begging you, let me go."

Ivonne thought about telling Rolf about the boy. It was the right thing to do. But who knows what kind of red tape would be involved with the arrest? Would Rolf making an arrest interfere with the wedding? Ivonne studied the child. A pang of pity shot through her.

What difference does the life of one ten-year-old Jewish boy make to anyone? I will tell the child to go, to get out of here tonight. If he is gone by morning I will never mention what I have seen in this cellar tonight to anyone.

After Ivonne warned the child that he must leave as quickly as possible, she took a jar of preserves off the shelf. Then she turned to the child again. "Don't take any food from here, or I will tell on you and have you hunted down. Do you understand?"

The boy's big black eyes looked massive in the dark. "Yes, yes, I understand. I will not take anything, thank you, thank you."

Ivonne went back to the house carrying the jam. She put two slices of bread and a knife on the table. Then she called Rolf into her parent's kitchen to join her. Everyone else was asleep. Rolf sat down at the table beside her. She took a spoon and fed him some of the sweet apples.

"Not as good as fresh," he smiled.

"It never is, is it?" she laughed. As she sat across from Rolf, she thought of the boy in the cellar.

Did I make the right choice? Well, no matter, I can't change it now. I am here with Rolf. Let him be happy and thinking about our future, not thinking about his work. And I know that child will be gone from our lives by morning.

She looked into Rolf's eyes and said, "Remember when we children, a whole bunch of us, would come back after our Hitler youth program to your parents' orchards and eat apples until we got stomach aches? They tried to keep the boys and girls separate, but we had our secret plans to meet after the group meetings were over."

"Of course I remember. You were in the Bund Deutscher Madels." He took another spoonful of the jam and put it into his mouth.

Ivonne squeezed his shoulder. Rolf touched her cheek but he thinking about Anne-Marie. When they were growing up Anne-Marie had been in the BDM, too. He remembered thinking how pretty Anne-Marie was in her uniform with her dark skirt and white blouse, her golden curls caressing her lovely face.

Damn Anne-Marie! When had she gotten so stupid as to allow a Jew into her life? What was she thinking getting involved with a Jew?

He knew the answer. Everyone knew the answer. The Jew was supposed to be brilliant. He was an excellent student. Anne-Marie was impressed, sucked into falling in love with him because of his mind.

Well, for certain it couldn't have been his looks. He was nothing to look at. Skinny, curly black hair, big nose. Typical ugly Jew. I outshone him in every way.

He was no athlete. The only thing about him was that—everyone had to agree—he was so damn smart. And that right there is exactly what Goebbels has been warning us about. These Jews are smart and they use their brains to manipulate us pure and good Aryans. Anne just couldn't see how devious he was. I know that Jews can't be trusted. And I also know that the Jew bastard tricked Anne-Marie into marrying him. I am convinced of it.

"You wanted to fly planes," Ivonne said, jolting him back to the present time.

"Yes, I did," he answered, shaking his head, trying to stop sickening thoughts from invading his mind. If he let his mind drift he could see visions of Anne having sex with that Jew.

"Did you ever fly?"

"No. I decided my career prospects were better in the SS than in the Luftwaffe."

"Were you sad?"

"No. I don't care about it anymore. It was nothing but a childhood dream."

"Well, you have certainly proved to everyone that you are a success, Rolf."

"Have I?"

"Oh yes. I am so proud to be marrying you."

He looked into her eyes and saw pure admiration there.

Who am I? I spend my days in that filthy ghetto. I spend my nights doing whatever it is that I do with Helen. Am I someone to be proud of? I don't know.

He knew that he could tell her about the Warsaw ghetto and his work there. There was no doubt in his mind that she would understand and even still admire him. She wouldn't doubt the importance of his work. She would never question whether what he was doing was right or wrong. She was like him in that she stood behind the Fatherland no matter what. But Rolf didn't want to tell her much about his job. At least not right now. Why spoil their moments together with the discussion of starvation, disease, and filthy Jews? As much as possible, he was enjoying his time with Ivonne. And although he still longed for Anne-Marie, for the first time in many years, he was content, if not truly happy.

Is it Anne-Marie I really want? Could I ever really be happy with such a woman? Or is it just that I want Anne-Marie to realize the mistake she made by choosing that piece of dirt swine of a Jew instead of me? Maybe all I really want is for her to come crawling to me, begging me …

Again Ivonne spoke, shaking him back to the present. "Did you know that I wanted to be a movie actress?"

"I knew. You told all of us at one of our picnics."

"I didn't think you would remember."

He laughed. "Of course I remember. You used to entertain all of us. You would tell jokes and make us laugh until our faces hurt."

She laughed a little. "Yes, I did."

"My mother used to like to watch you when you came to parties at our house."

"Did she really?" Ivonne's voice grew serious. "I'm sorry about your mother, Rolf. I know how close you were to her."

"Yes, my mother was always there for me. I will miss her."

"I'm glad you came back home … and I'm really glad you proposed to me." She cleared her throat. She was choked up with emotion. Looking up into his eyes she added, "I don't know if I should ask you this, but was it your mother? Was it your mother that wanted you to marry me? Or was it your choice?"

He hesitated. "My mother did want me to marry you. She always liked you. Does that change anything?"

"No. Not for me. I will be happy to be your wife on any terms, Rolf." There were a few seconds of silence. Ivonne did not look in his eyes; instead, she looked down at her hands that were on the table, twisting the tablecloth.

"I am not going to ask you if you love me, Rolf. I don't want to know. But what I do know is that I love you. And I promise that I will be a good wife to you. I will give you plenty of children for the fatherland. I will be a good German mother."

"I know this. And I want you to know that I care for you, Ivonne. You and I have been friends for as long as I can remember. We may not share the kind of love that little girls read about in fairy tales, but we do share the same ideals and you have always been my good friend. As time is passing, I am feeling that you are becoming my best friend."

"I can be happy with that," she said.

He smiled and thought *I think I can too.*

CHAPTER THIRTY-TWO

The wedding was charming. Ivonne's light brown hair was braided then wrapped around her head in the old-fashioned traditional German style. Her mother had intertwined tiny sprigs of white baby's breath into each of the braids. It didn't matter to Herr. Bauer or his wife, that they were draining their life savings for the wedding. They were so proud of Ivonne that they wanted everything to be perfect. On the glowing recommendations of friends and family, they hired a band that played everything from German folk music to Wagner. However, even though the band was expensive, the musicians were not always on key. In fact, they were obviously local musicians who had another job by day. Their performance was amateurish and mediocre at best. But they looked purely Aryan in their traditional German folk costumes, so it didn't matter. With Rolf's help, the Bauers stocked the bar, and most of the guests were drinking heavily. A crowded dance floor, more food than they had seen in years, and occasional explosions of laughter were enough to satisfy the Bauers. Herr Bauer gazed across the room. He was satisfied. That moment—the day his daughter would begin her future and carry on his legacy—was everything he'd hoped it would be. At that moment he decided that his own life had been a great success. His grandchildren would be the sons and daughters of a high-ranking SS officer. What else could a father hope for?

That night, Rolf made love to Ivonne for the first time. He wasn't surprised to find that Ivonne was a virgin. She was warm, tender, and willing the first time. But she winced in pain and when he got up to go to the bathroom he saw blood on the sheet. Confirmation that she was his alone, unspoiled by any other man. He came back to bed and took her in his arms. Just knowing that she was an unblemished flower excited him. He took her again. The second time, she was not only willing but she was even a bit aggressive.

"I am very happy, Rolf," Ivonne said after they'd finished.

"I am hoping you'll become pregnant right away," he said. "It would be good for my career if we started having a family. You know what the Fuhrer says ..."

"Yes, of course. It is an important duty for us to have as many pure Aryan children as we can. So, I too, hope I become pregnant right away. I want to be everything you want and expect in a wife."

"Can you cook?" he joked.

"Of course. I can sew and make clothes, too."

"Well then, all you need to do is give birth to plenty of Aryan babies." Rolf touched her face. "Thank you for tonight," he said, and gently kissed her lips. Then Rolf turned over and slept, satisfied. For the moment, he was at peace.

Ivonne lay beside him; a single tear of joy rolled from her eye to her white pillowcase. *I will make him so happy. I will make him love me. He will be so satisfied with our lives together that he will forget he ever knew Anne-Marie,* she thought as she drifted off to sleep.

All might have been well had Rolf not broken the handle off his suitcase. Both he and Herr Bauer had tried to fix it, but it was no use. Rolf would need to purchase a new valise in order to pack his things properly to return to Poland. Ivonne had a lot of work to do in order to prepare to leave. She was busy sorting through her things and packing.

"I am going into town to purchase a new suitcase," Rolf said.

"Shall I come with you?"

"No," he smiled and touched her face "You still have so much to do. I'll be back shortly." Rolf gently planted a kiss on Ivonne's lips.

She is such a good girl. My mother was right.

It was windy and cold outside, but Rolf didn't mind the walk into town. He enjoyed the crisp air and the sound of snow crunching under his boots. As he walked alone, finally settled down from all the excitement of the wedding, his thoughts turned to memories of his mother. He would miss her. Tears formed in his eyes as he entered the little square where all of the shops were located. His eyelashes froze. He quickly wiped his eyes with the back of his hand as he walked down the old familiar cobblestone streets.

Many of the little stores were just as he remembered. He had gone shopping often with his mother when he was just a little boy. It was hard to believe that they were still standing. Untouched. It was as if time had stood still there and for just a moment he could almost believe that there was no war going on. In fact, even with all the years that had passed, old Mr. Werner, the baker, had not changed the sign that hung above his store window. The sign was a little faded, and the wooden plaque's paint was chipping. But it was still there, still the same. Rolf smiled. Memories of holding his mother's hand as she took him from shop to shop brought back his feelings of loss with a vengeance.

Mama, I can't believe I will never see you again.

Rolf bit his lower lip to prevent the tears from starting again. It certainly wouldn't be fitting for an SS officer to be crying like a child. He was in the middle of town. There were people everywhere. What if someone saw him? He could never live it down.

The leather goods shop sold luggage, belts, custom-made shoes, handbags, and hats. It was located one street over from the main street and then another street to the left. He was heading across the road towards his destination when he saw her. Anne-Marie. She was coming out of the general store carrying a large fabric bag in both arms. He couldn't help but notice how tiny and delicate she was. It was hard for her to carry the heavy bag. How he wanted to rush over and take the bag and carry it for her. But he couldn't. Part of him wanted to run away and hide, not to face her at all. But from the direction in which Rolf was walking, it was impossible for him to avoid her. If he turned or crossed the street it would be too obvious that he was trying to evade her. He had to go forward. Destiny had it that they were bound to confront each other.

In fact, their paths collided head-on. His heart skipped a beat.

Just look at her. Anne-Marie ... she is stunning. Still. And she still has that same crazy effect on me. She makes my heart race, my pulse thunder in my temples. I want her so badly. And, my God!

It suddenly dawned on him.

I can't believe how much she looks like Helen.

"Rolf! How are you?" Anne said as they came face to face. Her voice was as soft and appealing as he remembered. "I hear congratulations are in order. Didn't you and Ivonne recently get married?"

To Rolf, Anne-Marie was breathtaking in her dove gray coat. He remembered seeing the same coat on a mannequin in the window of the local garment store just a few minutes ago. Anne-Marie had always been up on the latest fashion. He knew her family wasn't rich and he wondered how she afforded such a luxury. Before he went back to the Bauer's home he would go to that same store and buy that same coat for Ivonne. Anne-Marie would not own something nicer than Rolf's wife.

"Yes. Thank you for the congratulations," he said. "I wasn't expecting to see you. I thought you moved out of Germany?" Rolf couldn't keep the sarcasm out of his voice.

"I did ... for a while."

"It's true then. I heard that you married Sam Saperstein?"

"Yes, it's true. I married Sam and we left Germany together."

"A Jew, Anne-Marie. But why?"

"Because I always loved him. You knew that."

"I knew how you felt. But I couldn't understand how you could fall in love with swine …"

"Yes, I can imagine that you might feel that way. But, please, Rolf for old time's sake … don't call Sam bad names. It hurts me," she said, looking at his uniform.

"I'm Hauptsturmführer Boltz now." He smiled a wry smile.

"Hmmm," she sighed, snorting a little.

"I can see that you don't approve. I didn't think you would."

"Does it matter what I think? This is Germany now. I have very little to say about what goes on here."

"Is Sam back here in Germany? He couldn't be here and be married to you. It's against the law, you know."

"Don't worry, Rolf. He's not here in Germany. He's safe. Sam is in America. That's what broke up our marriage. I couldn't bear to live without my family. So your precious Nazi Party came between me and my happiness. Sam told me to come home. He refused to take me away from my loved ones. Sam was not selfish. He was never selfish."

"You are better off. You really should know that."

"I'm sure you think so."

"He is a Jew. His blood taints yours. If you had a child …"

"I don't want to hear any more about this. I've heard it all a thousand times. I have to leave. I can't stand to see you in that uniform, Rolf. We have known each other far too long and quite frankly, it makes me sick to see who you have become."

"You hate me, don't you?" Rolf put his hands on Anne-Marie's shoulders.

"I don't hate you, Rolf. You're confused. Something happened to you when you joined the Nazi Party. And now it seems to me that you can't think for yourself. They've sold you on their propaganda and you bought it. I am sorry for you."

"Don't you dare pity me."

"What are you going to do? Put me away in a jail or a concentration camp? I don't believe you have the heart to do that to me, Rolf. I won't believe it. I can't. If I let myself be convinced of such a thing then I have to say that I never really knew you at all. I am looking beneath that uniform and that swastika. I am looking for the man that I grew up with. I hope he is still there. Is he there, Rolf? Is he?"

Before he had a chance to say a word, she turned and walked away from him. He stood planted like a tree in the street with his face fallen and his mouth agape. He could punish her … easily. He'd have her arrested for treason. But Rolf knew he wouldn't … because he admired her courage. She was a slender, little bit of a girl and was usually shy and soft-spoken but not when it came to what she believed was right. Even when they were just children, she'd always stood up to defend the underdog. And when she was protecting something or someone she believed in, she was a tigress. She made him feel small and weak. But at the same time, he was filled with passion and desire for her. He would never hurt her, he couldn't. But he wanted to. Rolf wanted to slap her the way he slapped Helen, hard enough to make her head twist backward. He wanted her to know that he was more powerful than she would ever be and if she thought he was not man enough to stand up to her. Well, she was wrong.

All the joys of his new marriage slipped from Rolf's fingers like sand on the beach. He was angry. He'd been disrespected. Anne-Marie had not admired Rolf for his accomplishments. Ivonne did, but that didn't matter to him right now. The woman he truly wanted thought of him as nothing but a brute. He would have liked to teach her a lesson. His fists were clenched and his face was red with rage. He walked in and bought the suitcase, but when the shop owner tried to give him condolences about his mother, he didn't speak. Instead, Rolf just nodded, paid, took his purchase, and left. He forgot all about buying the coat for Ivonne. Instead, he walked for an extra fifteen minutes to try and calm his nerves. The last thing he wanted was for anyone at the Bauer house to be concerned about him or to ask him questions. Right now he would be annoyed, even if they were trying to be kind. And so rather than return home, he walked.

I am Hauptsurmfuhrer Boltz. I don't have to answer to anyone. No one here is my superior and certainly, no one here has the right to question me.

When he returned to the house, Ivonne ran to greet him. She reached up and kissed him softly on the lips. He didn't put his arms around her. In fact, he couldn't kiss her back. After seeing Anne-Marie earlier, Ivonne looked plain to him again. Anne-Marie's hair was so blond that it sparkled like gold in the sun. The blue of her eyes rivaled the blue of the sky. Yes, Anne-Marie's lips were a bit too full, as were Helen's, and perhaps her nose was just a little too long. Neither Anne-Marie nor Helen was truly beautiful but in Rolf's eyes, they were, although he would never want them to know that he felt that way. Both of them physically represented perfect specimens of Aryan women. But Helen was a Pole. She might look Aryan, but her bloodline was not. She could never be anything but a plaything. Anne had it all. She had the looks ... the bloodline. If he married Anne, his fellow officers would all envy him. They would be green to see that he had wed the ideal German woman. Ivonne, with her mousy brown hair and milky blue eyes, wasn't exactly what the others would covet.

What have I done to myself marrying Ivonne? Oh, Mother, you know how much I love you and how much I've always tried to please you. But it seems that this time it was a mistake to do what you asked of me. It's frightening. It seems to me that I might have doomed myself to living my life with a woman I don't love. After seeing Anne-Marie today and feeling the effect she still has on me, I know that Ivonne will never be more to me than second best. That's what she is… second best Ivonne. And the true love of my heart will never be mine.

That night, Rolf didn't touch his new wife. He could have at least tried but his heart wasn't in it. Her hand caressed his manhood and it grew hard and erect. Then just as quickly, it went limp. She lay very close beside him, rubbing her naked breasts against his arm, touching his face. It was obvious to Rolf that she trying her best to excite him. But it was no use. He was repelled by her. The very idea of making love to her made him feel unworthy of Anne, and that made him feel like he too was nothing but second best. When he thought about Anne-Marie at the same time he felt Ivonne's touch, he felt disgusted with himself. He turned away from her.

"Is something wrong?" Ivonne asked timidly. "Did I do something? Are you feeling all right?"

"No, nothing is wrong. I'm just tired. Very tired," he muttered, glad she could not see his eyes. Then, for several seconds, the room was eerily silent. Somewhere outside an owl hooted.

"I have been thinking," Rolf finally added. "Perhaps it would be a good idea for you to take a few weeks before you come to Warsaw. It would give you time to pack properly and say goodbye to all of your friends. Besides, I would like a little time to make some room in my flat for your things. I want to clean out part of the closet and a few drawers in my dresser."

"I can come with you now and help you clean."

"No, I would prefer to sort through my things alone. I'd rather you came in a few weeks." His tone was like the crackling of icicles.

"All right. I will do whatever you say. And, if this what you want …"

"Yes," he said. "It's what I want." He turned to look at her. "Goodnight," he said, almost apologetic.

The moonlight filtered through the window and he thought he saw a tear shining like a small diamond on her cheek, but he couldn't be sure. Rolf didn't want to think about how much he was hurting Ivonne. The more he thought about her and her feelings for him, the more repulsed he was.

How could I have done this?

Ivonne reached out and rubbed his upper arm. "Are you sure nothing is wrong?" She sounded so pathetic to him that he felt his stomach turn. He couldn't wait to leave this house, this woman, this bed, and get back to Warsaw where he could make believe that Helen was Anne-Marie.

"Yes, I'm sure," he snapped. "Let's stop talking. I'm tired. I'd like to get some sleep."

CHAPTER THIRTY-THREE

Rolf returned to Warsaw. He thought he would contact Helen immediately and bury his sorrow over Anne-Marie by sexually dominating Helen. But his heart was just not in it. Instead of contacting Helen as soon as he arrived, he fell into a deep depression. All he could think of was Anne-Marie and the fact that he'd lost her to a Jew. The day after his return, he reported to work in the ghetto. But as he was patrolling, he saw a young Jewish teenage boy washing a store window. The boy had curly black hair and although he looked nothing like Sam, Anne-Marie's husband, Rolf wanted to punish someone and the boy was there. So without warning, Rolf pulled his gun and shot the boy in the head.

I am a good shot. It's a good thing my father took me hunting so many times when I was a child. A woman walking by started screaming. Rolf shot her too. The street was suddenly a sea of blood. Rolf just stood there gazing at the scene with the gun in his hand. That's for you Anne-Marie. That's for you. I only wish you could have been here and seen it. If I could only get my hands on that bastard that you married I'd teach him a good lesson. Yes, Anne-Marie, that was for you… and for the future of our fatherland.

The power of killing another man, especially a Jew like Sam, made Rolf feel better, but only for a short time and then his misery returned. That night he drank to excess and forgot to eat.

However, the following day, when his superiors gave him their condolences and asked about his mother, he proudly told them that while he was back at home he'd gotten married. She was a childhood friend, and of course, she was a girl of pure Aryan blood.

"We are planning to have children as soon as possible."

His brother officers congratulated him on his success in Berlin and on his marriage. He should have been happy. But he wasn't.

CHAPTER THIRTY-FOUR

After two weeks of packing and attending small gatherings of her friends who kissed her, complimented her on the wonderful catch she'd made in Rolf, and then wished her well on her journey, Ivonne found herself riding a train on her way to Warsaw. As the train chugged over the tracks, she couldn't help but think about the last time she'd seen Rolf as he was leaving for Poland. He hadn't wanted her to go with him to the train station. Instead, he smiled and gave her a peck of a kiss goodbye at her home, not what a new bride expected. She'd hugged him tightly, but he had not returned the hug, and she'd been even more than disappointed. Ivonne was hurt. The night before he left he hadn't wanted to make love. He said he was very tired and had to travel early in the morning. She lay in bed beside him feeling sick, as if somehow something wonderful had flitted away like a firefly.

What have I done wrong? Everything seemed to be going so well and now he is so distant. I don't know what to do.

After he left that morning, Ivonne went back to bed. She laid down with her head on his pillow and wept.

Have I lost him? What if he sends me a letter saying he wants a divorce?

The thought made her anxious; she could hardly breathe. How had she lost Rolf's interest so quickly? A deep gash in her soul was bleeding. The pain was agonizing. But as the week passed, putting time between that hurtful goodbye and the present moment, Ivonne began to make excuses for Rolf. The excuses eased her mind. She tried to convince herself that Rolf was just jittery because he was anxious to get back to his work.

I can understand his feelings. After all, he has a very important position and between his mother's funeral and our wedding he'd been away from his job for so long. When I see him again everything will be wonderful, like it was in the beginning. I just know it. Everything will be fine again.

The train came to an abrupt stop. Outside she could see the placard Warszawa Główna identifying the partly damaged, modernist station.

The doors opened and Ivonne stepped off the train. She was a little nervous. She'd never been out of Germany.

Rolf's driver was waiting for her at the train station. He was holding up a card with her name on it. She walked over to him and said, "I am Ivonne Boltz."

"Welcome to Warsaw." He smiled.

Then he opened the door for her. She climbed into the soft leather back seat of the long black automobile.

"Give me a minute to load your bags into the trunk and we'll be on our way, Frau Boltz."

"You're Rolf's driver?" Ivonne asked as the car moved out into traffic.

"Yes, Frau Boltz. I am. Allow me to introduce myself, my name is Elberich Hahn."

"I am awestruck! Rolf has his own driver. And you are a German as well?"

"Yes, I am a German. Your husband is an important man; of course he has a driver. In fact, you will be happy to know that he has recently received a promotion. Has he told you yet? He is now Sturmbannführer Boltz. You must be very proud."

"He hasn't told me yet."

"I hope I didn't spoil the surprise. I would hate for Herr Boltz to become angry with me. He can be very difficult when he is angry. Oh, I shouldn't have said that. What am I doing? I am talking far too much Frau Boltz …"

"Don't worry. I won't tell him that you told me. I'll let him tell me himself," Ivonne said smiling. "You must be in the Party as well."

"I am but I am not an important man like your husband. I am just a driver."

"Do you enjoy your job?"

"Yes, I do. It is an honor to drive such an important man."

"My husband treats you well, I hope."

"He does the best he can, Frau Boltz. The Sturmbannführer is a very busy man. He doesn't have time for the likes of me. But ... please don't misunderstand. I don't blame him."

"It's all right, Hahn. You don't have to be afraid to talk to me. I will not repeat anything you say."

"You are very kind, Frau Boltz."

The black automobile slowly turned onto a driveway leading up to an amber colored brick structure.

"This is your home, Frau Boltz," the driver said as he got out and opened Ivonne's door.

"Thank you," she said, looking around with her eyes wide.

"You go on in and I'll bring your luggage." He smiled.

Ivonne had been expecting to move to Rolf's apartment when she arrived. Never in her wildest dreams had she realized how high her husband had risen in the Party.

Ivonne entered the house. Rolf had grown up in a wealthier family than hers, but this was far more magnificent than either of their parents' dwellings. Rolf walked into the room just as she walked in the door and Ivonne threw herself into his arms and kissed him. She could hardly contain her excitement.

"A house Rolf? I thought you lived in an apartment?"

"Yes, a house. My superiors in Berlin were very happy with my work here and also pleased that I have married. And of course, I spoke of your pure Aryan bloodline. You know how much the Party embraces children and family so they've given us a house to live in."

"It's beautiful. We will have lots of children." Ivonne smiled at him.

He wished she were a natural blond like Anne-Marie, and not so hefty and big boned. More delicate, like Anne. But at least he could tell the world that she was pure Aryan. And then, most importantly, although he wasn't pleased about it, he had fulfilled his promise to his mother.

"Oh Rolf, I can't believe this is ours. Would you just look at these furnishings? Did you put all of this together?"

"No …" He laughed. "It was this way when I moved in."

"I wonder who decorated it so beautifully? The artwork on the walls is breathtaking."

"I think it was owned by Jews then confiscated when they were arrested."

"Oh …" she said, the smile fading from her face for a moment, only to quickly return. "Well, it is very lovely. And we are so fortunate to be living here. We are lucky that we will raise our children in such a nice place."

"I am glad you like it. And, by the way, I have more good news."

"Go on, Rolf. I love good news."

"I have been promoted! I am now Sturmbannfuhrer."

"Oh Rolf, I am so happy for you! I am so proud!" she said, never letting him know that she already heard the news from his driver.

"Yes, I am very happy about it," he said.

"It certainly appears as if you are doing a good job and the Party is quite pleased with you. But of course, how could they not be? You are such a wonderful man ..."

His chest swelled with pride. He would have loved to hear Anne-Marie say those words.

"You will like it here in Warsaw. It is not our beloved Germany, but the Party takes good care of its own," he said, wishing he were happier to be with her.

"I know I will like it because I will be with you."

"I'm going for a walk," Rolf said a little abruptly.

Ivonne was taken aback by the quick shift in his personality. At first, he seemed happy to see her then he turned off all of his emotions and was like a stone.

"I know that you like to take walks," she stammered, "but it is rather chilly outside tonight."

"Yes, you're quite right, it is. I'll take a jacket."

"Would you like me to join you?" She could hear the hope in her own voice and felt ashamed that she was so needy for his affection.

"No, I need some time alone. I have business matters to consider."

"I haven't seen you for almost three weeks …" Ivonne stammered.

"Yes. That's true. We can talk again at dinner," he said, as he grabbed his coat off the rack and left the house.

She turned to the window to watch him as he walked away and again, Ivonne couldn't help but wonder what she had done to spoil things.

CHAPTER THIRTY-FIVE

Before Rolf left his office on January 17th, he was informed that he, along with several other SS officers, had orders from headquarters that on the following day they were to report to the Warsaw ghetto and round up seven thousand Jew for deportation. Not everyone involved knew all of the details, but Rolf did. He was told that the Jews were to be sent in cattle cars on transports that would take them to Treblinka. Treblinka was not a work camp—it was a death camp.

"Best not to think too much about it," Rolf's superior officer said when he read the telegram with the orders to Rolf. "This Jewish situation is a nasty business. I don't particularly relish the idea of mass murder, either. However, this is what must be done and one day the world will thank us."

Rolf nodded. He didn't care for the Jews anyway. But since Sam had poured his filthy seed into his dream girl and spoiled Anne-Marie forever, he had come to hate them.

"Yes, best not to think about it too much. We must clean up the world, rid ourselves of the sub-humans lest they spread their seed amongst the Aryan population. There are far too many mixed children already. We don't need anymore."

"I realize that seven thousand is a massive number for us to send on transports tomorrow. But the quicker we get rid of them, the sooner we can start rebuilding."

January 18th was a frigid morning. Rolf hated getting out of his warm bed on such days. He lay under the thick blankets, dreading the way the cold floor would feel against his bare feet. He tended not to feel as well in the winter as he did during the other seasons. Sometimes his back or shoulders ached from the chill. It seemed like the cold had a way of penetrating his skin and slithering inside of him. Turning over in bed, still languishing in the comfort, Rolf gazed out the window. It was a bright silver-blue morning, crystal-like icicles hung from the trees, shooting rainbows across the snow-covered ground when they caught the rays of the sun. It was so pretty; like a painting, but looks could be deceiving. Winter was a misery, for sure.

It was to be a full and trying day, and he wasn't looking forward to it. Not that he felt any compassion for the Jews. He'd killed them before. In fact, six hundred had already been exterminated in Warsaw. However, he knew by the frost on the window that it would be very cold outside and he dreaded that. But besides the chill, he dreaded having to contend with the filth and disease in the ghetto. Frankly, on a day like this, loading the swine into boxcars and trying to keep order was a real pain in the ass.

Rolf finally forced himself to get out of bed. He felt a shiver run through him. He realized he had awakened with a slight headache. If it hadn't been for the special orders, it would have been the perfect day to stay at home and rest. However, he knew that he had better go to the ghetto with the rest of his fellow colleagues and perform his duties. So he washed his face. The icy water stung his skin as he shaved. Carefully, he wet his golden hair then combed it neatly away from his face. Next, he took a clean pressed uniform out of his well-organized closet and got dressed. The clothing warmed him as he climbed down the stairs to the kitchen where the cook would prepare his breakfast.

Ivonne was still in bed, asleep, and he saw no reason to awaken her. He would rather not see her because sometimes seeing her made things that bothered him seem even worse. He found that when he looked at her he felt guilty for not being able to love her. He knew that the guilt stemmed from his love for his mother, but it was easier to stifle the remorse when he didn't have to endure the pathetic look of pure devotion in Ivonne's eyes.

He sat down at the table and waited. A loaf of white bread, a slab of butter, and a jar of jam were set down in front of him. He slathered a thick piece of the bona fide white bread with real butter then added some of the thick strawberry preserves. Gerlinde, his cook and housekeeper, poured him a cup of coffee, not the fake coffee that the rest of the world had to contend with, but authentic coffee, which he sweetened with genuine sugar. As he sipped the rich, dark brew he looked out the window at the snow-covered lawn and marveled at his good fortune to be a high-ranking member of the SS. Only men of his caliber had access to such rare treats. After he finished eating, he realized that his headache had begun to subside.

"Tell Hahn to pull the car around the front. I'll be out in a minute," Rolf said to Gerlinde.

"Yes, Herr Boltz. Right away."

Elberich Hahn had the car waiting when Rolf walked outside. The driver tried to talk to Rolf on the way to the office, but Rolf had no use for anything that someone so beneath him would have to say. After a few minutes of Rolf not responding, Hahn stopped talking.

CHAPTER THIRTY-SIX

The officers took several cars from their headquarters to the Warsaw ghetto. Rolf rode along with an old friend, Wolfgang Muehler.

Wolfgang and Rolf were chatting as they entered the iron gate to the Warsaw ghetto. Rolf happened to look up and noticed that small, diamond-like chunks of ice had formed on the barbed wire that surrounded the entire Jewish prison.

He and Wolfgang were discussing a local beer hall where they had attended a meeting a few nights prior. The beer had been flowing and the food was outstanding, all courtesy of the Reich. Wolfgang, who was still single, teased Rolf a little about tying the knot and Rolf laughed.

"You know that you can't wait to get married, Wolf. If nothing else it is a good mark on your name with the Party and can certainly help further your career."

"Yes, of course. I know you are right. I just have to find the right girl. I like to change them so often."

Rolf laughed. "You can still have others on the side. I didn't say you had to be faithful. Just married."

"Is that your plan, Rolf?" Wolfgang winked.

"Of course. I will have plenty of babies with my wife. And fun on the side."

They were about halfway inside the prison walls when a loud blast made Rolf jump. Rolf had heard gunshots before, but he wasn't expecting them. Again, more gunshots, even louder, rang through the ghetto. He froze on the pavement. The bullets were coming from somewhere overhead. Rolf looked up but could not determine where the shots were originating. Several Germans dropped to their unexpected deaths.

Rolf turned to look at his friend, Wolfgang, who had fallen silently to the ground with blood pouring out of his chest. At first, Rolf was so stunned he couldn't believe what was happening. He felt like he was dreaming. The nightmare had an unrealistic quality about it. Still, the gunfire continued. The bullets were coming from all directions and the Nazis could not determine where to run or where to find the perpetrators and stop them. Bullets rained down from an apartment in a building on one side of the road. The Germans ran up the stairs to the room where the shots had come from only to find it empty. Confused, they walked back outside where more gunfire attacked them from a completely different location. Bullets flew from so many directions that it was impossible to find the snipers as Nazis dropped like shattered rag dolls. The snow was stained crimson with their blood.

Rolf would never let on, but he was terrified. Jews were not expected to fight back like that. They never had. It was a terrible and unexpected surprise. The worst of it was that, no matter how hard he tried to find the shooters, he could not see his enemy. However, he knew that as long as he was wearing his Nazi uniform he was a target. Stunned and unable to fight back, Rolf ran as fast as he could out of the Warsaw Ghetto.

The entire group of Nazi officers who had been involved, Rolf included, were summoned to report to the closest police headquarters. He'd always hated the police department. It seemed like everyone was always trying to rise in the Party by bringing a fellow Nazi down. He walked in and the headache he had that morning immediately returned. Bright fluorescent lights shone overhead, making him feel dizzy. The tension in the room was so thick that it was like invisible quicksand. Everyone was talking at once. They were all trying desperately to place the blame on someone else. They argued in loud, angry voices as to what should have been done. The men who had not been present during the Jewish resistance all shouted their own surefire ideas as to how they would have efficiently handled the problem had they been there instead. And those who had been there in the ghetto that day were chastised harshly. Obergruppenfuhrer Ferdinand von Sammern-Frankenegg was on the telephone with Himmler, who was very angry that the SS had not had better control of the situation. He demanded to know how the Jews had been allowed to get out of hand like that. Where had they gotten guns?

Rolf was embarrassed and furious to be one of the men who had incurred Himmler's displeasure. However, he was relieved that he'd escaped without being shot. As he watched the rest of the men ranting and raving at each other, he was disgusted. They were like wild hungry dogs, all trying to eat each other to stay alive. He watched them but his thoughts turned to Sam. Sam Saperstein.

The audacity of that Jew. He had dared to touch and soil forever the most beautiful, sweetest woman I've ever known, and now those disgusting swine in the ghetto are causing all kinds of problems that are making me and the rest of the men who were with me look like fools in the eyes of my superiors. And no doubt the news of what happened today will reach the Furhrer. What are the chances that I will ever get another promotion after this? Those damn Jew bastards have ruined my life, not once, but twice. Right now it would be my pleasure to help with those systematic murders I'm hearing about.

There was a time when the idea of mass murder would have been horrific to him, but not now.

CHAPTER THIRTY-SEVEN

March 1943

Helen wanted to believe Rolf was gone from her life forever and that he was going to leave her alone. She wanted to believe that by some miracle he had lost interest in her. Perhaps he had met someone else. Or maybe he was transferred out of Poland. Even though she knew that God would never sanction what she had done with Rolf, she prayed for his forgiveness and begged him to make Rolf disappear from her life. It had been a long time since he'd left Poland to go home, and by now she was fairly sure that he had probably returned to work. But, for some wonderful reason, he hadn't called for her for a while and she thought that maybe her prayers had been answered. However, as much as she wanted to believe that he was really gone forever, a nagging voice in the back of her mind wouldn't allow her to feel free of him.

I cannot afford to let myself be too happy. Too many bad things have happened to me and I am scared to let myself feel good because at any time he could call for me … at any time things could go back to the way they were. And if I am happy the letdown will be even harder. If only I had somewhere to go far away from Warsaw, a safe place where I could take the children and hide. I would like to leave everything behind including Nik and all the mixed feelings I have when I look at him. But who am I kidding? I can't leave him. I've never been on my own. And besides, without Nik's salary, there is no money for us to live on.

Helen knew that her father would take her and the children in, even little Ela. Since her mother died he was alone and would welcome the company. But if Rolf came back into her life she would be putting her father in danger. He was an old and helpless man.

How can I even think about getting my papa involved in all of this? If anything happened to him I would never forgive myself. All she could do was keep praying that Rolf was gone for good. If only…

Before Rolf had gone home to see his dying mother, Helen had been too busy trying to balance meeting him with taking care of her home and children to pay much attention to Nik. It had been months since she'd even wondered what he was thinking or feeling. But now, with Rolf gone, Helen was at home with Nik and the children every night. She began to observe Nik more closely than she had in years.

One night, she watched him as he sat painting. He had begun painting more often. It seemed he could not communicate with her but he could put his emotions onto the canvas. His shoulders were slumped. Helen saw that the skin on his face had gone slack and tiny lines were carved around his eyes. His hair was beginning to go gray and had thinned considerably. It was oily and unkempt. How different this man was from the meticulous Nik she'd known in their early years. Nik's hand trembled slightly as he held the brush. She looked at the canvas he was working on and it shocked her to see how his paintings had changed. When they were first married he'd done lovely portraits of her, and then when Lars was born he'd painted him, too.

But the picture he was working on now was different. It was an image of a forest of gnarled trees. The sky was a charcoal gray with no moon or stars, and off in the distance, a decrepit house peeked through the intertwined branches. A face wearing a silent scream of horror was in the window of the house. It sent a slight chill through Helen. Although she couldn't say she loved him, it hurt her heart to see that he was looking so weathered and tired. For a long time, Helen had deluded herself into believing that Nik didn't care about being the head of his household. But, looking at him now, she could see that he felt powerless and it had taken its toll on him. As she watched him carefully mix paint on a pallet, she remembered how when Lars was a baby, Nick had been such a strong and virile man. He'd enjoyed coming home from work and playing with his son. In her mind's eye, Helen could see Nik lifting Lars high above his head until Lars giggled. Then Nik would turn to Helen and smile. Her life had been full then. In those days, which now seemed like a lifetime ago, she had believed in love, marriage, and happily ever after.

However, the Nazis had changed all of that and it was clear to see that, lately, Nik was irritated when Lars wanted to climb onto his lap. He would allow his son to sit with him for a few minutes before he stood up, pretending he had something to do, putting the child gently on the floor. He would not even touch Ela. If she came over to him, he ignored her as if she weren't there. It tore Helen up inside to see the gentle little girl trying so hard to make the only father she'd ever known care about her. But Nik wasn't having it.

And to make matters worse, Helen knew Nik was drinking heavily. Many nights he didn't come home directly from work, and when he did come home late at night he smelled of alcohol. Money was very tight, especially since she wasn't receiving any money or food from Rolf. They really couldn't afford for Nik to be buying so much alcohol, but Helen was afraid to mention his overindulgence. After all, the money he spent was money he'd worked for. But, more importantly, she was afraid that if she brought up his drinking, he might get angry and ask her some questions about things she didn't want to discuss.

And so they lived together, neither of them ever speaking their minds. Helen and Nik both tried to be overly polite to each other, but their hearts were separate, and their hopes and dreams were no longer braided together like the beautiful plait Helen sometimes wore in her golden hair.

On the other hand, Ela and Lars were growing up fast, and every day they did something that brought a smile to Helen's face. The two little ones were Helen's escape from all of the hellish realities surrounding her. They were children, and their innocence was like a spring day in the middle of a winter storm. Neither Lars nor Ela knew anything of Nazis or broken marriages. They were discovering the world around them, and their sweet awe inspired Helen enough to make her want to go on living. As each day passed, Helen's thoughts of

Zofia began to blur until she hardly thought about Zofia at all. Helen and Ela grew ever closer until Helen's attachment to the child became so deep she felt as if Ela were her own daughter and not a just a child who was living under her charge until her real mother could return.

Days turned to weeks, weeks to months, and the clock moved forward. Helen's neighbors got used to seeing Ela and Lars together and, with other things on their minds, people began to think of Ela and Lars as natural siblings. The women with children close to the same age trusted Helen to watch their children from time to time and they returned the favor by babysitting for Lars and Ela. With Ela's coloring being so similar to Helen's, people seemed to forget to question where she came from. They just accepted that Ela was Helen's daughter.

Helen found the winter to be cold and miserable, as most Polish winters were. But she did what she could to keep herself and the family warm. Slowly, the frigid weather began to thaw, the snow melted, and the spring rains came to wash away the slush, bringing with it the return of the green grass and colorful flowers. Bursts of bright sunshine gave Helen hope. She was beginning to accept that all was well. The very idea that Rolf was gone made her feel young and giddy, like a girl again.

On a muggy, gray and rainy afternoon, Helen had a terrible time getting the children to take a nap. They were both sweaty from the humidity and crabby. Finally, after reading them several stories, both children fell asleep. Helen would have loved to lie down, if only for a half hour. However, she needed the time away from the children to wash the floors. Lately, it had become impossible to wash the floors without the children running on them and slipping before they were dry. Then when they fell down the crying would start. That was the last thing she needed. She decided she must hurry before they awakened. Helen always started in the kitchen. She poured a bucket full of soapy water and got down on her knees with a scrub brush to begin her task. This was her least favorite chore, but it had to be done. She began scrubbing. There was a knock at the back door, which opened into the kitchen. Helen got up and dried her hands on her apron. She opened the door and there stood a young man with an envelope.

"This is for Helen Dobinski," he said.

She took the letter and nodded. He was waiting for a tip, but she didn't have enough cash to give him.

"I'm sorry," Helen said and shrugged. "I can't afford to tip you."

She closed the door. Walking around the bucket and scrub brush and taking care not to trip on any spilled water, she walked into the living room. Her heart sank as she tore the envelope open and saw the signature. Helen had hoped that it wasn't from Rolf but, of course, as soon as she saw the letter she knew that it was.

"I will see you tonight at seven but the place we will be meeting will be changed from now on. Do not come to my apartment. I don't live there anymore. Instead, you will go to the Polonia Palace hotel. When you arrive, go and see the desk clerk. Tell him you are to be meeting Sturmbannführer Boltz and then give him your name. He will have a room key waiting for you. Come upstairs and knock. I will be there. Rolf."

A shiver slid like a snake up her back.

I knew it was too good to be true. I knew he wasn't gone forever. The Polonia Palace? That's the fancy hotel where all the Nazis meet. Why would he want to meet me there? I have never even been inside of that place and I am terrified of all the Nazis that will be in there. They are so cruel and I am a woman alone.

Oh dear God, why?

Why can't this man just let me be and get out of my life? Now I have to go into a hotel full of these terrible men and face all of them before and then again after I commit this horrific sin with Rolf.

What am I going to do? What can I do?

Helen wept a little but knew that she had no other option. She must go to him. He still had the power to destroy her and everything and everyone she loved. Helen had been taught not to hate anyone, but she felt so much hatred right now towards Rolf that she hardly recognized herself. Lars came out of the bedroom. He'd hardly napped.

"What are you doing out of bed?" Helen snapped loudly. "Get back in that room right now."

Ela came out with her thumb in her mouth. She was crying.

I must have woken her up. They have never heard me yell at them like that. I have to compose myself. It's not their fault; they are just children. Damn it. Rolf is back in my life and my floor is not clean.

Tears began to sting her eyes.

"Come on you two, back to bed with you." She tried to sound firm and in control, but she wanted to fall on the floor and weep.

"Was someone here? I thought I heard someone at the door," Lars asked.

"No, no one was here. You must have dreamed it," Helen said.

CHAPTER THIRTY-EIGHT

"Nik, I am going back to work again. The old lady who I work for was staying with her daughter for a while. Now her daughter is leaving Warsaw. The daughter has contacted me and asked me to return to work. She wants me to come back again and do her mother's housework twice a week. The extra money was good for us. I've agreed to take the job."

"Yes. It's a good idea. The money helped," Nik said emotionless. He never looked up from his bowl of soup.

Just look at him eating. He doesn't have a clue about anything. He is happy for the extra money. That's all that matters to him. If I am working he will have more money to piss away on drinking. He couldn't care less about me.

"I'm going to start back to work for her tonight."

"Put the children to bed first."

"I will," she said, the words sticking in her throat.

CHAPTER THIRTY-NINE

Helen took the tram and then walked several blocks before arriving in front of the hotel. She walked inside. The palace was as beautifully decorated as she'd imagined. The floor was white marble, veined with light and dark gray. A large crystal chandelier hung from the ceiling. A mahogany bar with a bartender wearing a tuxedo was to her left. The bar was adjacent to a fancy restaurant with white-gloved waiters holding silver trays. Helen couldn't help herself; she had to take a quick peek inside the restaurant. Wide-eyed, she watched ladies dining in beautiful gowns. Most of them were sitting across from men in their Nazi uniforms, at tables with white linen tablecloths illuminated by the soft glow of candles. As she suspected, there were Nazi officers, Gestapo, and SS of every rank standing in groups and chatting in the lobby. They were sitting at the bar laughing and talking.

It all seems so civilized. But I know better. I know that these men, these Nazis, have no hearts.

It was as if she was invisible. No one even seemed to notice her. The heels of her shoes clicked on the marble as she walked up to the desk. A slender, middle-aged man, well groomed, with thinning dark hair and deep-set dark eyes greeted her.

"How may I help you?"

"My name is Helen Dobinski. I am here to pick up a key which has been arranged by Sturmbannführer Boltz."

"But of course." The man smiled. "Excuse me for a moment," he said then turned to a board on the wall. He took down a key and handed it to her.

"Room 248. The Sturmbannführer has already arrived. He said to tell you he is upstairs waiting for you".

"Thank you."

She took an elevator to the second floor and then walked down the hall to room 248.

I can't believe I am going to a hotel room with a man who isn't my husband. When will this nightmare end?

She knocked on the door.

Rolf opened the door, looking glad to see her. He smiled brightly when she walked into the room. In the glow of the overhead light, his teeth were so white that they looked almost pale blue. As he leaned over to plant a kiss on her lips, his tooth shimmered and it made her think of Little Red Riding Hood and the wolf.

"You look well," Rolf said. "I think you might have put on a little weight. That's a good thing. You've always been far too skinny, you know."

She felt her lower lip tremble as she tried to smile.

"I hope I am wrong. But from the look on your face, it seems to me that you are not really very happy to see me. I should think you would have missed me. If not me, then at least the extra food?" he asked, cupping her face with both hands.

"I'm sorry. Of course I missed you."

"Little liar," he snorted, shaking his head and pushing her away from him. She hit the wall with a thud. Her eyes opened wide.

Did I hurt her or is she afraid of me? Perhaps it's both.

Rolf was in a terrible mood. Ivonne had been grating on his nerves. Her adoration of him to the point of worship had begun boring him. In fact, it had gotten so bad that he hated being around her. When he'd contacted Helen again after so many months, he believed that seeing her would make him feel better. But even that wasn't working. Helen challenged him, like Anne-Marie, and he liked that. But, until tonight, he'd somehow deluded himself into believing that Helen actually cared for him.

However, as he stood there with his gaze meeting hers, he knew the truth. Her eyes told him what her words could not … she despised him. She was not at all grateful for the things he'd done for her. This affair they were having was not consensual. He'd made himself believe that it was. But looking at Helen now, he knew the truth. The thought that she found him repulsive made him feel undesirable and, at that moment, he hated himself.

To make matters worse, things had not been going well for him at work. The Jews in the ghetto were still acting up. The home army was getting out of control. And he had to face the truth. After he'd gone home and seen Anne-Marie again, he knew that he'd lost her forever. Up until their last meeting, he'd somehow in the back of his mind kept a small window of hope open. That window was now closed and sealed forever. It was the death of a dream. A dream he still mourned. He would have liked to punish Helen for what Anne did to him. And if his feelings of inadequacy didn't go away, he just might.

So, Helen, you don't love me. You find me disgusting. I don't care. It doesn't really matter how you feel. You will see me and I will do as I like with you for as long as it pleases me because I still have the power to destroy you. Yes, if I have nothing else, I have power.

"Please don't get angry, Rolf. I did miss you. I missed you very much …"

"Well, it doesn't really matter anyway, now does it? I have quite a few things to discuss with you. So why don't you sit down and I'll get you a drink."

The room seemed to go black. Helen was dizzy, short of breath.

I hope I don't faint. What does he want to tell me? Dear God, please nothing bad. I don't trust him. I am afraid of him; he thrives on cruelty.

"Drink up." Rolf handed her a glass of vodka. His eyes twinkled.

Helen shivered. Her face scrunched up but she swallowed the shot in one eager gulp.

"My mother passed away." He looked away from Helen and walked towards the window. Instead of looking into her eyes, Rolf moved the shade just enough so that he could stare into the darkness at the shadows of the city below.

"I'm sorry about your mother …" Helen said.

"So am I. More than I can say. But enough about that. I didn't bring you here to hear about your sympathy. What you need to know is that we will be meeting here at the Polonia Palace from now on. I like this room. It's lovely here, don't you think so?"

There was a long silence. Helen felt her skin turning hot and she wondered if she was breaking out into a rash. Her nerves were on end. If only she knew what he was going to do next. He was so unpredictable, and she knew he got pleasure from controlling her like a puppet.

She nodded.

"Don't worry. I'll handle everything. I'll give you money to pay for the train so that you get here twice a week. You can tell your husband you've gone back to work and I'll pay you, just like before. But, from now on, you will use another name when you check in to the hotel. And I will also call you by that name. I think it's best. This way there will be no trace of your meeting me. You see …" he laughed a bitter laugh. "I think of everything." He gave her a wicked smile then lit a cigarette. "From now on, there will be a room waiting for you at the desk under the name of Anne-Marie Hofmann."

When he said the name, Anne-Marie Hofmann, she heard a strange soft and gentle tone in his voice. That name meant something to him and she couldn't help but be curious.

"That's a pretty name. But can I ask why that name?"

"No, you cannot ask why …" he snapped at her. "You ask nothing. You ask no questions of me ever. Do you understand?"

"Yes," she said as she sucked in a sharp breath.

"But I do have something I have to tell you," he added. "I am sorry if I am breaking your heart." Again, he gave a bitter bark of a laugh. He wished he was breaking her heart but he knew she couldn't care less. She looked so much like Anne-Marie. "I am married. I got married when I went home."

"Oh," she stammered. "Why then, Rolf? Why continue this thing with me? Why not try to build a good marriage with your new wife?' Her voice was pleading. If only he would consider her words.

"Don't make me tell you not to question me again. You try my nerves, Helen. Do you think I take orders from a woman? I don't. In fact, I don't take orders from very many people. And you are certainly not my superior." He folded his arms across his chest and paced the room. Then out of nowhere he walked over to Helen and slapped her across her face. Her head spun and she gasped. Then suddenly she exploded into uncontrollable weeping.

"Stop it right now. Do you hear me? I have no time to listen to you whimper like a child. You will meet me twice a week here at the Polonia Palace. I will call you Anne-Marie and you will tell me how grateful you are for all that I do for you. Even if it's a lie, you will tell me that you love me. And you'd better make sure you are a convincing liar. Then you will tell me that you are impressed with how strong and powerful I am. You will do as I say. Is that understood?"

Helen nodded her head. Blood dripped from her lip onto her skirt. She wiped it with the back of her hand.

"We can begin calling you Anne-Marie right now. This way you can get used to your new name. Yes?"

"Yes," she said, barely above a whisper.

"While I was away I thought of you and I brought you a gift, Anne-Marie. Are you excited to see what I brought?" He smiled.

She was terrified of him. Her eyes and face must have shown her fear. "Yes, excited. Yes…"

"No need to be afraid, Anne-Marie. Smile." It made him feel better to call her Anne-Marie. He was enjoying this game of pretend. "Let me get you a towel for your lip," he said. Then he walked into the other room and came back with a wet rag. Gently he blotted the blood from her lip.

Helen tried to smile, but her stomach was in knots. She felt bile rising in her throat. Swallow. Don't vomit. He'll kill me if I vomit.

Rolf went to the closet and took out a coat. It was a lovely dove gray coat. The same one he'd seen Anne-Marie wear.

"It's very fashionable. In fact, it was in the window of the nicest women's clothing store in my hometown." Rolf had gone back to the store on his way to the train station and purchased the coat. But he had not gotten it for Ivonne, he'd gotten it for Helen. He wanted to see Helen wearing it and to imagine she was Anne.

"Thank you, Rolf. It's lovely."

"I am fairly sure that I got the size right. You are the same size as an old friend of mine. I just asked the shop owner what size she wore, and that's how I knew what to do when I bought it."

Helen nodded.

"Put it on."

"Now?"

"Now."

"But my lip is still bleeding. I will get blood on the coat and besides, I am not going outside."

He tilted his head to one side. "Hmmm. I suppose you're right. Well, very well then. Don't put it on now. But be sure to wear it every time you come to the hotel."

"I will," she said, her fingers squeezing the fine fabric of the coat.

Why can't you just be with your wife and be happy and leave me alone?

"Take off your clothes, Anne-Marie," Rolf said.

Anne-Marie. Now I'm Anne-Marie. I can only imagine who she must be. Dear God he is getting crazier as time goes by. What will he want next?

CHAPTER FORTY

April 1943
The Warsaw Ghetto

Rolf was told by his superior that Himmler was beyond livid. Himmler could not believe that the Jews had taken over the Warsaw ghetto in January and were still maintaining control. The men in charge were incompetent, he said, and the whole incident was nothing but an embarrassment to the superior race. It was now April, and Himmler made it clear that he wanted the entire ghetto liquidated completely by April 20th as a gift to the Führer for his upcoming birthday.

The demand made Rolf a nervous wreck. Going into the ghetto was treacherous now, and he and his colleagues discussed the situation further. Was it possible that the Jews could continue this fiasco forever? They had no food, and they had to run out of ammunition at some point. But it was impossible to determine when. What if the Poles in the home army were helping the Jews acquire what they needed? There were so many variables that the SS was having difficulty deciding what to do.

It is impossible to win with the way that these devious Jews are fighting. It is just like them to behave this way. They are not like men of character at all. I feel that when we enter the ghetto we are going into battle against ghosts. Unseen monsters out of a childhood nightmare. Bullets come from everywhere, but there is never anyone to be found firing the guns. Not one of them is man enough to step forward and fight.

Rolf shivered as he reiterated Himmler's demands. April 20th. Hitler's birthday. Himmler wants the ghetto liquidated by April 20th.

However, Rolf knew that April 20th was not only Hitler's birthday but that year it was also the first night of Passover. Passover commemorated the night when the angel of death passed over the Jews and killed the firstborn in every Egyptian household. He'd heard the story and until now he hadn't paid any attention to it. But, the truth was, he was afraid of the Jews. There was something akin to black magic about them. The Jews had been slaves to the Egyptians for centuries. And then came their prophet, a man who was called Moses. He boldly asked the Pharaoh to set the Jews free from bondage but the Pharaoh refused. Moses told him that God demanded that he set the Jews free. Again the Pharaoh refused. The Pharaoh became angry and in his anger, he called for the firstborn of every Jewish household to be murdered that night. But what the Pharaoh did not know was that God had other plans, turning the Pharaoh's curse on his own people. The Angel of Death passed over all of the Jewish households. Rolf wondered if the angel of death was right around the corner, ready to kill the Nazis.

Rolf heard two SS officers talking. They said that one of Himmler's men went to Himmler and told him the Bible story about Moses.

"What nonsense," Himmler said as he shook his head.

"I don't believe in such a ridiculous thing as an Angel of Death. But, if I did, I could promise you that this time the angel will not pass over a single Jew. We are going to eliminate all of the Jews. The gift of the Third Reich to the world is a Europe free of Jews, with our Aryan race as its rulers. Germany will win this war and change the world. Mark my words," Himmler said.

Rolf secretly trembled inside when he heard the account of the Himmler story.

CHAPTER FORTY-ONE

The Jews were fighting back. They seemed to know what the Nazis had in store for them and they were fighting hard with the strength of a people who had nothing to lose. Rolf felt this made them even more terrifying.

"The trains to transport the Jews will have to be running constantly with the cattle cars filled to capacity in order to accomplish such a daunting task. They will have to stand for the entire two-day trip crowded together like sardines. Women with children, especially babies, will be forced to hold their children in their arms or they will be trampled. We will put a single wooden bucket inside each train car for human waste. When it overflows, the prisoners will be forced to stand in their own urine, vomit, and feces. With luck, many of them will die before they reach their destination. As for those who survive the transport, when they arrive there will be a selection process. The ones who can work will be sent to slave labor, the others will go directly to the gas chambers," Rolf's superior officer, SS Oberführer von Sammern-Frankenegg, told him as they sat in Rolf's office one afternoon.

Rolf nodded. He swallowed hard and lit a cigarette. He was trying to appear emotionless, but the visuals that were being described to him were revolting and the fight that lay ahead to force the Jews into submission was frightening.

"The transports have already been taking place. They have been running for a while now. Of course not since January, not since the Jews have taken over. I just don't know how we are ever going to regain control of the ghetto," Rolf said.

"We will. We must. Himmler says he has an idea. Once we have recovered our stand we will up the number of people we are sending to be executed. These ungrateful Jews should never have acted up the way that they did. We gave them food, lodging. What more did they want? Everything, they want everything. That's what is wrong with those sub-humans. They are never satisfied. We have to stop wasting time with them and finish our work. Get rid of them completely, like cockroaches."

"I see…" Rolf said. "Who will be accompanying the transports?"

"I am not sure. Do you want to do it?"

"No." Rolf said, "I'd really rather not."

"I can understand. You've always been a good man. I will do what I can to spare you from this particular assignment. I will put in a request that they use some of the others."

"Thank you." Rolf sighed with relief. "The smell alone will be enough to make you want to puke."

"Oh yes, that is for certain. And we expect that there will be plenty of dead ones once the train cars are opened. That will be quite a mess. However, in the end, it won't be entirely my decision and I am hoping that neither of us is selected to escort the trains. I, too, would rather not be there to smell the terrible stench when they unbolt that train car to find all those dead and rotting bodies, the unwashed Jews, the human waste. Disgusting."

Rolf's superior officer shook his head. "But it has to be done. So what difference does it make if they die on the transport or in the camp or the gas chamber? Either way, they will all be dead eventfully."

"I am still not sure how we are going to get them to cooperate now that they have gotten so violent."

"Himmler knows what to do. And once we've calmed them down we will tell them that they are being resettled in work camps."

"But we told them that before."

"Yes, but they will be subdued and they will want to believe what we tell them. So they will get on the trains."

Rolf couldn't help feeling strange about what he knew. He wouldn't tell Helen anything about the plans for the rapid mass extinction of the Jews, knowing that Zofia, Ela's real mother, was in the ghetto. He could, if he felt like torturing her for not loving him, but why? She would still be powerless to reject him.

It was none of her business. She was merely a plaything for him and he would use her to pretend Anne-Marie was in love with him. He tried to convince himself that he should feel no guilt towards her. She was nothing but a Pole, and all the Nazis knew that the Poles were put on earth to serve their superiors, the Germans.

Rolf was proud of his country. The Reich had designed and constructed the most efficient facilities in order to solve the very distasteful Jewish problem. After all, in the building of these facilities, they had accomplished a monumental task. Their efforts would enable them to obliterate large groups of people and dispose of massive piles of dead bodies as quickly and efficiently as possible. In fact, Rolf was impressed when one of his fellow colleagues told him that the Reich had ingeniously designed special gas chambers that used Zyklon B and were now able to systematically murder 4,500 people every day—all sub-humans like Jews, gypsies, and homosexuals. They made disposal of the bodies equally as convenient by erecting crematoriums that they built very close to the gassing facilities.

"It's just like us Aryans," Rolf answered when it was all explained to him. "Very resourceful we are. We do get the job done, don't we?" He smiled and said, "I am proud to be a member of the superior race," but inside, he still wondered how Himmler was going to regain control.

I shouldn't be worried about this. After all, we are the smartest people, the best athletes, the most talented. In fact, the Führer has assured us that we are the best and brightest of all human beings. Still, I hope that I can somehow avoid going back into the ghetto, Rolf thought, trying to reassure himself by going over all of the messages he'd been taught in the Hitler Jugend.

But even so ... there were the dreams. Rolf began having horrifying nightmares. He would fall asleep only to be terrorized by visions of heaps of dead bodies, a terrible stench unlike any he'd ever smelled permeating the air. Sometimes the bodies came to life, their mouths frozen open in screams of horror, their eyes burning holes into his soul. They chased him until he awakened with his heart racing, his head throbbing, sweat covering his brow, and bile rising in his throat.

Rolf was hoping that whatever Himmler had planned, it would work. It would be a relief to have this mess over with. He admitted that at times, especially early on, he'd enjoyed the power. But lately, he just wanted to be done with it all.

Himmler was clear about his disappointment and his loss of faith in the men who had been handling the situation in the ghetto. Rolf was ashamed, but he had no idea of how to fix things. Then, in mid-April, Himmler made his move. He contacted SS Major General Jurgen Stroop. Rolf heard about the strategic move Himmler was about to make, and he knew his superior officers were angry at the slight. But Stroop was confident that he could do a much better job than his predecessors and assured Himmler that he would have the job done by the end of the day. And so command was taken away from SS-Oberführer von Sammern-Frankenegg and given over to Stroop.

Stroop arrived, leading his soldiers into the ghetto in tanks. Stroop was confident that with all of his equipment and men, he would overtake the Jews rapidly. Even though the Jews knew that they were bound to lose, they would not give up the fight.

They attacked the tanks with explosives. Within minutes, two of the tanks had burst into flames. The red fingers of fire reached to the sky. Gray smoke billowed upward and filled the streets, blinding the Nazis. The roar of the fire was Hitler's birthday song.

CHAPTER FORTY-TWO

Stroop could see that the task of regaining control of the Warsaw Ghetto was not going to be as easy as he had originally anticipated. He requested more manpower and additional weapons. He was given two battalions of Waffen-SS, one hundred army men, several units of Order Police and one hundred Security Police. Not only did Stroop have manpower but his troops were heavily armed. In fact they were given more tanks. All of this was necessary for one of Hitler's top Major General's in his fight to subdue seven hundred and fifty Jewish fighters armed with seventeen rifles, less than one hundred pistols, and Molotov cocktails.

Once these supplies were granted to Stroop by Himmler, Stroop took his men and returned to the ghetto. Even though the Polish resistance sent them some supplies, the Jews were running out of ammunition. Still they fought, the men, the women, the children. They fought against what they knew were impossible odds. The Jews were willing to die rather than go passively the way they had when the Nazis first imprisoned them. They fought and they died. But they gave the Nazis one hell of a fight.

Then, sadly, on May 16th the Jews of the Warsaw ghetto uprising were defeated. Stroop announced that the fighting was over and he planned to burn the Great Synagogue, which was still standing in the Jewish sector of town outside the walls of the ghetto. He did this as a symbol of the Nazi victory. Stroop then proudly proclaimed that the Jewish quarter of Poland no longer existed. Some of the inhabitants of the ghetto escaped into the forests during the uprising but anyone still left within the stone walls and the barbed wire of the Warsaw ghetto was transported to Treblinka, the death camp where seven thousand of them perished. However, this was a memorable moment for the Jewish moral. The Jews fought gallantly, holding their enemy at bay for 27 days, with only a handful of desperate, half-starved freedom fighters, very limited weaponry, and the will and heart to fight back against an enemy bent on their destruction.

CHAPTER FORTY-THREE

January 1944

Helen might have gone on forever bearing her burden of Rolf's abuse in silent misery, had she not seen Eryk outside the bookstore one chilly afternoon. It was a strange day for Helen. She'd desperately needed an hour alone away from the children, which was a rare occurrence for her. However, between her responsibilities at home and the pressure from Rolf she had begun to feel as if she might crack. She asked one of her neighbors to watch Ela and Lars for a short time. Helen had done similar favors for this particular neighbor and so the woman readily agreed.

It felt good to Helen to have an hour to herself as she walked alone down the cobblestone street. She was on her way to the grocer's shop. In the past, she'd always had the children with her so she never paused to window shop; her attention was always on the children. But today she stopped in front of the bookstore window to admire a beautifully bound book. It was in the reflection of that window that she saw Eryk walking by. She remembered him. How could she forget? He'd made such an impression on her at the meeting she'd attended with Artur and Marci. Then once he'd helped her when she'd forgotten her ration cards. They had only spoken a handful of words and even though she didn't know anything about him, from his voice and the way he carried himself she made believe that he was everything Nik was not. It was a fantasy and Helen knew that, but she enjoyed dreaming about Eryk being a strong protective man. Silly, childish daydreams. Silly, yes, but also very pleasant. Purely on impulse, she turned around.

"Hello," she said.

He looked in every direction as if he wasn't quite sure she was speaking to him.

"You don't remember me," Helen laughed. "We met at a meeting once. Your name is Eryk. I remember you. You work for the sanitation department."

A deep wrinkle formed on his brow.

"I don't know what you are talking about. Meeting? I don't know of any meeting," he said, cocking his head.

"Yes, of course, you do. But I wasn't thinking straight. Of course, we shouldn't talk about such things here in the street. Let's walk."

He stared into her eyes. Then he rubbed his chin with his thumb and nodded. "All right. Let's walk."

The snow crunched beneath their feet and their breath was white in the frigid air. After several minutes Eryk turned to Helen. "Who are you and what do you want?" His voice was harsh.

"I'm Helen Dobinski. We met at a meeting … a long time ago. I want to help the cause."

"Help? Help what cause? I don't know what you're talking about."

"Defeat those bastard Germans," she whispered. "I want to do whatever I can to get them the hell out of Poland."

He looked at her with a shocked expression then he laughed. "I'm sorry to laugh at you. It's just that you are such a proper looking petite girl that I wasn't expecting those words to come out of your mouth. "

"I hate the Nazis."

"I don't blame you," he said in a half teasing voice.

"I don't appreciate your tone. This is not a joking matter for me. I have my reasons for wanting to do this."

"And exactly what meeting are you referring to where we met? I still don't have any idea what you are talking about."

"Artur and Marci Labecki took me to a meeting of the Polish home army…"

"All right," he said with conviction, his voice suddenly serious. "That's enough talking.

"You are right; it is not safe to discuss these things on the street. We should go somewhere private where we can speak freely. I don't mean for this to sound forward, and please don't take it the wrong way. However, with things being the way that they are, it is best for us to go to my apartment. We must always be careful when we are talking. There are enemies all around us. And, quite frankly, Helen Dobinski, you just never know who we can trust."

Helen nodded. She could see in his eyes that he was skeptical about trusting her. She didn't blame him. But she was going to do this. No matter what the danger, she was going to do this.

"Let's go to your apartment then."

She shivered from the cold. Her coat was hardly warm enough to combat the chill but she walked quietly, following Eryk for several streets until they were in a lower class neighborhood very similar to her own. He led her into a tall brick building that was in need of repair, and she followed him up three flights of creaky wooden stairs until he stopped in front of a door.

"This is it," he said turning the key in the lock. "Come in."

The apartment was sparsely furnished with a lumpy sofa and a single lamp on a small lonely desk. There were a few books on a shelf and an unpainted wooden table with two chairs. Not much sunlight came through the window.

"Please sit down," Eryk said. Helen sat on the sofa. One side of her hips was higher than the other because of the bulges in the couch.

"All right, go on now. Finish what you were saying earlier. It's safe, we can talk here," he said

"I saw you at a meeting that I attended with friends."

"What friends? Tell me their names again."

"Artur and Marci Labecki. I told you their names earlier."

"I wasn't listening. I was looking around to see if anyone else was watching us. You have to be very careful what you say and who you talk to. How do you know the Labeckis?"

"Artur and my husband, Nik, have known each other for years. Do you know them?"

"Yes, I do. Not very well, but well enough," he said, and then seemed to relax a little. "Yes, now that I am looking at you, your face does look familiar to me."

"Artur brought us to the meeting because he wanted my husband to join the home army. But my husband is afraid. I am not afraid. I don't know how to use a gun or how to fight but I want to help with the resistance, and I can learn."

"I think I remember an incident between you and me that had something to do with some potato starch. It happened a few years ago." He smiled. She couldn't help noticing that the dimple on his left cheek made his smile look very sweet and enticing.

"Yes, you helped me. I was at the store and I had forgotten my ration cards at home. I was desperate because they were running out of flour and if I had gone home to get my cards, there would be nothing left by the time I returned."

He smiled. "Actually I do remember that."

"You were very kind to me. And I was very grateful to you for your help."

Eryk studied her for several minutes. It was as if he were sizing her up, deciding whether to trust her or to throw her out. Then he cocked his head and cleared his throat. "I am going to ask Artur about you and your husband. But I am sure you realize that I must do this."

"You can ask them all about us. But please don't tell them that I am planning to work with you. Nik would never approve."

"I am going to question them about your character. About whether they think we can trust you. I am hoping that we can"

She nodded. "I understand."

Eryk cleared his throat then his voice became deep and serious. "I'm sure you know that if you do this you will be putting yourself in grave danger. If you are caught, you must never reveal the names of anyone else you've ever worked with in our organization." He watched her carefully, calculating the expressions on her face. Then he said, "I don't know if you working with us is such a good idea."

"Why? Why do you say that?"

"Helen. It is Helen, yes?"

"Yes, Helen Dobiniski."

"Helen, you seem like a delicate sort of woman to me. And the truth is I am not sure that I trust you completely. How do I know you're not a spy?"

She laughed bitterly. "Oh, believe me, I am not a spy. You'd be surprised if you knew what I have endured at the hands of the Nazis. I've suffered plenty. Now I want to do what I can to force them out of our country. Please allow me to help the resistance."

He sighed then shook his head as if he were still not convinced. "You want a cup of tea?"

"No, thank you," she said.

"All right then. Give me a day or two to think this whole thing through. I want to talk to Artur. Then in two days you can come back here to my apartment. At that time we will discuss this again and I'll give you my decision."

CHAPTER FORTY-FOUR

As per Eryk's request, two days passed before Helen returned to his apartment. Once again, she asked the neighbor to watch her children for her. Then she took the tram early in the afternoon. When she arrived at Eryk's apartment, he was ready for her to begin working with the resistance. Helen decided that he must have spoken with Artur, who told him that she and Nik were good Polish citizens and would never be German spies.

"I've decided to trust you," he said. "Don't make me sorry I did. Do you understand me?"

"Yes."

"All right. Now listen closely. This is what I expect you to do. You will take these books back to the library for me." He handed her a pile of old hardcover books. "When you get there, you will look for the female librarian with the blond hair who wears thick black rimmed glasses. She is about forty years old. Her hair will be pulled back into a knot at the nape of her neck. Look for a pin on her blouse in the shape of a bird. She should be wearing a pink skirt with a white blouse. Her nametag will say Christina. When you find her, you will say to her, 'I enjoyed these books very much.' She will answer you, 'I am glad to hear that. It's wonderful when you find good books.' Once she says that you will hand her the pile. Make sure that you do not give these books to anyone other than this woman. Do you understand me perfectly?"

Helen nodded. "Yes. I understand."

"Do not open any of these books. Your job is only to get them to the library as quickly and safely as possible," Eryk said. Helen trembled, she was suddenly afraid. The books were heavy, but she didn't say a word. She'd decided that she was going to do this and she would go through with her decision. She turned and began to walk out the door.

"Be careful," Eryk said.

"When should I return here to your apartment?" Helen asked, just as she was about to leave.

"Come back in three days," he said.

Helen's unsteady knees trembled as she walked towards the library. She wanted to know what Eryk had stashed inside the books she was carrying. They were books that were obviously Nazi-approved literature. Two were about travels in Germany's great countryside, one was about Vikings and another about Hitler's greatness. Not one of the books would raise the slightest suspicion. However, she knew that Eryk had a reason for her to take them, but she was afraid to stop and open them to find out what it was. The quicker she got them delivered, the better. She decided it was best to curtail her curiosity because she had no secret place to open them. If she did so in the street she would be risking the possibility of someone else seeing what Eryk was clearly hiding, even from her.

As Eryk had promised, Christina was sitting at the front desk when Helen walked into the building. She knew for sure that it was Christina immediately. The black-rimmed glasses, the blond hair pulled back, the pin. Helen glanced around her quickly to see if anyone had followed her or if anyone was watching her. Nobody seemed to be paying any attention. Still, Helen couldn't stop biting her lower lip. Anything could happen. The Gestapo could be hiding behind one of the bookshelves. They might be waiting for her. She felt the sweat begin to pool in her armpits. Her hands were trembling as she approached the desk.

"I don't recognize you," Helen said. "I come here often. What is your name?"

"Christina."

Helen nodded. "I enjoyed these very much." She stammered, trying to smile.

"I'm glad to hear that. It's wonderful when you find good books," Christina answered. Helen noticed she wore the silver pin shaped like a bird like Eryk said she would.

Helen forced a trembling smile. Then she turned and walked quickly out of the library. She was moving so fast as she walked down the stairs that she slipped, but a Nazi officer in a dark coat caught her before she fell. She felt the blood pump through her temple.

Did he see me give that woman the books? Does he know what I just did? Was he waiting here to catch me? Oh dear God help me, please …

The officer smiled at her. "You almost took a spill."

She nodded. "Yes, almost. Thank you for catching me." Her heart was beating in her throat.

Every nerve ending in her body was tingling with fear. She wanted to run, but she forced herself to smile and walk away slowly.

After walking for several minutes she glanced behind her. No one was following her. It was difficult to catch her breath but she thanked God that she'd gotten that far safely. When she arrived back at her apartment building, she went upstairs to the neighbor's to collect Lars and Ela.

"I thought you went to the market. Where are your purchases?" Frau Kalmuski, the upstairs neighbor asked.

"I did go to the market," Helen lied. "But I went to my apartment and put the food away before I came here to pick up the children."

"I was afraid you weren't able to get any food. I am glad that you did. I just wanted you to know that little Ela is such a pleasure. She is like a miniature mother to my little Mikey."

"I'm sorry if Lars was difficult."

"He's not really. He's just a typical little boy. And he and Ela keep each other entertained. I am so glad that they play with Mikey, too. It gives me a chance to get some things done in the house."

"Can I give you some money for watching them?" Helen asked.

"Of course not. You watch Mikey for me all the time. We help each other. It's good to have a friend to share the burden of child-raising. Heaven knows that men are no help. That's for sure, isn't it? Ela is more like a babysitter than a child who needs watching."

Helen laughed. "Yes, she is. Ela is a big help to me. In fact, she loves to grab a dust rag and imitate me when I clean."

"By the way, I was going to ask you if you would watch Mikey for me next week? I want to go across town to see my mother, but the weather is too cold for me to bring him with me. He's so little and he tends to get sick so easily," Frau Kalmuski asked.

"Of course. It would be my pleasure."

CHAPTER FORTY-FIVE

May 1944

Helen's meetings with Rolf at the hotel were even more uncomfortable for Helen then the encounters at his flat had been. The hotel lobby was filled with people, many of them Nazi officers. When she walked in she kept her head down, her face was always red with shame. But twice a week, Rolf demanded that she meet him and she could see no way out. She would go to the desk clerk who had come to know her. He would smile a knowing smile that made her feel dirty and vile, then he would hand her the key that Rolf had left for her. Twice-a-week she went up to that little room where, against her will, she tolerated Rolf's sexual demands. He gave her gifts of money, food, and little trinkets that he bought for her and the children. Sometimes he could be very kind. But when he had a few drinks, any small thing could set him off on a tangent of madness and he would hurt her. From their first meeting at the hotel, he called her Anne-Marie. Never again did he call her by her real name, Helen. She knew better than to complain or admit that she wished to be free of him and beg him to let her go. She tried a couple of times but it had only enraged him. Since then she had to submit to his will. In secret, she joined the resistance and did what she could to defeat him and the Nazis.

Eryk knew where to reach her. He would send a message in a code that they had agreed upon and when she received the message she would go to him and he would hand her another stack of books. Helen asked no questions, she just took them to the library and delivered them to Christian, just as she was told to do.

March meandered into Poland slowly. The bitter cold began to subside and the coming of spring began melting the frost of winter. Helen used the frigid weather as an excuse to leave the children with Frau Kalmuski, her neighbor when she went to the market. But in another month, the weather would be warm enough for Helen to easily take the children into town with her.

"Soon I won't be able to come to your apartment anymore during the day to pick up the books because I will have the children with me. I am thinking that I can take Lars and Ela to the park and while they are playing we can meet there. I will sit on a bench. You can sit beside me. You bring the books and leave them on the bench. I will take them to the library with the children."

He grunted. "The risk will be even greater for you with the children."

"I know. But I think that maybe I will be less suspicious with them."

"If you are caught …"

"Don't even say it."

"Helen, I have to say what is on my mind. If you are caught, the Nazis are heartless. They would not think twice about shooting two little children. You do realize this?"

"Yes, I know. But I must do what I can. We, the Polish, must risk everything to get them out of our country." She sighed.

"How soon do you think we will have to change our plans and meet in the park?"

"Perhaps we can get away with continuing like this until late April. But things will have to change by early May. Yes, definitely early May at the latest."

"I don't think this is a good idea, Helen. I couldn't live with myself if you were caught. I really don't want you to do this …"

"I know. But I want to do it. I must do it."

For several minutes he just sat on the sofa looking at her without saying a word. Then he shook his head.

" A woman like you should never have to face anything like this. But unfortunately, this is what we have been reduced to," Eryk said sadly.

"I know, Eryk."

"I feel guilty allowing you to undertake this with two little children in hand. It was bad enough when it was just you."

"It is my choice. Please respect it."

He nodded. "All right, then we will meet in the park."

She nodded.

"You know, I worry about you. Every time you go on one of these missions, I am frantic until I hear from either you or Christina that you have been successful and that you are all right. You're a brave soul, little Helen."

"No, I am not. I am an angry woman, Eryk. I am hurt, angry, and afraid all the time. I have a terrible secret that drives me to want to kill those Nazi bastards."

"You can talk to me. You can tell me why. Maybe it will help you if you unburden yourself."

"I can't."

"Yes, you can." He put his hand on her shoulder. "Talk to me."

She looked into his eyes; they were a deep rich shade of brown, the color of topaz, but more importantly, they were kind. "You want me to tell you my secret …"

"Yes. I want you to share your secret with me."

"You will hold it against me."

"I will not. Helen, I care for you."

"But I have done something terrible."

"We have all done terrible things; it is the times we are living in. Our circumstances force us to act in ugly ways. And we all have secrets …"

"I'll tell you mine if you tell me yours." She smiled.

"I agree. Tell me."

"My daughter. You know, my Ela?"

"Yes, the cute little girl who has your golden curls?"

Helen laughed. "Does she? Does she have my golden hair?"

"She does."

"No, Eryk, she doesn't. I am not her real mother. Actually, that golden hair of hers comes from her father who was an American. He is long gone; he abandoned her mother when she was pregnant. No one knows where he is. But Ela's birth mother is imprisoned in the Warsaw ghetto. She is a dear friend of mine, and she is Jewish. Her name is Zofia Weiss. Ela's real name is Eidel. Ela was smuggled out of the ghetto as a baby. I am raising her as my own child."

"You've been hiding this, of course."

"Yes."

He nodded. "That's not a terrible thing. Why would you think I would hold such a kindness against you?"

"Because it is not all I have done. There is more to my secret. But, now that I've told you an important part of my life, it's your turn. You tell me one of your secrets."

"I am involved with an organization that is smuggling Jews out of the ghetto through the sewer system. That's why I work there. I am part of a group of partisans that wreaks havoc on the Nazis. We have connections with the Soviet army. We blow up railway stations." He smiled at her. "Dangerous work to be sure. The books you are delivering for me … they contain falsified papers. These papers are like magic; they turn Jews into Gentiles." He smiled as if this were a casual thing. Then he winked at her and shrugged his shoulders. "After you give them to Christina, she brings them to a safe house. All of these little miracle papers are tucked inside of the books."

"Inside of the books? How?"

"Yep. We carve out a square and fold the papers then put them inside."

"You act as if this were easy. Nothing to it at all."

"Easy?" he laughed. "Nothing about it is easy. But the allies are winning and the Nazis know it. They are losing the war. We'll get them out of our country. It's only a matter of time."

"So you said you did something bad …"

"I've watched men die because of the bridges I've blown up. I killed a man with my bare hands once. I choked the life out him. I watched his eyes pop, his face turn red. It was horrible, Helen. I never thought I was capable of such cruelty. But this is what I have become."

"You only did what you had to do."

Helen liked him. How could she not? He was everything she wished Nik would have been. Nik was weak; Eryk was strong. Nik was a coward; Eryk was a hero. In her life, Helen had experienced very little happiness. Very little. She got up and walked over to Eryk. Reaching up she cupped his face in her hands.

"Kiss me," she said.

He looked into her eyes. Then he put his hands on her shoulders and gently pushed her away.

"This sort of thing is not a good idea for us. It complicates our situation too much. You're a married woman. I have no time for a lover. I am dedicated to a cause. I could easily be killed tomorrow …" he rambled.

She looked down at the floor. "I'm embarrassed. I don't know what I was thinking. I'm sorry." Her face was hot and she knew her skin was crimson.

His hands fell to his sides.

"I should be going," she said, not looking at him.

"Yes," he said. "Be careful. Perhaps it is a good idea that we start meeting at the park right away instead of here at the apartment. Yes, I think that is best." He seemed unnerved by her actions. "Our next meeting is scheduled for next Tuesday afternoon. There is a bench at the north end of the park, the one that is across the street from the Bloomski's bakery. Is two in the afternoon, all right?"

She nodded, still not able to meet his eyes. "Yes, all right. I'll be there."

She picked up her handbag and slipped on her jacket, but as she was walking towards the door Eryk stopped her. Without saying another word, he took her in his arms and kissed her. Then he kissed her again. Lifting her easily, he carried her into the bedroom. She didn't resist. For the first time since the early days of her marriage, Helen was sharing herself with someone she wanted. She was making love to a man of her own choice. Her body was not being used by her husband to clean and cook and her sex was not being taken against her will by Rolf. This time, everything was on her own terms.

After they made love, Eryk caressed her shoulder as she lay in his arms. "I haven't been with a lover for many years," he said. "I have purposely avoided involvement. But I couldn't help myself with you. When you touched me, I wanted to push you away but I couldn't. I've been attracted to you since that first day I saw you at the meeting."

"So you did remember me? Why did you pretend you didn't?"

"I didn't want you to know that you'd made such an impact on me. I guess I was trying to avoid this."

"You mean becoming my lover?"

"Yes. In my line of work, so to speak, it's best not to care about anyone too much."

"But then what is the point of living?" Helen asked. "I want to care. I want to care and be cared for." The words choked in her throat.

"Your husband?"

"Nik? He is complex, for sure. When we first got married, I thought he loved me. But he is selfish and he loves the bottle more than he could ever love anyone or anything. Sometimes I feel so alone."

They were both silent for several minutes. The only sound was a flock of birds chirping outside the window.

"Helen . . ."

"Yes?"

"I've never admitted this to anyone before. And it's hard for me to tell you this now. But, Helen, most of the time I too feel very alone. I suppose when I act like I don't care, it's out of fear. You see ..."

He hesitated for a moment.

"The real truth is that I am afraid of how much I do care. I'm terrified of becoming too close to anyone because of the constant threat of loss. Of losing them or knowing that they may have to cope with my death. You understand?"

She nodded.

He continued, "It's the way I survive. If I don't care about anyone or anything then nothing can hurt me. But the reality is I long for someone to love, for someone to share my life. I must sound like a real old-fashioned sap, and even as I am speaking I can hear how foolish I sound. But I've never said these words before."

Helen touched his chest. She ran her fingers up and down, feeling the warmth of his skin. She felt so close to him, closer than she'd felt to anyone in a very long time. She longed to unburden herself and to tell him about Rolf. It felt wrong to be hiding her terrible sin from him. But she could not bring herself to open that Pandora's box. She was afraid she would lose him. If Eryk knew that her body had been penetrated by a Nazi he might not want to be her lover anymore. And she couldn't blame him. Even though the sex with Rolf was never her choice, it still might be enough to repulse him and send him away from her forever.

CHAPTER FORTY-SIX

Not only did Helen want Eryk in her life, she needed him. He was her friend and her lover. He was all that Nik should have been but was not.

Before Helen's affair with Eryk began, the only thing that kept her going was the children. Otherwise, every day she awakened feeling like she was trapped in a dark cage and she could not find any escape. If not for Lars and Ela, she would have probably committed suicide. But they were so young and needed her so desperately that she could not leave them and trust them to Nik. There was no doubt in Helen's mind that if she were no longer around, Nik would find a way to rid himself of Ela. She imagined him taking Ela away on a train and then leaving the child alone in some strange and far away location. He would probably just leave her on a park bench somewhere and disappear. The very idea sent shivers up Helen's spine. She thought that he might try to raise Lars alone, but since he'd been drinking so heavily, she doubted that he was capable. With his long work hours and drunken nights, it was hard to tell what would become of Lars. No, suicide was out of the question. Helen had two children to think of and, as miserable as she was, she felt she owed it to her babies to care for them until they were old enough to care for themselves. That was the way her life had been until she and Eryk had fallen in love. Now, even in the darkest time of Helen's life, her face still had a rosy glow.

It was wonderful to share things with another adult and to talk about everything imaginable. And that was what Helen and Eryk did. Their relationship was physical but it was so much more for both of them. Before they'd found each other, neither of them had anyone else they could lean on. Now they had each other. The time they spent together was precious. They drank the terrible bitter stuff that had become known as coffee since the beginning of the war and shared all of the dreams they'd had as children. Both of them had lost the last of their parents during the past seven years and they shared memories of their childhoods. Eryk told Helen about his sister who had married and moved to France before the war began.

"She was ten years older than me. I was a surprise baby for my parents. They weren't expecting to have another child so late in life. Then my mother became pregnant and there I was," he said, shrugging his shoulders. "I've tried to make contact with my sister. I sent letters but received nothing in return. There was no response to my telegram. It is impossible to reach her. I don't know if she is alive or dead. Sadly, Germany has her tentacles around France, too. And, to make matters even more worrisome, my sister's husband is a Jewish professor. So God only knows what's happened to them."

"Well, all we can do is pray for them," Helen said.

Helen continued to insist on helping the resistance by delivering the books. But the more entwined she and Eryk became as lovers, the less he wanted her involved with the partisans. Helen knew he was afraid for her. She wanted to go with Eryk when he was involved in blowing up a train, but he adamantly refused to take her. While he was gone, Helen was sick with worry.

But nothing changed in her life. Helen was still forced to go to the hotel and meet with Rolf to endure his repulsive demands. When she fell asleep, she often had dreams of killing Rolf. One night, she dreamed of stabbing Rolf in the eye with her sewing scissors. Bright red blood spewed out of the hole where his eye had been. The dream was so real that when Helen awakened she was shaken to the very core. She lay in bed and begged God for forgiveness. Because of the dream and the hatred she felt for Rolf, she was afraid that God would punish her. She didn't care if the punishment was taken out on her alone, but her biggest fear was that because of her evil thoughts Eryk would be killed during his mission.

Time was passing and she had not seen or heard from Eryk. He was gone for almost two weeks but, just when she was sure he was never coming back to her, he returned. For the first time in her life, Helen felt truly grateful to God. That night, she went to Eryk and stayed with him much later than she'd ever stayed with Rolf. She ignored the curfew, telling herself that if she were caught on her way home she'd use the note Rolf had given her for their meetings.

That night, Helen and Eryk made love for hours before either spoke at all. Once they had finished and were both covered in sweat, Helen felt a tear drop from Eryk's eye onto her neck.

"I was so worried," Helen whispered in his ear.

"I thought of you every minute." He kissed her. "Divorce your husband, Helen. Marry me. I'll be a father to your children. You are not happy with Nik. If you were, you wouldn't be here with me."

"No, I am not happily married to Nik. But there is something that I must tell you. I don't know how you will feel about me once you know and I am terrified that I will lose you. But I can't lie to you anymore. I love you too much to keep secrets."

Helen had been worried every day that Eryk would find out about Rolf before she had the nerve to tell him. If he did find out on his own he would feel betrayed, and how could she blame him? She knew that the Polish partisans and the Soviets had spies everywhere. What if one of them had seen her going to meet Rolf at the hotel? She wasn't sure who was watching her and who might deliver that information back to Eryk. The spies for the home army and the Soviets seemed to know everything and every day they were growing more powerful and more informed. If someone told Eryk that they saw Helen going to meet Rolf, not only a man but an SS officer in a hotel room, what would Eryk think? He might be convinced that she was a spy and never trust her again. No, he must not learn about her situation with Rolf from anyone else. The truth must come directly from her. If this was to be the end of their love, then so be it. She would be devastated, but at least she would know she had been truthful with him. He deserved that.

"You are not going to like what I have to say." Helen sat up in bed and turned to look at Eryk, who was lying on his back.

"Helen, what is it?" He sat up in bed and smoothed her hair out of her face. "You should feel free to tell me anything. I won't leave you. I love you." He took her in his arms. "I've never told anyone I loved them before. I take those words very seriously. Now, please, tell me … whatever it is."

"Eryk, I love you too." She was crying softly.

"Then go on and tell me. Trust me. Please."

Helen sucked in a deep breath and told him all about Rolf. Everything. She told him how they'd met, how he'd threatened to take Ela if she did not succumb to his demands.

"He is a Sturmbannführer, a high-ranking officer, Eryk. He has power and he is dangerous. When I first met him, he was working in the Warsaw ghetto. That's where Ela's real mother was imprisoned. God help her. I have no idea what has become of her."

"What is his name? This Sturmbannfuhrer?"

"Rolf Boltz"

"I know him," Eryk said.

She went into more detail about how Rolf told her that he knew the truth about Ela being Jewish.

"Rolf even knew that Ela's mother's name is Zofia Weiss. He had the power to destroy me and my family then, and he still does. I did what I had to do. Forgive me, please." By the time she finished, Helen was sobbing uncontrollably. Eryk let her cry. When she finished, the room was silent. Helen felt a chill rise up her naked back. Eryk got up and left the room. Several minutes passed. Helen was sure that he was done with her. Suddenly, she wanted to leave, to run out of the apartment and be away from the pain she was feeling. The pain in her heart was far worse than any beating that Rolf had inflicted upon her. Helen got up and began to put her clothes on when Eryk walked back in the room. There was a deep crevice between his brows and his face was lined. She couldn't tell if he was angry or concerned until he put his arms around her and held her close to him.

"I love you. Don't blame yourself. It's not your fault," he whispered.

Helen wept again. Gut-wrenching sobs left her throat and if Eryk was not holding her she would have fallen to her knees. Her body was limp in his arms.

"I love you. Thank you for your forgiveness," she whimpered.

"Now that I know everything, will you consider leaving your husband and marrying me?"

"Yes. Yes, I will, Eryk. But even if we are married, you must know that I still can't get rid of Rolf. I pray every day that he will tire of me. Or worse … sometimes … I am ashamed to say it, but I pray he will die."

"I'll get rid of Rolf. I'll kill him," Eryk said matter-of-factly.

Helen was trembling. "No, Eryk. No, not murder. Please. Besides, he's an SS officer. If you are caught …"

"I've blown up trains filled with Nazis. If I'd been caught, I would be dead. I've taken chances, serious chances, before. But this bastard and I have a personal issue. It will be a great pleasure for me to end his life."

Helen looked into his eyes. "I am scared for you, Eryk. And I am afraid to condone this. It is breaking one of God's sacred commandments."

"You don't have to condone it, Helen. I am a grown man. I will do what must be done with or without your permission. When does he expect you to meet with him again?"

"Next week. Wednesday night."

"I'll see you before then. I will tell you what I want you to do."

"Eryk, you don't expect me to kill him, do you? I couldn't."

"Of course not. I am just hoping that I will be able to arrange things so you don't ever have to see him again. Not even next week. But I am not sure I can get everything I need to finish this off in time. However, I'll do my best."

"Eryk." She whispered his name and her heart hurt as she held him close to her chest. "I am afraid for you. I am so afraid. Now that I've found you I can't bear the thought of losing you."

"And I can't bear the thought of that bastard putting his hands on you again."

"I shouldn't have told you. Now I've put you in danger."

"I've been in danger since the Nazis came into our lives." He looked outside. "It's getting late. It's past curfew. Let me walk you home."

"No, I have a note from Rolf that makes it safe for me if I am found outside after curfew."

He looked away. "So that's why you never let me walk you home. I thought it was because of Nik."

"No, it's because I am safer alone. And you are not safe with me at all."

He looked away. "A man is not a man if he can't take care of the woman he loves."

"Eryk, stop, please. You are only making this worse." She touched his cheek. "I really should go now. If I am any later Nik will ask questions."

"Wait. I want to give you something. I brought you a present." Naked, he walked into the kitchen. She watched him. Helen had never thought of any man as being beautiful until she met Eryk.

He makes me so happy. I don't know what's right or wrong anymore.

He came back into the room and handed her a cloth sack. "Be careful with that," he said.

"What is it?"

"A dozen eggs and two soup bones." He smiled. "You deserve so much more but it was the best I could do."

"You got it from the black market?"

"I received it as a gift from our Soviet friends, and of course I wanted to give it to you."

"Did you save any food for yourself? You need food too, Eryk."

"I have plenty."

"The one egg a month the Nazis ration us? That's enough for you? I don't think so," she said as she gazed at him "Here, at least take half of this."

"I have friends, Helen. They get me what I need. I am not starving. You have two children to take care of. I insist that you take these small offerings. They are for you. Now, take it, please."

She smiled at him.

"Oh, and take this too. Just in case you need it." He took a gun out of the drawer in his nightstand.

"I wouldn't know how to use it," she said.

Eryk gazed at Helen for a few minutes. "Then it's best you don't take the gun. You might be in more danger with it than without it."

CHAPTER FORTY-SEVEN

Ivonne Boltz opened her eyes and stretched like a contented cat. She'd slept much later than usual. When she looked at the clock on the wall, she was shocked to see that it was eleven a.m. Her entire body tingled with excitement; she had slept very well. It was the first time in weeks that she wasn't awakened before nine due to the morning nausea, which had always resulted in her jumping out of bed and racing to the toilet to vomit. Rolf had already been gone for hours. She knew that he always left for work no later than eight-thirty. The house was serene and quiet, save for the birds chirping outside her bedroom window. She looked out and saw a spider building a web in the tree just a few feet from her window. Stretching again, she smiled to herself.

Tonight, everything has to be just right because tonight is going to be very special.

She bit her lower lip and giggled at the joy she felt. When she got out of bed, Ivonne would instruct Dericka, the new cook she had hired last week, to prepare all of Rolf's favorite dishes. Although Ivonne would never tell Rolf, she'd hired Dericka because Dericka was unattractive and Ivonne felt safer having her in the house with Rolf.

Why tempt him if I don't have to? Dericka does a good job of cooking and she is also an excellent housekeeper.

Ivonne ran her fingers over the embroidered and lace quilt that covered her bed and sang to herself. It was an old German folk song she had sung as a child. She had something wonderful to tell her husband. The news was sure to make him very happy. And she had grand hopes that it would turn their lackluster marriage into the fairytale romance she always knew, always believed, that it could become.

"Dericka," Ivonne called out in a melodious voice. "Dericka, come here to my bedroom please."

Dericka Fischer was a heavy-set young girl with a face marred by blemishes and frizzy brown hair that seemed to jump out of the bun she wore. She came rushing into Ivonne's room.

"Yes, Frau Boltz?"

"I want you to have Elberich drive you to the market. Once you get there, I want you to purchase a chicken, a white bread, or some flour to bake one, and some butter. Never mind. Here, take this list I made for you of the dishes I want you to prepare and just purchase what you need. You know where to go. Tell the shopkeepers that you are buying these goods for Sturmbannfuhrer Boltz. If they are able, they will get them for you. You may have to go to a few different shops, but I want this done for tonight."

Ivonne got out of bed and went into the drawer where she kept her lingerie. Hidden under her silky slips was a piece of paper. She handed it to Dericka.

"These are all of Herr Boltz's favorite foods. Take extra care in your preparation; make sure they are delicious. I need them to be hot and ready to eat before you leave here for the evening."

"Yes, Maam."

"Don't forget to set the table with my mother's lace tablecloth. Use the good china and crystal … and Dericka … make sure there is absolutely no dust anywhere. Rolf hates filth."

"Yes, Maam."

"Go on now," Ivonne said to Dericka. Then she called out, remembering that her mother always told her to be nice to people. "Dericka ... thank you."

Rolf should treat the servants more kindly than he does. He is very hard on Dericka and Elberich, and all they really want to do is please us. Ah, well, I can't bring such a thing up to him. Rolf wouldn't want his wife telling him how he should behave towards servants. And I can't blame him. After all, he is the man of the house.

Ivonne got out of bed and went to the bathroom to wash her face and hands.

I am going to do it.

She shivered nervously as she took a bottle out of the cabinet. She had been hiding the hair lightening mixture that she'd bought for this special evening. Ivonne turned the box over in her hands and read the label. 'L'Oreal.' Before she had decided to try to lighten her hair, she'd talked to several other women about the possibility of it actually working. They all had recommended that she buy this product to do the job. She'd never done anything like this before and was a little afraid to try a chemical on her hair. What if it fell out? So before she bought the hair color she did plenty of research. She found out everything she could about the company that made this miracle product. She learned that the hair lightener was invented in Paris by a man named Eugene Schueller. He owned the large and very reputable cosmetic company called L'Oreal. Not only was the company considered a good choice for hair products but Schueller also had a good reputation amongst the Germans. He was a good man and he'd financed the main fascist movement in France.

She opened the box. There were two bottles that had to be mixed together then the mixture was to be applied directly to dry hair. The product had cost her a pretty penny but it would be well worth the money if it worked as promised. She knew she would have to color the roots when her hair began to grow in brown, but as a blonde she would be Rolf's Aryan ideal woman. And if there was anything Ivonne wanted, it was to please her husband in every way possible. Ivonne watched her reflection in the mirror as she applied the liquid.

I'll just put this in my hair and sit in the sun for a few hours.

Her hands were trembling. Even though she had done plenty of research, she was still nervous. But she had to do it. She wanted the results so badly.

Before Dericka left to go to the market she'd prepared a light breakfast for Ivonne that she left on the table. When Ivonne climbed down the stairs and entered the dining room, she found a lovely tray with two thick slices of white bread, a hunk of cheese, and two hard-boiled eggs waiting for her.

Dericka is such a good girl. If Rolf will allow me to, I would like to give her a gift. Some chocolates perhaps. She would like that.

Ivonne ate her breakfast while waiting for the color to process in her hair. Her scalp began to burn, but at first the burning was mild. She took her breakfast and went outside to sit on the porch. Finally, it was time to see the results. Her knees trembled as she got into the bath where she shampooed out the chemical. When she was finished she wrapped herself in a towel and then she looked in the mirror. Ivonne's hair wasn't exactly the color of wheat; instead, it was more of a strawberry, brassy gold. However, her hair was much lighter than it was before, so she was pleased with the results.

Taking a thick towel off the bathroom shelf, she dried her hair vigorously and then twisted it into tiny pin curls. It wasn't very thick, so it would be dry long before Rolf arrived back at home that evening.

CHAPTER FORTY-EIGHT

Rolf was detained at work that night. He didn't call for Elberich to pick him up until seven forty-five. The sun was setting and the evening was just on the horizon.

"Frau Boltz has been preparing a special evening for you, Herr Sturmbannführer. She will be disappointed that you are so late," Elberich said.

"Mind your own business," Rolf snapped at his driver.

Who the hell is he to tell me how to manage my wife?

Rolf was in a foul mood. He'd hoped to have peace for a while now that the Jews were gone. But he'd received information that day that there was more trouble with the home army.

Damn those fucking Poles. This is certainly not what I need right now. The incident in the ghetto in April when the Jewish swine had caused all that trouble is still hanging over my head. I still look like a fool because of it and it will take years before I am taken seriously again.

His superior, Obergruppenfuhrer von Sammern-Frankenegg, was publicly embarrassed by the fact that Himmler had been forced to call Jurgen Stroop to replace him. It was a blow to all of von Sammer-Frakenegg's staff, Rolf included. They looked weak and incompetent because they had been unable to get those Jews under control and on the trains. Although no one had mentioned it yet, Rolf knew that he had fallen down a notch in the eyes of the Party. It didn't matter that liquidating the ghetto hadn't been easy for Stroop, either. He had done the job and that was all that the senior officers would recognize. And because Rolf was part of von Sammern-Frankenegg's staff, it meant he could kiss the idea of any more promotions goodbye, or at least until he could find a way to prove himself worthy again.

If that was even possible.

Ivonne knew how much pressure Rolf was under. He told her often and, even worse, much of the time he was in a terrible mood. But she had a way of getting under his skin. He hated himself when he was mean to her but sometimes she could be so childlike and stupid. She would tell him jokes and try to make him laugh when the last thing he felt like doing was laughing. Everything she did was to please him and he knew that. He wished that he had the patience to be kinder to her. It would be nice if he could even find a way to enjoy some of her efforts to make him happy.

But things at work were growing more difficult for him by the minute. Now, with the partisans and the Soviets closing in, he had far too much on his mind to be excited about silly things like the bouquets of sunflowers that she would proudly show him or her new negligee.

CHAPTER FORTY-NINE

When Rolf walked through the door, he could see that the house was set up for a celebration. He bit his lower lip to keep from saying something unkind. Rolf knew that Ivonne meant well, but right now he found her to be nothing less than an annoyance. The table was lovely, set for two, with their best china and crystal. A candelabra with white candles burning softly stood in the center of the table. He couldn't imagine what they would be celebrating and at the moment he didn't care. There was nothing in his world right now that felt deserving of a celebration.

Well, at least it appears that Ivonne hasn't invited any of our friends. That at least is a good thing. I am certainly in no mood to be bothered with people.

Ivonne came gracefully down the staircase. So delicate was her footing that it seemed as if she walked on air.

"Rolf." She kissed him. "I'm glad you're here. Dinner is ready." Her face was glowing.

"You've changed your hair," he said.

"Do you like it?"

"Yes, actually I do. You look lovely as a blond."

Still not as pretty as Anne-Marie or Helen with their wheat-colored hair but, I have to admit, it is better than her natural brown color. And it is obvious that she is trying hard to please me. I must try to control my temper.

"I am sure you are tired, my darling. Sit down, have a glass of wine."

"It's just the two of us tonight, yes?" he asked.

"Yes … go and get undressed. I want you to be comfortable. I have some news for you."

"Good news, I hope." He was walking towards the stairs feeling exhausted and a little defeated. His shoulders slumped and climbing the stairs felt like an effort.

"Yes, very good news. I think you'll be very pleased."

When he got to their bedroom upstairs, he undressed down to his underwear and white tee shirt. Then he went into the bathroom and splashed cold water on his face. As he was reaching for a towel he glanced in the mirror. His eyes caught a glimpse of the tattoo of his blood type that the SS had put under his arm when he'd first joined.

I can still remember the day I got this. I had so many dreams, so many aspirations.

Rolf touched the tattoo.

Now I don't know if I'll ever be promoted again. I am so afraid that my career is ending. I hate taking it out on Ivonne, but I am so angry, so frustrated.

Every instinct inside of him made him want to lash out at someone. And being that she was the only person who was there with him, she was vulnerable. However, he forced himself to think about his promise to his mother. Mother liked Ivonne. She wanted this marriage.

I have to try to treat my wife as gently as possible even if she doesn't excite any passion in me. I'll force myself to find a way to be civil as I sit through this dinner with her. Then I'll excuse myself and go upstairs.

Elberich was often the one he would take his bad mood out on, because Elberich never knew when to be quiet. He grated on Rolf's nerves with his endless talking and constant questions.

When Rolf came down the stairs in his robe, Ivonne smiled brightly.

He is so handsome. I can't believe he is really mine. He is my husband.

"Sit down, please. I had Dericka prepare all of your favorites," Ivonne said.

The food was wonderful. Ivonne knew how much Rolf loved Chicken Schnitzel with sauerkraut and white bread slathered in real butter. As per Ivonne's instructions, Dericka had gone from shop to shop until she found everything that she needed, and she'd also purchased wine and vodka. Dericka did a good job; everything was perfect. Ivonne sighed with satisfaction.

Watching him eat, Ivonne was sure that her husband was enjoying the delicious meal. And as he ate, he seemed to be in a better mood. It was as if he were allowing himself to take a little time to forget his problems at work.

After dinner, Ivonne brought an apple strudel out of the kitchen and cut him a thick piece. She poured him a cup of real coffee with milk. Then she sat back down beside him. She could hardly contain her excitement as her face burst into a wide smile. Rolf turned to look into her eyes. Seeing the joy on her face, he tried hard to return the grin.

"So, my little imp … what's your secret?" he asked.

It had been so long since he'd spoken to her in such an endearing way that she wanted to jump into his arms and flood his face with kisses. But she knew he wouldn't like that. So she sat still and remained as dignified as possible.

"I'm pregnant, Rolf. You're going to be a father."

His face lit up. He cocked his head. "Really? Are you sure?"

"I am sure. I am showing all the signs."

Rolf reached over and touched her belly.

He'd always used protection with Helen and with the other Polish girls with whom he'd had sexual intercourse, so he didn't know how long it would take him to impregnate his wife. But to his delight, Ivonne had conceived quickly. He was going to be a father! The very idea made him feel strong and virile. He'd heard of couples trying for years before succeeding.

This is really an honor, both to me and to the fatherland. My superiors will be happy to hear the news.

"Have you seen a doctor?"

"Yes. He thinks from the symptoms that I have been having that I am close to two months pregnant."

"I am happy … you were right, this does please me. This is good news. Very good news." He turned to her and took her hand and brought it to his lips. His mother was right, Ivonne was a good wife and at that moment he felt a sudden wave of tenderness towards her. He'd treated her badly. He knew it. Sometimes he had been short with her. Rolf had also been unfaithful, both in his heart and in his bed. Right at that moment in time, he was sorry. But he knew that as soon as that old fever of passion stirred in him, he'd be taking his need for Anne-Marie out on Helen again.

However, he decided that he must treat Ivonne with more tenderness. She deserved it. In fact, tomorrow, he would bring her a little gift. It was a shame that he couldn't go to that seamstress friend of Helen's—the one who had been in the ghetto—and have her make a dress for Ivonne.

Zofia Weiss.

He even remembered her name. The irony of it brought a crooked smile to his face. The poor Jewish girl, she was probably already dead or waiting her turn at Treblinka. Zofia's affair with the Kapo had kept her safe for a while. But that Kapo was on his way to Treblinka now, too.

Ah, well. It would have been nice to have the dress to present to Ivonne, however, the sooner we get rid of all of the Jews the better. Zofia Weiss, she really was quite talented as a dressmaker. It's a shame, it would have been a nice gift and I wouldn't have had to pay a penny for the workmanship.

CHAPTER FIFTY

July 1944

It was dusk. The sun, after an exhausting day of keeping the earth bright, had begun her descent from the sky. A soft golden glow followed, then it was as if a paintbrush of pale indigo, fuchsia, and orange fell like a curtain over the heavens and the moon began to peak her silver head out of the semi-darkness.

Eryk waited for night to fall. He sat hidden behind a few mature oak trees where he could see Elberich and Rolf as they drove up to the house. Eryk watched as the driver opened the car door and Rolf got out of the back seat. He cringed when he heard Rolf's voice. That bastard forced himself on Helen. Eryk's hands clenched into a fist.

Control yourself. It's not time yet. At least I know that Rolf has arrived at home. Soon I will make sure that Helen will never have to endure his disgusting advances again.

Eryk's heart was racing. He wanted to run up to Rolf and plunge a knife into the Nazi's heart.

Be patient. It's not time yet. Wait until nightfall, he told himself.

I must contain myself until every light in every window in Rolf's house is dark. Then I can begin to put my plan into action.

His breathing was ragged. But he stayed hidden and kept his eyes fixed on the scene in front of him. He stared in through the glass picture window and saw the elegant living and dining room. Rolf was sitting at a table across from a young slender woman with strawberry blond hair. She seemed quite jovial, constantly smiling, throwing her head back and laughing. The table was filled with food and drink, the likes of which Eryk had not seen since before the war. Eryk continued to peer into the window as he held on to the tree bark to control his anger. When Rolf took the woman's hand in his and kissed it, Eryk spit on the ground. A talon of anger filled with a need for revenge gripped Eryk's heart, crushing it as he whispered a curse in Polish.

CHAPTER FIFTY-ONE

Once they'd finished dinner, Ivonne went upstairs where she took her time getting ready for bed. Gently, she removed the gold comb from her hair and studied herself in the mirror. There were places where her hair was lighter than other places. In some spots, the red was more vivid, in others the blond was a bit brassy. But, all in all, she was glad she'd lightened her hair. She was no longer a mousy brunette; she was a blonde. And that was what Rolf wanted. And she was pregnant with his pure Aryan child. But most importantly, Rolf finally seemed pleased with her. For a few moments at the table that night, he acted the way he did in the very first days of their marriage. It was wonderful. She had such hope for their future that it brought tears to her eyes. Ivonne hummed softly to herself as she slipped on her nightgown. It was a long, silky blue dress with a slit up the side that hung softly over her curves. She'd paid more for it than she'd wanted to but she hoped it would entice her husband.

Rolf came into the room and took her into his arms. Tears of joy and relief overcame her. Ivonne was beginning to believe that Rolf might someday actually fall in love with her. Perhaps he'd just been preoccupied for a while. The reason he had been distant didn't matter to her. She would forgive him anything. All that Ivonne cared about was right now, this very moment. At that moment in time, she felt like she was floating on air.

CHAPTER FIFTY-TWO

Eryk still sat on the hard ground. He felt his buttocks tingling from a lack of circulation. At least the unrelenting heat of the summer day was starting to subside. He'd been sitting against the tree in Rolf's yard for over four hours. The bark had begun to grind itself into his back. However, all of the lights in the house had been off for an hour. He wanted to wait a little longer to be sure everyone was asleep. If he acted too quickly, his plan would fail.

At a little after two in the morning, Eryk began his work. He moved quickly and purposefully. Taking a hose out of his pocket he began to siphon the gasoline out of Rolf's automobile into a bucket he'd brought with him. It made him smile to see that the tank was full. Damn Nazis.

Of course he has a full tank of gas. No one else does. But right now, I am glad that the Nazi bastards take good care of themselves. Well, this particular SS bastard is about to regret having a full tank of gas. He'll wish he'd been a little less generous with his own needs, and been more concerned with the war effort, Eryk thought to himself and smiled.

Eryk had purposely worn several ratty old shirts that night. He took them all off except for one and laid them in a pile. Next, he took his whittling knife out of his pocket and began cutting them into pieces. Quick and light-footed, he spread the fabric rags around the house. Then he poured the gasoline over the rags and lit a match.

CHAPTER FIFTY-THREE

Since Elberich was a boy, he'd always had trouble falling asleep. At night when he was alone and not busy, he had time to think. And for as long as he could remember, he was always drawn to thoughts of how he'd been underprivileged in every way. He was not a handsome man, not athletic or particularly intelligent. Elberich had no talents to speak of, and since he'd gotten his job he was terribly envious of the Sturmbannführer. Rolf Boltz had everything a man could wish for, a beautiful wife who only wanted to please him, a high position in the Party, a beautiful home, servants, and plenty of money. Besides all of that, Rolf Boltz was a son of a bitch who treated him terribly. Many nights he lay awake in his bed, discontented and wallowing in his misery as he gazed out his window, watching the trees sway in the breeze until dawn.

That night was no different. It was two in the morning and Elberich was still looking out the window of his room, which was a small area just off the kitchen, when he noticed that there was a man outside. Curious, he sat up in bed to take a keener look. It was dark and for several minutes he wasn't sure what the man was doing. But as soon as he realized that the man taking the gas out of the auto, Elderich knew that something was amiss.

However, he wasn't sure exactly what the man's intentions were.

Is he stealing gasoline? Or is he going to start a fire? If he starts a fire, I must be ready to run to get out of here. But … I don't think I am going to awaken the Sturmannfurrer.

Elberich's entire body was trembling, as he quickly got dressed. He grabbed his gun, still keeping his eyes on the window.

Ah ha, I was right!

That man is pouring the gasoline all around the house. He is planning to assassinate the Sturmbannfuhrer. I should awaken them, for Ivonne's sake. I like her. But it is a pity that she will have to be sacrificed for having married that bastard Boltz.

I am not in any hurry to stop the burning of this house. I just have to be sure to get out in time. This is an opportunity, and I am not about to let it slip away. This is my chance, finally my chance, to prove myself. I have bigger plans for myself than saving Boltz.

Elderich thought for a minute about Ivonne. She'd always treated him kindly. Poor thing, she'd just been in the wrong place at the wrong time. For a single moment, Elderich felt a slight pang of regret for what he was about to do. But he had ambitions and he'd learned that no one was going to help him. No one ever had. If he was ever to be anything but a driver, he had to prove himself worthy of being promoted. He had to gain respect from his superiors in the Party. And that was just what he was going to do.

Quickly and quietly, he slipped out a side door and hid, waiting for the fire to take on a life of its own. He watched for a moment as the flames turned into a giant red monster with an insatiable appetite to consume all in its wake. The monster began to rise and quickly devour the house, the Sturmbannfuhrer, and with it Elberich's career as a failure and a nobody.

CHAPTER FIFTY-FOUR

By the time Rolf and Ivonne awakened they were both choking and coughing. The fire had taken hold and the house was already ablaze. Their bedroom was located on the second floor. Rolf got out of bed, but he was coughing so hard that he couldn't catch his breath and he was disoriented. The room was filled with smoke, making it impossible to find the door out of the bedroom let alone the staircase to the first floor. Rolf's eyes were burning and tearing profusely. Somewhere within the room he heard Ivonne hacking and crying out for him, but he couldn't see her.

I can't find my way in my own bedroom. I can't see, I can't hear, I can't breathe. I know Ivonne needs me, but right now I don't care. I just have to get out of this house.

"Rolf," she called again, but the crackling of the fire was too loud for him to determine where she was. Then he heard a loud noise; something had fallen. He somehow found the door and ran out of the room, hitting his cheek on a piece of wooden board. Blood poured down his face, but he didn't feel any pain. The fear he felt was all consuming. Then he heard another terrifying noise but Rolf couldn't determine what had caused the loud crash.

He had no idea that it was Ivonne. She had found her way out of the bedroom and to the stairs. Gripping the railing, she tried to get to the first floor when the wood of the rail gave way. She kept her balance for a moment, but then the stairs collapsed and she tumbled like a rag doll to the ground. She'd broken her neck and laid there, dead. Smoke as thick as a velvet blanket covered every room in the house.

The windows cracked.

Rolf felt a deep pain whenever he tried to breathe. It was as if his lungs were burning up with the house. He was desperate for air. In a panic, he inhaled too deeply. The pain that shot through his chest knocked him to the floor. A wood beam, red with fire, fell from the ceiling right onto Rolf, pinning him beneath it and, in seconds, the powerful Sturmbannfurer Rolf Boltz was consumed by the flames of hell.

CHAPTER FIFTY-FIVE

Once Eryk could see that the fire had grown to where it would easily consume the house, he began walking quickly away from the scene. He hid behind a cluster of bushes and watched for just a few moments. It was after curfew and he knew he must not be caught outside but he stood mesmerized by the fire. He had to wait until he was sure that he did not see Rolf escape. From where Eryk stood, he could hear the big picture window in the living room burst. He saw shards of glass flying across the lawn, lit like glass daggers in the light from the flames. Thick clouds of black smoke billowed out from inside the house and flew up to the sky, growing denser by the minute. It was time to get away. Eryk considered escaping into the sewer beneath the street before the authorities arrived to put out the fire, but he knew that one of the partisan organizations of which he was a member had been hiding Jews in that sewer, and he didn't want to jeopardize any of their plans for their safety.

No, he would move through the shadows until he arrived back at his apartment. It was a long walk, but he had been through much worse and he'd survived. He would persevere this time, too. Every few minutes he looked back to be sure he was alone and no one was following him. Everything seemed to be going as planned. No witnesses. As Eryk turned a corner into an alley way he heard the commotion of automobiles and sirens all headed towards Rolf's house. His nerves were stretched like rubber bands. Eryk knew he should stay calm and walk, but it was as if he couldn't stop his legs, and he began to run.

He stayed in the back alleys as long as possible. Then, when he was forced to come out to the street, he hugged the building and stayed out of the light. Finally, breathing heavily and covered in sweat, Eryk arrived at his apartment. Once inside, Eryk leaned against the wall and sucked in deep breaths of air and a smile came over his face.

Helen, my sweet Helen, is free. That man will never take her against her will again. I will sleep well; my conscience is at rest because I have rid the world of a bastard tonight.

CHAPTER FIFTY-SIX

Elberich Hahn had escaped before the fire had begun to climb the walls of the Sturmbannfhrer's home. Hahn had gotten out of the house through an employee door that let him out in the back of the garden. He followed Eryk home without ever being spotted. Once Eryk was inside his apartment, Hahn looked at the bell downstairs to discover Eryk's name. Eryk Jaworski. Apartment #3B. Elberich took a pencil and paper out of his pocket and wrote down the name and address. Then he left and headed for the police station. His lanky legs easily navigated the streets and he arrived at his destination quickly. The fire at the Boltz home was still raging when Elberich walked into the police station. He walked up to the officer at the desk and said, "I know who it was that started this fire."

He leaned forward on the desk as he continued.

"You see, I was the Sturmbannfuhrer's driver. My name is Elberich Hahn. I saw everything, but I was too late to stop it, so I came here to you."

"What did you see?"

"I saw the man who did it escaping. I was looking through my bedroom window. Of course, the first thing I did was try to get upstairs to rescue my employer and his wife, but the smoke was too thick so I ran out of the house. To my surprise, the criminal was still there, watching the fire. I hid until he left, then I followed him home. That's how I got his name and address. I have them right here for you."

"What's his name?"

"Eryk Jaworski."

"Give me his address," the policeman said.

CHAPTER FIFTY-SEVEN

Once his heart settled down to a regular rhythm, all Eryk could think about was seeing Helen. He knew she was married. Although he had very little respect for Nik, he still wouldn't dare go to her window in the middle of the night. Instead, he would wait until her husband had left for work. He longed to tell her that she would never have to feel the hands of that filthy Nazi on her body again. Eryk poured himself a glass of vodka and downed it with one swig. He wiped his mouth with the back of his hand and lay down on the sofa, too tired to undress. He planned to sleep until eight in the morning then go to Helen's house and share the good news with her. Exhaustion overtook him as his eyes fluttered shut. A smile drifted across his lips as he thought about how happy Helen would be when he told her that Rolf was dead.

CHAPTER FIFTY-EIGHT

There was a thunderous knock and Eryk was jarred awake out of a deep sleep to see the door of his apartment crashing down. Five armed Gestapo agents rushed inside with their guns pointed at Eryk.

I am a dead man.

His heart was thumping in his throat. He jumped up. Eryk was light-headed from standing up right out of a dead sleep. He moved too fast and felt as if he might faint.

How did they find me? I must have been followed but I didn't see anyone.

Eryk tried to run to the back door, but he was too late. One of the Gestapo agents pulled him back and hit him with the back of his gun, catching Eryk across the cheek and forehead. Blood gushed into his eye, blinding him on his left side. His hand went up to his face instinctively as if he might somehow protect himself from the next blow that was already being delivered. Eryk heard a crack of bone inside his head as the Nazi hit him across the nose. He was unable to breathe as a river of blood, running like the rapids, rushed down the back of his throat. Eryk began choking and coughing up blood, which spewed from his mouth onto the floor, while the remainder ran down his chin. He reached for his gun, which was on the coffee table right next to him, but his inability to catch his breath had disabled him and he could not get to it fast enough. One of the Gestapo agents grabbed it.

When he first awakened his mind had been blank. His only thoughts were of the moment, of survival. But as he spat out more of the blood and was able to fill his lungs with air, a flood of thoughts filled his mind.

What the hell is wrong with me? Why didn't I reach for my gun as soon as I woke up? I must have been really sleeping deeply. Well, there was another gun in the drawer of the desk. It was just a few feet away.

If only he could just get over to it. Eryk was still clumsy due to his injuries, but he lunged for the desk drawer and pulled it open. But before he could grab the gun, one of the agents plunged a knife into his hand. Pain shot through him. He had been too feeble to succeed at his attempt to secure the weapon. Instead, one of the Gestapo agents laughed and picked up the gun. All Eryk had left to defend himself with were his feet and his fists. Blood ran down his throat and he coughed and spit. His hand was a mass of bloody tissue and he could not make a fist, but Eryk began to fight. He hit one of the Gestapo agents with his good hand and punched another. However, these men were armed, healthy, and strong, and if they were angry when they arrived, now that Eryk was fighting back they were livid.

It was five against one, and they grabbed him and cuffed his hands with tight metal cuffs, his stabbed hand throbbing with pain. Eryk kicked as they cuffed his feet together. All five of them began beating him at once with their fists and their guns. Eryk tried to use his head to butt one of the bastards in the face but he was unsuccessful. Finally, with a bloody face, a massacred hand, a broken arm and leg, blood pouring from his broken nose and out of his mouth from a kick in the abdomen, Eryk was pushed down the stairs of his apartment building. He was thrust into the back of a black automobile. The siren blared and he was on the way to the local police station.

CHAPTER FIFTY-NINE

July 1944

They beat him again when he arrived. It was a miracle that he didn't die.

"We know you started the fire at the home of Sturmbannfurrer Boltz. We want to know who else was involved."

Eryk would not answer.

This angered the Nazis and they tortured Eryk more. But still, he would not give them any information. The Nazis were having trouble with the home army and this incident stunk of Polish resistance.

The bastard with the shiny black boots who interrogated him promised to stop torturing Eryk if he would just give them the names of the others in his group. Eryk remained silent. He would never give them anything, and most of all, they would never know about Helen and Rolf. He would make sure that none of this mess would ever put Helen in harm's way. Eryk knew he was going to die. There was no doubt in his mind that soon his life would be over. But with his last breath, he would protect Helen.

The Nazis decided to hang Eryk in the center of the city as an example to anyone who would dare to plot against them. Before they killed Eryk, they announced the hanging by putting up notices all over the city. They even offered slices of bread to those who attended the event.

Helen was on her way to the market. She had the children with her as she went from shop to shop in search of whatever food she was able to find. Lars was holding one hand, Ela the other, when Helen looked up and saw the paper announcing Eryk's hanging, posted on the side of a building. "Stop! Wait, children. I must read this before we go on," Helen said, her voice trembling.

"But, Mama, it's hot and I want to go home," Lars complained.

It was scorching hot. Helen felt a bead of sweat trickle down her back and another down her forehead. The heat made the children tired and cranky.

Ela looked up at her mother. Helen was shaken and she couldn't help but catch Ela's gaze that seemed to be saying, *Go ahead, Mama. Read the sign. We can wait a few minutes. I will watch Lars.*

Helen thought *Ela's eyes are so deep and dark. She is just a young child but she has the eyes of an old woman. How is it that she seems to understand so much more than is possible for her age?*

Ela took Lars' hand and sat down, propped against the building. Lars finally took Ela's lead and sat beside her.

Helen felt a lump in her throat as she looked at the sign. Before she began to read it fully, she glanced down to be sure that the children were all right. They were sitting quietly; Ela was showing Lars an ant hill.

"Be careful, don't touch that," Helen said.

"Yes, Mama. It's all right if we just look at it, isn't it?"

"Yes, just look."

Helen took a deep breath. She was afraid to read the notice but she knew that she must find out what it said. She began to read the poster, which said that Rolf was dead. Eryk had killed both Rolf and Rolf's wife by starting their house on fire. Then she reread the words that had sent a bolt of terror through her heart—Eryk was to be hanged on July seventeenth.

Three days from now. Oh dear God, no. Not Eryk. Not Eryk. I have to see him. I must find a way to see him.

She was having a terrible time trying to catch her breath. Helen would have liked to go home and lie down. The strength had drained out of her. But they had no food. She had to find food. So she waited in line at the store, her mind full of fear, her hands trembling. She felt chilled.

I need help. There must be someone who can help Eryk. Or at least there must be someone who can help me get to see him. Oh God, what am I going to do?

Standing on wobbly legs, waiting … waiting … she couldn't concentrate on anything. Helen was paralyzed with the thought of losing Eryk forever. When Lars ran off to play with some broken bricks, Helen left her place in line and went over to get him. But instead of picking him up and bringing him back into the line with her, she spanked his behind hard, much harder than she would ever have in a normal situation. Lars let out a scream but Helen had no patience for him right then. She couldn't bear to stand in line another minute. Even though there was no food in the house, she couldn't waste precious minutes.

Let them all starve. Right now, I don't care.

"Come on, children," Helen said. Lars was still wailing from being reprimanded. Normally, she would have comforted him, but not that day. Instead, she scolded him and pulled both children by the hand.

"Where are we going, Mama?" Ela asked.

"To the library."

"Can I take out some books?" she wondered.

"Not today."

Helen hurried the children along. Her palms were sweating. She had to find the woman, Christina, the blond with the bird on her sweater who in the past had been her contact. Perhaps that woman could help.

Few people were in the library that day. Helen walked in so quickly that she was practically dragging the children. She rushed to the front desk and looked everywhere, but the woman was nowhere to be found. Instead, a young man with a slender build and short brown hair sat at the front desk where Christina had always sat.

"May I help you?" he asked.

"I am looking for Christina," Helen answered, trying not to sound hysterical. "Is she here today?"

"I don't know anyone by that name," the young man said, his eyes blank, revealing nothing.

"But she used to work here. She is a blonde with black-rimmed glasses."

"I don't know her, I am sorry. There is no one working here by that name." The man began to nervously shuffle papers on his desk.

"Is there someone else I can speak to?"

"No. There is no one here but me. There is no Christina working here. I have been here for years and I have never known anyone by that name," he said. Helen noticed that his hands were shaking slightly.

"But I am sure …"

"No, you are mistaken. I am sorry." The young man shook his head. Then he got up and began putting books about the glory of Germany into piles. The Reich had restricted so many books that it was no wonder the library was almost empty.

"Good afternoon," the librarian said and walked away.

Helen had no choice but to leave.

What am I going to do now?

She opened the door and led the children outside. The sun weighed heavily on her shoulders like the hot hand of the devil. Holding tight to both children, she began to walk. Lars had stopped crying but both he and Ela were overheated, their faces were beet red. Helen knew that soon they would complain about being hungry.

I have no choice. I must get back in that food line. But what am I going to do? How can I get to Eryk? Is there anything I can do to help him? I must do something.

Exhausted, terrified, and overheated, Helen began to make her way back towards the general store. A pounding headache had begun behind her eyes.

"Mama, I'm thirsty," Ela said.

"I'm sorry. I don't have any water."

"I'm thirsty, too. And I'm hungry," Lars said.

Helen felt like she might break down at any moment. "That's why we have to get back in line and buy our food. Then we can go home and I'll give you both food and water."

"Why did we go to the library?" Lars asked.

"Because I needed to speak to a friend."

"But why?" Lars asked again.

"Because. Stop asking questions," Helen snapped. She saw Lars and Ela look at each other and she felt bad for them. They were just children.

Helen was so worn-out and frazzled that she allowed the children to play in a pile of rubble while she stood in the long line. They were only a few feet away from her and if she hadn't been so distracted by her circumstances, she would never have allowed them to play in such a dangerous place.

What am I ever going to do without you, my love? Eryk, you can't die. You must not die …"

Then something clicked in her mind and she thought, *Artur! He may be able to help. I don't know for sure, but maybe he can. It doesn't matter to me anymore if Nik finds out. I will do anything to help Eryk. I'll ask Artur if there is anything he can do. If he can't save Eryk maybe he can arrange for me to see him. Artur will be shocked. After all, Nik and Artur are best friends. But I must do it.*

I see no other way.

I'll try to tell Artur that Eryk and I work together in the resistance and that is why I must see him. I don't know if he will believe me since Nik told Artur that he and I were not going to work in the resistance. Of course, Artur would think that Nik was in control of me and he'd have all kinds of questions. It doesn't matter; I don't even care what happens between Nik and I. I must find a way to get to Eryk.

CHAPTER SIXTY

Helen dropped the children off with her neighbor and went to the factory where Artur worked with Nik. She waited until the workers came out of the building at the end of the day. At the end of the street, Artur went left and Nik went right and that was where she stopped Artur.

"Artur."

"Helen. What are you doing here? Nik is on his way home. I just left him."

"I know. It's you I want to speak with."

"Me?"

"Yes. I am looking for someone whom you might know. He's been arrested. I think perhaps you can help me see him. His name is Eryk Jaworski." Helen felt the sweat on her face.

"Eryk Jaworski? You want to see Eryk Jaworski? How do you know him?"

"I work with him, Artur. I've been doing work for the resistance."

"Jesus, Helen. Does Nik know?"

"He doesn't. He would never approve."

"We shouldn't talk in the street. Come to my apartment," Artur said.

Helen followed Artur. Neither of them spoke until they arrived at Artur's flat and were securely inside with the door locked.

Marci was standing in the living room. She and Helen had been friends for years.

Again, Helen explained that she had been working for the underground. She told them that she worked directly with Eryk and that she knew he was being held in prison and soon would be hanged.

"I must see him," Helen said.

"You never told us that you were working for the resistance," Marci said.

"I know. I couldn't because of Nik."

"There is nothing you or anyone else can do for Eryk anymore," Nik said. "The Nazis have him. They plan to use him to make a statement to the Polish. He is to be an example of what happens when the Poles fight against their oppressors. It's very sad. I feel bad for him. He was a nice fellow …"

"No one is going to try to rescue him?" Helen said, her voice cracking as she spoke. But she knew the answer before she voiced the question. Tears threatened to fall from her eyes. She hoped she was wrong.

Artur shook his head. "We can't try to save him. It would put too many people at risk. Eryk knew the danger. He knew what would happen if he were to be caught. Just as you must know the danger? You do realize?"

She nodded. "But can I somehow speak to him? Isn't there something you can do to help me, please?" She felt panic rising in her stomach.

"I'm sorry Helen …"

CHAPTER SIXTY-ONE

The next day when Nik came home from work, he looked haggard. His brow was lined and his eyes were glossed over with pain.

"Artur told me. How could you do it? How could you work for the resistance when I told you that I didn't want you to do it?"

"I'm sorry."

"I knew you were up to something. Oh God, Helen, you've put our family in jeopardy again. Again!"

"I know. I am sorry."

"You keep saying you're sorry. But if the Nazis catch you, sorry isn't going to be enough. We will all be killed. Why don't you realize this, Helen? Do you ever use that little brain of yours?"

"If we don't fight against them Nik, then who will?" she snapped at him, crossing her arms over her chest.

"I was afraid you had taken a lover. I was afraid that was why you were always gone and so distracted," he said, almost in a whisper.

"But you never asked me. You never said anything. Did you even care, Nik?"

"Of course I care. I care more than I can ever tell you. I was afraid to ask. Afraid you might say yes. You might tell me that there was someone else. Then you might ask for a divorce. And I don't want to lose you. I love you, Helen."

"Oh, Nik. You say you love me. I am not sure I believe you. If you really loved me and you thought I had a lover, you should have fought for me. You should have fought for us."

"I couldn't. I have nothing to give you. I can't even protect you. I don't even earn a decent living."

"So you thought I had another man and all you did was just look the other way? Ignore it? Ignore me?"

"Yes. I know it was a weak man's way out, but I hoped and prayed that by some miracle you would just come back to me on your own. I didn't want to risk losing you. I kept my mouth shut when you came to bed smelling like men's cologne."

"To me, it felt like you didn't care …"

"You are so wrong. I do care. I care too much. Artur mentioned a man … a freedom fighter."

"Yes, there is a man," Helen said, putting her hands over her face. "Oh Nik, so where does this leave us?"

"I don't know. Helen, I still want you …"

He looked pathetic and small.

"There is so much more to all of this than you know."

"Do you love him, this freedom fighter?"

"Yes."

Several seconds passed in silence. "Are you going to leave me?" Nik asked in a small voice.

"Not if you don't want a divorce. But there is still something I have to do before this is all over."

"You are involved in the resistance. I am afraid for you."

"I can't help it. I am sorry. I will leave or give you a divorce, if that is what you want. But I must finish what I started."

"Do you plan to keep seeing this man?"

"No. Not after this week is over. He is to be executed. I must see him one more time."

"My God, Helen. You are going to see him at the execution? Are you crazy?"

"Nik, it is not going to do you any good to keep questioning me. I am going to see him. That is all there is to it."

"I hope that you are not arrested when you are there."

"If I am, then so be it."

"What about the children? What about me?"

"I can't say anything except that I am sorry. But no matter what the cost, I will be there for him. When it's all over, if you still want me, we can try to make what's left of our marriage work. I don't know that there is very much to build on. But I will try if it's what you want."

Nik looked down at his shoes. At first he didn't speak. He just kept nodding his head. Then in a small voice he said. "Yes, it's what I want, Helen."

CHAPTER SIXTY-TWO

Helen's heart ached but she knew that she would have to be at the hanging for Eryk's sake. Although she knew she would not be able to speak to him, she would use her eyes and send messages to him with her mind to let him know that her soul was linked to his and perhaps it would give him some comfort. Even though it would be unbearable to see him suffer, Helen would stand in the front row.

Eryk must be able to see me at least this one last time. Dear God, let it give him strength to know I am here. Let him see that I am with him in his final hours. I know I have sinned; I have sinned terribly. Please God, forgive me. I am weak. I need you to carry me even though I am a sinner. My heart aches with love for him and I am so afraid of being without Eryk now that I have found him. The loss I know I will feel after his death is terrifying me. I can't help it; I am selfish, thinking of myself. But, God, please help me. I can't stop being afraid.

It was the morning that the hanging was to take place. Helen fed the children. She had not slept or eaten since she'd learned of Eryk's fate. Nik never again mentioned the fact that she was attending the execution. However, he did not go to work that morning. "I will stay with the children," he said.

She could hardly speak. It was so unlike Nik. It was so unselfish that she thought she might weep. Then she cupped his face. "Thank you."

He nodded. "Go then, if you're going."

"Yes, I should go." Helen swallowed hard. On legs that felt like rubber bands, she left her apartment and walked to the center of town. There was a large gathering of people in the square.

Why would anyone want to see the terrible thing that is about to happen? I wish I could run away and make believe forever that this is not happening and that Eryk is safe. But I cannot. I must be strong for him. I must stand here and wait to make sure he knows that I am with him in heart and soul. When he looks out into the crowd, he must see me. It is essential that he look into my eyes.

She walked to the front of the crowd. It felt as if she were the one who was going to die there that day. Helen knew for sure that at least a part of her was about to die. Her hair was askew and dark puffy circles rimmed her red eyes. But she stood in the front of the crowd of onlookers, holding her handbag in both hands, gripping it with white knuckles.

Two SS guards wearing gray uniforms brought Eryk out, and Helen felt her entire body shudder. She could no longer hear the crowd or see them. Everything but Eryk was black. It was as if the world had gone dark and he was the only flicker of light she could see. And soon, very soon, the Nazi's were going to extinguish that tiny flame.

I must not faint.

It was hard to catch her breath but then Eryk looked down and saw her and their eyes met. Helen's mouth was dry and her throat felt like sandpaper, but she managed a sad smile. Eryk smiled back. Then he winked as if to say, "Everything is fine. I am fine." She tried to hide her shock and horror at seeing how badly bruised his face was. Tears filled her eyes. She tried to hold them back for his sake.

They've tortured him.

Helen felt like her soul was breaking into a million pieces.

This poor man, my dear love Eryk. He loved me so much that he killed a man to protect me. And now they are going to use him as an example.

She stared deep into his eyes and tried to speak to him without words.

I know you can hear me. Our hearts, souls, and bodies have been one so I know you can hear me. Eryk, I love you. I never wanted to hurt you and yet my love was a curse to you. You are suffering as a result of my sins. It was me who went against

God's commandments. I committed adultery with you and, even though I wasn't willing, with Rolf. And now…."

Eryk was pushed up the stairs to the high platform. He tripped, but he climbed the stairs.

His hands were bound but one of the guards still held him tight while another put a rope around his neck. He didn't try to fight. He stood tall, looking out at the crowd with pride and defiance. Helen imagined that if they gave him a moment to speak, he would say how proud he was to be born Polish. He would have denounced the Nazis. The guard tightened the noose. Helen dropped her handbag as she felt the breath leave her body.

Dear God, I can't believe this is really happening. In a few minutes Eryk will be dead.

Helen felt as if she might faint, vomit, or scream in protest. But for Eryk's sake, she must not. He looked at her. His eyes were fixed on hers. Again he smiled. She felt a pain in her chest.

Helen thought she could hear his voice speaking to her in her mind. *I can hear you. I know you love me. And I love you. I have no regrets, Helen, none.*

Then, just one second before they kicked the step out from under him, Eryk blew Helen a last kiss. She bit her lower lip so hard that she tasted the salty taste of blood.

He didn't die immediately. It took several terrible minutes that felt like hours. Helen watched Eryk's legs tremble as he dangled in the air like a rag-doll . His eyes bulged. Then he gasped. Next Eryk gurgled and made a horrible choking sound. And then … he was silent.

For Helen, the silence was peaceful; at least he no longer suffered. However, it was also unnerving because now he was truly gone.

The crowd began to dissipate. Helen whispered under her breath, "Goodbye my love." Her whole body was unsteady, but she knew she must go, leave, walk away, even though her legs felt glued to the ground. Helen's stomach ached and she knew, even as she turned to leave, that she would never forget the way Eryk's face looked as he hung dead in the center of town.

At first, Helen felt numb inside. All she could do was try to remember to breathe. She walked slowly for several streets, holding onto the side of buildings. But then out of nowhere, great heart-wrenching sobs poured from her lips, and she covered her face with her hands as she continued to try and make her way back home.

CHAPTER SIXTY-THREE

August 1944
The Polish uprising.

Helen lost the heart to work with the Home Army. She was so tired that she could hardly pull herself out of bed in the morning. Her skin was a translucent pale ivory and most of the time she had trouble catching her breath. She thought of Eryk often. It was both her greatest joy and her deepest pain. She thought about the time they spent together and felt guilty for the sin of adultery. Still, she knew if she had the opportunity to see him for just a few minutes she would, even if it meant an eternity in hell. No matter what happened in her life from now on, she would always love him.

It was August and the summer days were long and tedious. The children made her smile, but little else did. Then she remembered that Eryk had told her that an uprising of the Polish home army was planned for the month of August. The war in the streets that had been brewing for a long time would erupt any day now. The Soviet Union, he told her, had promised to do what they could to help the Polish. Eryk had believed in the Russians and, because he did, so did she. There was to be chaos, fighting all around her. Helen was aware of all that was to take place and yet she was in such a deep depression she could not grasp the reality until it fell upon her like a bomb. When she and Eryk were together, he had made plans for her to take the children and go underground into the sewers until the fighting was over and it was safe to be outside again. But she'd been too distraught to follow his plans. She'd done nothing to prepare for what was about to happen.

The fighting began; death and destruction surrounded her. It was as if Helen were awakened from being asleep and she found herself terrified for her children. Nik still staunchly refused to take part in the uprising of the Home Army. He was firm in his belief that the Soviets would not be any better to the Poles than the Nazis had been. But when the Nazis began setting the apartment buildings in their neighborhood on fire, Nik finally agreed that they must take the children and go into hiding.

She and Nik discussed how they were going to go about escaping. They decided it was best to try to get away during the night. So after the sun went down and darkness covered the streets, Helen carried Ela and Nik carried Lars as they made their way through the fires and shootings in the city. Helen held Ela close to her chest. The little family was surrounded on every side by bullets and flames. There were Soviets, Poles without uniforms, and Nazis. The noise was deafening. The children were terrified, screaming and crying as Nik and Helen raced through the turmoil carrying them. Helen's heart was beating hard in her chest and for the first time since Eryk's death, Eryk wasn't on her mind. All she could think of was saving the children.

"Hurry, Nik. We have to get underground as fast as we can."

Helen saw Nik's head turn. He was checking in all directions before the family went down into the sewers. They must not be seen. But, fortunately, there was so much confusion everywhere that no one noticed them. The loud blasting of gunfire was earsplitting. Helen's head throbbed. As they reached the sewer they heard a thunderous blast. Somewhere very near them a glass window exploded. Lars let out a piercing scream. Fire and smoke made their eyes water and their noses run. All around them people were falling to the ground with their arms, legs, or heads blown off. Blood pooled and ran like a river in the streets. Ela tucked her head into Helen's chest.

"Is this the right one?" Nik asked Helen as he lifted the top of the manhole.

"Yes. This is the one. Be quick. There are other people down there already hiding in the sewers. It's not fair to them for us to risk their getting caught."

"I'm doing my best, Helen," he snapped.

Nik strained as he lifted the heavy cover and held it as Helen quickly took Ela down, then she reached up and Lars practically jumped into her arms. His small body was trembling. Nik followed and grunted from the weight of the cover as he reached up and closed it over them, leaving them in darkness.

The smell of human waste made Ela gag. She vomited.

"Did anyone see you?" Helen asked Nik.

"No, I don't think so," Nik said

Lars vomited too. Helen felt herself gag.

"It stinks down here," Lars said. He was out of breath from throwing up.

"Quiet," Nik said.

Then they began to wade through a river of awful waste until they found the others. For over two months, Helen, Nik, Ela, and Lars lived like rats underground, surrounded by filth until they became accustomed to it. They huddled in the disease-infested sewer while the battle raged in the streets overhead. The polish underground brought food when they were able. However, although the adults became accustomed to eating very little the children were always hungry and constantly asking for food. Still...they were alive.

In October, after a brave attempt to recapture their beloved Poland, the home army succumbed to the Nazis. The Dobinski family returned home to find that their apartment building had not burned down. It had suffered some structural damage, but it was still standing. Their flat had been looted and left a mess. What little they had of any value was gone.

CHAPTER SIXTY-FOUR

January, winter of 1945

The only thing that helped Helen assuage the guilt that constantly lingered in the back of her mind was reading the Bible. She longed for the world she remembered from her childhood, and a big part of that world and her memories had to do with her Catholic upbringing. If only she could go to confession and unburden her heavy heart. But the Nazis were determined to destroy the church. They had killed so many priests that it was far too dangerous to openly attend any kind of service; the only way to go to church was to go underground, and Helen just didn't have enough strength to do that. She felt the children were all she had left in the world and she was no longer willing to put them in danger in any way by going to church. What she'd gone through with Eryk had sobered her. Until she'd actually seen Eryk die, she had somehow believed she and her loved ones were invincible. Now she knew better. She was not as reckless as she had been in the past.

Both children needed as much of her time as she could give them. Lars had grown into a rambunctious seven-year-old while Ela, who was the same age, was far calmer and loved to help her mother cook and clean. At night, Helen secretly read the children Bible stories. Lars wasn't particularly interested. He wanted to learn to go hunting and fishing. Nik was working too many hours to take Lars on outings very often, but he tried as often as he could. On the other hand, Ela loved the stories and it gave Helen peace to read to her from the Bible.

Helen loved to reminisce. She enjoyed telling Lars and Ela stories about going to church and how much she had loved it when she was a young girl. She talked of the kindness of Jesus and told them about his birth, about Christmas Eve, and described the beauty of midnight mass. Ela seemed to be mesmerized by the very idea of all that Helen described. Lars was excited about presents on Christmas morning. It made Helen smile that he was such a typical boy. However, even as Helen told the children the stories, she also made sure to warn them to be very careful not to let anyone know that she was teaching them about Jesus or Catholicism.

"The Nazis don't approve of this. It must be our secret. You must never tell anyone that we are reading the Bible. Do you understand?" Helen asked Lars and Ela. They both nodded. "We understand," they said in unison.

At the start of that year, both Ela and Lars began their formal education as it was imposed by Poland's German conquerors. They attended a primary school called a Volksschule where they would take classes for the next four years. Helen had to walk them to different schools as they were separated by gender.

On the morning of the first day she, Ela, and Lars walked together, arriving first at Lars' school. He was eager and excited to be attending school and couldn't wait to meet and play with boys his own age. He kept talking about how he was "All grown up now." But not Ela. She hugged Helen tightly. "Mama, I don't want to go and leave you. I want to go home with you. I'm scared."

"I'm sorry, darling. You have to go to school. You'll learn to read and write and you'll meet lots of little girls your age to play with." Helen felt she might cry, too.

"But I am learning to cook and clean and sew from you. I don't need to go to school. I am happy at home ..."

"You will learn to love it here. You'll see. You must stay and I must leave. I'll be back later today to pick you up."

"Do you promise?"

"Of course I promise. I will be here at the end of your day."

Ela released her grip but tears ran down her cheeks. Helen leaned down and kissed Ela, then she walked out of the room. Strangely enough, it was easier for Helen to let go of her hold on Lars than it was to be separated from Ela. The first day of school, Helen stood outside the building where Ela was in class. She leaned against the wall and took a deep breath. Her chest hurt and she felt a terrible sense of loss. Her children were growing up. Soon they would not need her anymore.

The nightmare of what happened between Rolf and Eryk was still fresh in Helen's mind, and there was no doubt that she was changed. She wanted to repent for her sins, and she felt that if she expected God to forgive her, she must also forgive Nik for all she had blamed him for. And so, as the days passed, she made an effort to be kinder to Nik. She forgave him for his weaknesses and tried to be gentle and understanding towards him. Often, she found herself looking at him and thinking that in many ways she pitied him. Then, as the months passed, Helen and Nik became more like old friends than lovers. Eryk's death and her still heart-wrenching love for him had poisoned Helen's desire for intimacy with anyone else ever again. If it had been possible for her, she would have liked to become a nun. But of course, considering her circumstances, that wasn't an option. Nik made no demands on her for physical intimacy. It seemed to Helen that he too had lost all the feelings of passion they'd once shared. Sometimes, Nik stayed out late, well into the night, leaving Helen thinking he'd probably taken a lover. It was strange to feel the way she did, but she hoped he had someone who cared for him as a lover. She knew that she could never feel that way towards him again. It was sad, in many ways, but it was a fact. Helen knew that what she and Nik had shared on the day they married was gone forever.

However, as Lars grew older, his bond with his father deepened. They did not go hunting. Nik didn't have the heart for it. But they went fishing and sledding together. Helen felt bad that Nik never thought to invite Ela, but Ela seemed content to stay at home with her mother. And Helen was glad that Lars and his father shared things. When Nik gave

Lars a knife so that he could teach his son to whittle, Helen protested, saying Lars was too young to own a knife. But Nik insisted and they spent hours together with Lars learning his father's hobby of making small wooden boats or animals. Nik taught Lars to paint, marveling at the imaginary talent he saw in his son. Helen never wondered if Ela felt left out because she and Ela had so much fun together. Helen taught Ela to bake, to sew, to love Jesus, and do good deeds whenever possible. To impress her mother, Ela learned all of the Bible stories that Helen told her and she was able to recite them by heart.

Then on a miserable, snowy January evening, Nik did not return from work. He was off work the following day and Helen thought he might be with a lady friend. But when he still had not returned by late afternoon the next day, Helen began to worry. In all the years of their marriage, he had never been gone that long without telling her in advance. Another day passed and Nik still did not come home. Helen was going to go to the factory in the morning to see if Artur could give her any insight as to where Nik might be.

However, Nik arrived home that night. Helen could see by his appearance that he was obviously ill. His eyes were milky and glassed over, and his skin was hot and deep burgundy. His whole body looked as if it were bruised. He came into the house and never said a word. Instead, he ran to the bathroom where, through the door, Helen could hear him vomiting.

Perhaps he is drunk. I won't ask him any questions. He never questioned me. I owe him the same respect, she thought.

But Nik wasn't drunk. He was very sick. When he told Helen that he wasn't feeling well enough to go to work, she began to worry. In all the time that she'd known Nik, he'd never missed a day of work, except for the day of Eryk's hanging when he'd taken off to help her with the children. He'd even gone to work when he was recovering from a very bad hangover. Now he was lying in bed and he could not move or get up, not even to go to the bathroom and vomit.

"Helen … please, bring me a pot."

"A pot?" she asked, but he didn't answer. She took the soup pot off the stove and brought it to him. Her stomach lurched as he vomited into the pot. She couldn't look at the contents, but she sat down at the edge of the bed. "What's wrong?"

He shook his head. "I feel terrible."

"Your stomach?"

He nodded. "Terrible, my stomach, my head, I am freezing …" he whispered.

She touched his forehead. It was hot with fever. "I'll get a doctor."

"We can't afford to spend money on a doctor," Nik said, retching again. Helen turned away. The sound of his gurgling and hacking made her feel like she might throw up, too.

"I'll go to the doctor and see if he'll come over and see you. I'll beg him to allow us to pay him when we are able."

"Go if you'd like. I can't tell you what to do. But he probably won't come. He knows that we have no money."

"How can he know that?"

"Because men who work at jobs like mine live from day to day. There is no money left over for luxuries, like doctors."

"Nik, I can't just sit here and watch you like this. I am going to ask one of the neighbors to take the children for a half hour and then I am going to go to the doctor and beg him to take pity on us."

Nik shrugged, looking small and weak under the blanket. "Do whatever you want to," he said.

Everyone in the building was too busy tending to their own family to help Helen out by watching Lars and Ela. Nervously, she went from door to door asking if someone would keep an eye on the children even for just a half hour. But she couldn't find anyone that night. She was almost in tears as she headed back to her flat when one of the young girls who lived upstairs came out of her apartment and yelled to

Helen from the banister.

"I'll do it if you pay me with rations," the girl said.

Helen looked up. The girl offering to babysit was a child herself, who appeared to be around eleven years old.

Maybe it would be best if I bring Ela and Lars with me. But they slow me down so much and I want to get to the doctor's office as soon as possible. If I go alone, I'll be back in a half hour. With the children, it will be at least an hour before I can return. Maybe more. I don't really have the rations to spare to pay this girl to babysit. But I owe this to Nik after what I have done …

"All right. I have some bread. I'll give you a slice," Helen said.

The girl put her hands on her hips. "One for me and one for my sister."

"Very well," Helen said. "But I have to hurry. I must get to the doctor's office. Do you want me to bring the children up to your apartment?"

"No. I'll come downstairs to yours with my twin sister. My mother's boyfriend wouldn't want a couple of little children running around."

"Thank you," Helen said.

"Sure." The girl disappeared into a doorway. Then she returned with an identical twin and they both trotted down the stairs.

"Please watch them carefully. I am depending on you," Helen said to the two girls. "I am trusting you …"

"We will take good care of them," one of the twins said.

After Helen explained to Lars and Ela that she had to go out for a very short time, she left.

Her head was spinning with guilt as she ran to the doctor's office.

Is this happening to Nik as punishment for my sins?

As she arrived at the doctor's office, the sky opened up. Talons of lightning came ripping through the sky and black rain fell in sheets.

Helen took this as another sign from God that he was angry with her.

"I am sorry," the doctor said. "The office is full. I can't leave to make a house call. There is some kind of influenza that is going around."

"What can I do? Please, you must help me."

"All I can tell you is to keep him comfortable. Make sure that he drinks plenty of liquids …"

CHAPTER SIXTY-FIVE

Helen walked home in the rain. The thunder crashed like cymbals around her head. By the time she arrived at her apartment building, her hair and clothes were soaked through to her skin. Teardrops fell down her face, mingling with the rain. Even though she was sick with guilt about what she had done, she couldn't help but think of Eryk. How she missed him! How she missed his tenderness and having someone to lean on. But, as soon as she thought about how much she still loved Eryk, she would immediately be consumed with guilt. Then because of how much she blamed herself, she would see Eryk in her mind's eye as he looked the last time she saw him on the day he died. How his eyes were red and bulging, his legs twitching as the life was forced out of his body by the noose around his neck.

She wanted to scream.

God! Help me! I know I have sinned. I know I have done things that are terribly wrong. I broke your commandment and committed adultery. But I am begging you, Jesus, please have mercy on me. Please try to understand, Eryk was my only chance at happiness. I was weak and selfish. I couldn't help myself; I loved him. I still love him. Please, I am begging you, please forgive me and don't punish Nik for my sins.

When Helen arrived back at her flat, the girls she'd hired to babysit were asleep on the sofa. Ela had fallen asleep on a blanket on the floor. Where was Lars? Panic began to rise in Helen. She ran to the children's room but Lars wasn't there. As she was racing back to awaken the babysitters and ask them to help her find Lars, she quickly glanced in on Nik. And there was Lars, asleep with his head on top of his father's chest.

Oh, no. I pray that this illness that Nik has is not contagious.

Gently she lifted Lars out of Nik's arms. She held her son close to her and kissed his forehead. Then Helen said a prayer that Lars would not come down with Nik's sickness. Lars stirred awake. He looked into his mother's eyes and then fell back to sleep again. Tenderly, Helen carried Lars to his own bed. She undressed her son and put him into night clothes. He awakened again, but only for a moment and said, "Mommy?"

"Yes, my love."

"I am glad you're home."

"Yes, Lars, I am here."

"Daddy is very sick."

"I know."

"Will he be all right?"

"I hope so …"

Lars nodded. He seemed to be satisfied with Helen's answer. She tucked him into the covers.

Then she went into the living room and lifted Ela up from the floor.

"Mommy, I was worried about you," Ela said. "I was afraid you wouldn't come back."

"Of course I came back. I would never leave you."

Ela hugged Helen tightly. The child was trembling.

"Do you feel all right?" Helen asked.

"I am just scared. You were gone and the two girls who you left to look after us kept going back and forth to their apartment upstairs. Lars told me that Daddy is really sick. He said that one of the babysitters said daddy might die. I don't want him to die. But I really don't want you to ever die. Promise me you won't die."

"I am not going to die, Ela." Helen stroked Ela's hair and finally Ela released Helen from the tight hug she'd had her in. Then Helen kissed Ela and whispered, "Everything is fine. I am home now. Let me help you get ready for bed."

Ela nodded and then she hugged her mother again. Her little face was wet with tears.

After both children were tucked into their beds, Helen told the babysitters that they could go home. The girls left. Helen would have liked to reprimand the girls for not watching the children properly but she was too exhausted. Fighting was too draining and it would serve no purpose.

When the flat was quiet, Helen took a candle with her and looked in on Nik. He was asleep, so she didn't want to turn a light on. He looked peaceful, but his breathing was very shallow. She could see the blue veins through the translucent pale skin on his forehead.

"Oh, Nik," she whispered. "How did things go so wrong with us?" Gently she touched his arm, but he didn't awaken. "We had so many hopes and dreams when we were first married. Who would have ever thought we would turn out like this?" She touched his cheek. It was cold.

Helen got undressed and went to sleep on the living room sofa. She had a dream that was so crystal clear it seemed to be real. In her dream she was transported back in the time to the days when she and Zofia were designing her wedding gown. Both she and Zofia were very young then. They were laughing and making plans for Helen's wedding. Helen woke up shivering. She had been transported back.

Neither of us had any idea what the future would bring. Zofia was pregnant then. She was a single mother living with her friends Fruma and Gitel. Little did I know at the time that the day would come when the child Zofia was carrying would become my Ela. And how could either of us ever have imagined that Zofia would be locked up in a ghetto like an animal in a cage? Only God knows where Zofia is now that the ghetto has been liquidated.

The reality of all that had happened since that happy day when

Helen and Zofia were trying to decide whether to put pearls on Helen's wedding gown shook Helen to the core and she began to weep. She cried for Zofia, for Eryk, for Nik, for Ela, for herself, and for the uncertain future.

CHAPTER SIXTY-SIX

In the morning, Helen went into the bedroom to check on Nik only to find his body lifeless. Somehow, Helen had known he would be dead even before she entered the room. Even though she expected it, waves of shock still shot through her when she found his limp body. She fell to her knees.

Oh, Nik! Goodbye, my old friend.

But before she could even absorb the magnitude of Nik's death, Ela came running into the bedroom.

"Mommy, Lars is sick …"

Helen jumped up and ran to the bedroom. Her son lay on his back. His breathing was ragged and his face was as white as a powdered geisha.

"Lars, my darling little boy," Helen fell at his bedside. As she looked at Lars, she felt sure he was going to die. This was to be her most painful punishment for breaking God's commandments. "No …" Helen cried out. Her eyes were wide and she felt as if she were losing her mind.

"Mommy?" Ela said with fear in her voice. "Mommy?" Ela began to cry.

Helen picked Lars up and began to rock him in her arms. She was weeping and calling out, "God please forgive me. Take me not him. I am the one to blame for breaking your laws. Not this child. Please, not this child."

Ela backed into the corner of the room. Even though she hadn't sucked her thumb for years, she did so now. Her body was trembling.

"Is Lars dead, Mommy?" she asked in a small voice. But Helen didn't answer. It was as if Helen was in another world, another place, another time. She didn't seem to hear Ela at all. Ela began to rock back and forth, sucking hard on her thumb.

"Lars is going to die. I know it," Helen finally said as she looked over at Ela. "All I can do now is pray that God will spare you."

Ela was petrified. "Are we all going to die?"

"Come here. Come," Helen beckoned her; her voice suddenly quiet and eerily calm.

Ela walked over to her mother. Helen took the little girl into her arms. "I wish I knew where to find an underground church. It is time. I must go to confession and beg for forgiveness."

"Today, Mommy?" Ela asked. She was sweating and sucking her thumb.

Helen watched her daughter. *She is nervous. I am nervous too. But I must be strong. I couldn't bear it if she became ill, too.*

"I can't go to find a church. I can't leave Lars and the doctor isn't able to come." Helen tried to find her way back to sanity. "Maybe we can pray together and he will be all right." She was trying to comfort Ela, but it was difficult to pretend she believed that Lars would survive.

Helen tried to wake Lars but he slept too deeply. His skin was clammy and his face was flushed and hot.

Helen stayed at Lars' bedside on her knees in prayer for the entire day. Every few hours she shook him but Lars never awakened. By mid-afternoon, his face was no longer red. In fact, his skin had gone pale gray and felt cool, almost cold, to the touch. Because his breath was so shallow his chest did not move. She put her ear to his lips to see if he was breathing. Barely. By the following morning, he was dead.

That day, two bodies were removed from the Dobinski home—the bodies of Helen's husband and her son. Helen felt as if she might lose her mind with grief and guilt. Everywhere she looked she saw memories of better times. She remembered how excited she and Nik had been when Lars was born. How happy they were in those early days of their marriage before the Nazis had ruined Poland and ruined her life along with it.

Her mother had warned her about sin and angering God, and she knew that she had done bad things. Helen had sinned with her body with that vile creature, Rolf, and then she'd sinned again in her heart with Eryk, a man whom she loved more than her husband. Helen held her daughter in her arms and wept. Now Ela was all she had left in the world and she was terrified of losing her. She'd raised this precious little girl and had come to love her deeply. But she had to face facts. Ela was not really her daughter. Ela was Eidel and she belonged to another woman. The very thought sent chills up Helen's spine. She couldn't bear to lose Ela, too.

If Zofia is alive, she will return for Eidel. There is no doubt about that. She will take her child, my child. I will be forced to let Ela go with her rightful mother. The very idea is unbearable. I love Zofia. Many years ago, she was my dearest friend. And yet I am a horrible woman because, secretly, I can't help but hope that Zofia has died. Only death would keep her from her daughter. Who am I? Who have I become? How can I wish something so terrible on someone who was so dear to me? And yet, God help me, God forgive me, but … I do. I do hope she is dead.

Helen spit three times on the floor.

CHAPTER SIXTY-SEVEN

It became apparent that Germany was losing the war and the Russian army was advancing into Poland. Helen was glad to be rid of the Germans but the uncertainty of what the future would bring weighed heavily on her mind. Nik had constantly warned her that the Soviets would not be much better than the Nazis. But many of her friends were optimistic about the possibility of a communist government being a good thing for Poland. Stalin was making promises to the Polish people that the conditions in Poland would improve. Helen was trying hard to be hopeful, but she had her doubts.

CHAPTER SIXTY-EIGHT

And then in the spring of 1945 … it finally happened.

"The Nazis have surrendered!" People were running through the streets shouting, "It's over. We are free of them! The Nazis have surrendered to the Allies."

Hitler and his terrible Reich were no more, but the aftermath of what they had done had yet to be revealed to the world.

When the Russian soldiers marched through Poland they found evidence of the death and destruction that the Nazis had left behind—the piles of dead bodies, the gas chambers, the crematoriums, not to mention a raped and pillaged Poland. The poor souls still in camps, who by some miracle had survived Hitler's attempts to annihilate them, were liberated as the Russian soldiers came through. Everything might have been perfect but it wasn't because Poland was once again under the rule of another country. A communist government was established and called The Polish People's Republic. However, as many of the Polish had feared, the Soviets were not kind and benevolent rulers. On their way through the Poland countryside, they took what little was left. They stole livestock and produce. The Russian soldiers were conquerors who pillaged the land and raped the women. Helen hid in her apartment with Ela, both of them cowering in terror while mayhem filled the streets of Warsaw.

You were wrong about the Soviets, my love, my Eryk. Actually, Nik was right. They are as bad as the Nazis were. The only difference between the Nazis and the Russians is that they wear different uniforms. Will Poland ever be free? Helen wondered, as she sat on the bed with Ela in her arms. *I pray that they don't come here and find Ela and me.*

The bond between mother and child was strong. Ela became Helen's reason for living. They both loved the evenings that they spent together reading Bible stories. It was the same ritual that had begun when Ela and Lars were very young. But now, after Lar's passing, it became more important to both of them. Every night, Ela would climb into her mother's bed. The two would cuddle together as Helen told Ela a story. Ela had favorites that she would ask Helen to recite to her, even though she knew them all by heart. For Helen, sharing the stories she'd heard as a child helped her to feel closer to God and to God's forgiveness.

With no one else in the apartment, Helen and Ela became so close that Helen knew what Ela needed or wanted before she even asked. And when they were outside, Helen clung to her daughter with the fear that only a mother who had lost a child could understand. Helen was careful, so careful, always afraid that something could happen to take Ela away from her. Ela had to bundle up warmly if they left the house during the winter. Helen insisted that she eat her meals even if she wasn't hungry. Life had taught Helen to be very careful with everything she loved. It was difficult for Helen to allow Ela to go to school; she would rather have had Ela at home with her where she could be sure Ela was safe. But the government forced every child to attend school and so Ela attended. Then one day when Ela was at school, Helen decided to clean the drawers in Ela's dresser. She wanted to be sure to keep Ela's clothes clean.

The day before, when Helen was waiting in the doorway for Ela to come home from school, she'd heard one of the children who lived just down the hall coughing. At first, Helen hadn't thought anything about it but then during the night, she awakened in fear. She was suddenly very afraid that the child down the hall had an illness that was contagious.

What if that child has something life threatening? What if Ela catches it?

Helen emptied the drawers in a panic. She was going to wash everything Ela owned to make sure no germs were harboring in the clothes. As she emptied the contents of one of the drawers at the bottom she found the most unexpected thing—a pile of pictures that Ela had drawn. The pictures were of Ela and Lars together. Helen sat down on the edge of the bed and slowly looked through the drawings. Tears threatened.

I have been so selfish. I haven't even thought about how hard all of this is for Ela. She is suffering too. She has lost her brother. And just look at these pictures. I can see that she misses him deeply. I never realized it, but Ela has no friends. I have been keeping her away from other children because I am afraid she will get sick or somehow I will lose her. This must be terrible for her. I have to stop this. I have to find a way to help her have friends even though the idea is so frightening to me.

That night, after Ela fell asleep, Helen got an idea. When Nik died, he had left them very little money to live on. In order to survive but at the same time help Ela make friends where she could still keep watch over her, Helen got a job working in the office at Ela's school. There, Helen met other mothers who had children the same age, many of them widows as well. She forced herself to make friends with these women and thereby their daughters became friendly with Ela.

The other mothers took a liking to Helen. She was kind to the children and they felt they could trust her. Many asked her if their children could join her and Ela when she walked Ela to school in the morning and so Ela became very popular in her class. Every day after she and her mother returned to their apartment building, Ela would quickly do her homework, then race outside. Helen held her breath with worry when she saw Ela go outside to play but she could see that Ela enjoyed having friends. The child was happier, more carefree than she'd ever been. Unless it was raining, all of the girls in the neighborhood who were close in age were outside in the courtyard playing jump rope. They held contests to see who could jump the longest, the highest, the fastest. In the spring, summer, and early fall they made dandelion necklaces for the winners—a double strand for the winner, a single for the first runner-up.

It was a crisp fall day. Ela quickly finished her homework and was getting ready to go outside and participate in a jump rope competition.

Helen was relieved to be able to look out her window and see the children. She watched them often. If she needed Ela to come upstairs, all she had to do was open the window and call outside for her daughter. Helen took out a bowl of dough from the cabinet and then poured flour onto the clean wooden table and began kneading the gooey mixture.

"Button your coat, sweetheart," Helen said. "And don't forget to wear your scarf."

"It's not that cold, Mommy."

"It doesn't feel cold, but if that brisk air seeps in around your neck you're bound to get a sore throat."

Ela tied the wool scarf that her mother had made with yarn salvaged from several old, worn-out sweaters around her neck. Helen smiled.

"Better safe than sorry …"

"Yes, Mommy," she said. "Can I go now? Please."

Helen crouched down to Ela's height, put her hands on Ela's shoulders and looked into her daughter's eyes. "I'll call you when dinner is ready. Don't leave the courtyard. You understand? And make sure you don't talk to strangers. If anyone you don't know comes up to you and asks you to go with them, you yell for me. Then you run right home."

"Yes, Mommy. I know all of this. You have told me many times."

"I realize that you know, but I like to remind you. There are bad people out in the world. You must always be very careful. Always. And you know that I tell you this because I love you."

"Yes, Mommy, I love you, too. Please, can I go now?"

Helen nodded. Ela kissed her mother's cheek. Helen's love for the child felt as if it might overflow as she gently caressed Ela's cheek. "Today is an important day for you, am I right? You are competing in the jump rope contest, yes?" Helen winked at Ela.

"How did you know that, Mommy?"

"Because I am always listening to you. I heard you talking with the girls on the way to school this morning. You think I am not paying attention but I am always paying attention."

Ela smiled." I am excited but I'm very nervous. I've never competed before. I've always stayed in the background. I was too afraid that I would do so badly that everyone would laugh."

"I've watched you outside. You can jump rope very well."

"You think so, Mommy? This is a contest to see who can jump for the longest time. I would love to win. But, I don't know."

"If you do the very best you can then you are a winner, whether you can jump twenty or twenty-five times in a row. It doesn't really matter if someone else can jump more. Never try to compete with anyone but yourself. Do a little better today than you did yesterday. That's how you win in life."

"I love you, Mommy. Will you watch me when it's my turn? If I call your name will you look out the window?"

"Of course. I always do. And I'll be cheering for you …"

Ela gave her a wide smile as she walked out the door.

She's growing up so fast. Too fast, Helen thought as she mindlessly kneaded the dough. One of the mothers whose daughter walked to school each day with them had given Helen a few apples as a way of thanking her for watching over her daughter each day. Helen was considering making a pie with the apples and the dough.

Yes, I think I will make a pie. Ela would love that.

With a small paring knife, Helen began peeling one of the apples. A few minutes later, Helen heard Ela's voice. She looked out the window where she saw her daughter enter the circle of girls who were already practicing their rope jumping in the courtyard. Helen heard the girls counting the jumps in singsong-like voices. She turned her chair so she could watch them while she cooked. Baking was always calming for her. The steady repetitive yielding of the soft doughy mixture in her hands, along with the sound drifting up to her of the little girls counting in their sweet high voices, were almost memorizing. Helen opened the window.

The cool fall air felt good.

"Anka, it's your turn," one of the girls outside said loud enough for Helen to hear. Helen smiled. She had watched this scene enough to know that of all the girls, Anka was the best jumper. Anka took the rope and made a little curtsy. Helen saw Ela bite her nail, and she knew by Ela's facial expression that Ela was nervous. Anka began jumping and the girls began to count. The girls sang, "One for fun, two for blue, three is free, four to score."

A loud knock on the door startled her, and Helen got up quickly. Even though the war was over, loud noises still had a frightening effect on her. Her heart beat in her throat. She knew there was little to fear, yet she'd lived with terror for so long that it had become second nature to her. Still, a feeling of dread came over her as she wiped her hands on her apron. She had no idea why she felt so anxious.

The visitor is probably one of my lady friends who live in the building. It's probably Jasa again. She always needs to borrow something.

Helen shivered, she suddenly felt cold. Reaching up, she pulled her sweater down from the hook on the wall where she kept it and put it on.

Helen opened the door.

"Zofia …." she said. "My God. Is it really you?"

Of course, it was her. Older, more weather-beaten, but it was definitely Zofia. Helen was overcome with a million contrasting, confusing, and devastating emotions. She leaned against the wall trying to catch her breath.

"Helen." Zofia put her arms around her old friend.

"Come in," Helen stuttered. There was a man with Zofia. Helen didn't recognize him, but she assumed he must be Zofia's husband. "Please, both of you. Come in."

"Helen, this is Shlomie. He is a friend of mine," Zofia said.

Helen nodded. Barely able to speak, she said, "How are you Zofia?"

The day that Helen had been dreading had arrived. After today, everything would change forever. Little Ela would become Eidel again, and then she would leave Helen forever and go off with her real mother.

Zofia shrugged. "I am all right. It has been hard." She cleared her throat. "Helen … is Eidel here? Did she survive the war?"

The sound of children counting could be heard in the background. The dough lay limp on the table. Helen's hands trembled.

There was fear in Zofia's voice. At that moment, Helen realized that she could lie and tell Zofia that Eidel was dead and Zofia would never know the truth. She would leave and be gone from their lives forever.

How can I think such things? I love Ela, but I can't do this to a mother … to a friend.

"Yes. She's here. She's alive. But she has no idea of who she really is. She knows nothing of her past. She thinks I am her mother."

Zofia nodded. "I expected as much. You could never have trusted a child with such dangerous information during the Nazi occupation. One wrong word would have resulted in the death of your entire family. And I am sure she thinks your husband is her father and your son is her brother."

Helen turned away. "My husband and son are dead. They died of the fever. It is just Ela and me now."

"Ela is Eidel?"

"Yes. I had to give her a Polish name. She has never heard the name Eidel. If you call her Eidel she won't understand."

"Can I see her?" Zofia's voice sounded soft and strained.

"Come here. Look out the window," Helen said, pointing to the group of girls jumping rope. "That's her. The one with the red coat and the thick scarf."

Zofia gasped. Her hand went to her throat.

"She is so beautiful." Tears came to Zofia's eyes. "The last time I saw my child she was just a baby. Now she is a little girl with long golden curls." Helen could see that Zofia was weak and wobbly. Shlomie put his arm around Zofia to steady her.

"Would you like to sit down?" Helen asked.

Zofia did not answer. Her eyes were glued to Ela, who was jumping rope right outside the window.

"One is for fun, two is for blue ..."

All the little girls were counting as Ela jumped rope. Zofia put her fist over her lips. She looked at Helen. "She is happy? And she has friends here in this neighborhood?"

Helen nodded.

There was a long silence as once again Zofia stood gazing out the window, watching. Then in a voice barely above a whisper she asked, "Do you love her?"

"Yes, I do love her. I feel like she is my own child, my own blood," Helen said. "We became very close over the years."

The children were laughing outside. It was a musical, sweet sound.

"Can I meet her?"

Helen closed her eyes and nodded. She was sick with trepidation. Soon Ela would know the truth. Zofia was about to reveal everything and then take Ela away with her. It was as it should be and yet, for Helen, it was as if the world was coming to an end.

"Ela, come inside. There is someone I want you to meet," Helen called out the window.

"Yes, Mommy. Did you see the contest? I won, Mommy. I won!!!! I did even better than Anka. I did four more jumps than Anka!"

"Yes, sweetheart. I saw. I am very proud of you," Helen said, trying to muster a smile, but her heart was heavy. "Please, come upstairs."

"I'll be right there."

Helen had to sit down. Her world had already been turned upside down so many times and now it seemed it had stopped turning and was coming to an end. She was powerless to stop it. Helen looked into Zofia's eyes and as much as she wanted to resent Zofia, she couldn't. All she saw when she looked at Zofia was a woman who missed and loved her only child.

"Zofia," Helen said. Her voice was ragged and strained. She knew her eyes were pleading and she was about to open her mouth and beg Zofia not to take Ela away. But before she could utter a single word the door to the apartment opened and Ela ran inside.

"Did you see the whole thing, Mommy? I can't believe it! I beat Anka. I have been practicing every day for so long!" Ela's voice was light and airy with excitement.

"Yes, I saw the whole thing, sweetheart. You really did a wonderful job of winning," Helen said, but she felt the tears begin to leak from her eyes.

Ela looked at her mother. She cocked her head in confusion then Ela noticed the woman with dark curly hair standing in the middle of her living room and the strange looking man who stood next to her. The woman was gripping an old handbag in front of her with both hands. Her knuckles were white, her skin was pale, and her eyes were bloodshot. When the dark-haired woman smiled at Ela, the corners of her eyes broke into tiny lines. Something in the smile made Ela feel warm and comfortable. But in a strange way, Ela was also a little frightened although she couldn't say why.

Helen saw the bewilderment in Ela's face. She had to comfort Ela; no matter what, she had to make everything all right for her little girl. Helen forced a smile then she cleared her throat and went over to Ela. She bent down and put her arms around the child she'd sacrificed so much for.

"This is my friend Zofia. We knew each other before the war. I would like you to meet her," Helen said.

How am I going to tell her everything? Perhaps I will just let Zofia explain. Then I will be here to help Ela understand.

"Good afternoon, Ma'am," Ela said. "It's nice to meet you."

"Hello, Ela," Zofia said. Her face was strained. "You are so beautiful." Zofia walked over to Ela and touched her hair. Then Zofia's hand went to her own lips as if she wished she could kiss the child's hair.

"Thank you," Ela said, backing away a little. It was clear to Helen that Ela was a little unnerved by this stranger who seemed to be so intense. Ela's lip trembled as she tried to smile at Zofia. But even as Ela was smiling, she turned to look at Helen for validation.

"Are you a good student?" Zofia asked, her voice breaking. It sounded as if she were on the verge of weeping.

"Yes. I get good marks," Ela said, moving instinctively toward Helen.

"Those girls outside, the ones you were playing jump rope with, are your friends?"

Ela nodded.

"Are you are happy here?"

Ela titled her head to a side. It was clear to Helen that Ela Zofia's question.

"Mommy?" Ela said, leaning against Helen's leg.

"It's all right. Everything is all right," Helen said, smoothing Ela's hair. Then she turned to Zofia. "My friend Zofia has something she must tell you."

Ela curled into Helen as if she knew that whatever it was Zofia had to say was going to be something serious and maybe even scary. Helen automatically put her arms around Ela.

Zofia didn't speak for a moment. A tear slid down her cheek that she didn't bother to wipe away. Helen held her breath and braced for what she knew was about to happen. Ela curled into Helen even tighter then Zofia smiled.

"There is nothing to be afraid of, Ela. I only came here to see your mother and to meet you. Your mother had told me so much about you and about how much she loves you."

Another tear ran down Zofia's face. "That's all I have to tell you. There is nothing else. Nothing at all. But you see, I brought a little shirt I made for you. I hand-embroidered it. I made it a long time ago, but I think it is going to be too small for you now." Zofia took a tiny garment out of her purse and held it up. She let out a pained laugh. Shlomie put his arm around Zofia and squeezed her shoulder. Zofia handed the shirt to Ela who took it, but the child's eyes never left Helen's face. "Can I have a hug from you as a thank you for the shirt?" Zofia asked, her voice sounding as if she were pleading.

Ela turned to Helen. "Mommy? What should I do?" Helen could see that Ela was afraid.

Helen nodded. "It's all right sweetheart. You can go ahead and give Zofia a hug. Then you can go back outside and play with your friends."

Gingerly, Ela walked over to Zofia. Zofia scooped Ela into her arms and held her tightly. She buried her face in Ela's hair. When Ela squirmed a little, Zofia let go.

"Thank you for the shirt, Ma'am," Ela said. "I think it will fit my doll."

"Oh, that's very good," Zofia said. She was crying, tears running down her face.

"Mommy, please, can I go back outside now?" Ela looked at Helen with her eyes wide. "Please, Mommy?"

"Zofia?" Helen said. "Do you have anything else that you want to say to Ela?"

There were a few long seconds of silence. Helen's heart was beating so loud she felt that everyone in the room could hear it.

"No, there is nothing else. I would just like to say that it was wonderful to meet you, Ela." Zofia cleared her throat. Her voice was strained. "You are as lovely as your mother described." Zofia turned from Ela to meet Helen's eyes. Helen knew at that moment that Zofia had decided to sacrifice her own happiness for the happiness of her child.

Helen felt a chill pass through her. A million thoughts passed through her mind.

Oh God, thank you, thank you. I believe you have forgiven me. You have blessed me this day. You have given me the child that I have come to love with all my heart. God, please bless Zofia. She is a good woman, a good mother. If it were Lars, God rest his soul, would I have the courage to put his happiness before my own? Zofia ... Zofia ...

"Yes, it was wonderful to meet you too, Ma'am," Ela said smiling, but her lips trembled and Helen knew Ela was a little leery of Zofia. Ela turned her head back to Helen. "Mommy? Can I go now?"

Helen walked over and touched Ela's hair. She bent down and kissed her. Then she said, "Very well. You may go outside. And as always, be sure to play where I am able to see you through the window."

"Yes, Mommy. I will."

After the door closed, Zofia and Helen stood looking at each other in silence. They heard the girls outside cheering when Ela came to join them. "Here she is! It's Ela Dobinski, the winner!!!"

Zofia bit her lower lip and then looked out the window. For several minutes she stood there with Helen and Shlomie by her side. Finally, she spoke. "You love her very much. I can see that."

"Yes." Helen tried to control her shaking hands. "Very much."

"She has a whole life here. She has friends," Zofia said, more to herself than to the other people in the room. "She is no longer my Eidel. Her name is Ela. Ela Dobinski." Then Zofia looked Helen square in the eye. "You saved my daughter's life. She survived the war because of you and I am sure you made many sacrifices to protect her. However, in order for her to live, I had to lose her. She is your daughter now. I love her too much to take her away from the only mother she has ever known. I won't hurt her like that."

"Zofia," Helen said, tears of relief flooding down her face. "You are sure that you are not going to take her?"

Zofia shook her head. "I can't be that selfish. As much as I want to …"

"Zofia … how can I ever thank you? How? Ela is my life. She is my everything. I feel like I gave birth to her."

"You have already done so much for me, Helen. You put your self and your family at risk to save that little girl that we both love. Take care of her. I know that you will." Zofia reached out and hugged Helen. It was a stiff hug. Helen felt Zofia's tears brush her cheek and mingle with her own.

"Will you be back?" Helen asked.

"Never. It's best for Ela that she never sees me again. Let her be happy. That is what matters most to me. That she is happy." Zofia croaked out the word. "Goodbye, Helen. And thank you."

Zofia took Shlomie's arm and they walked out the door.

For Helen, everything seemed to be moving in slow motion, like a dream. The door creaked as Helen closed it. She could hear the footsteps on the stairs. And … finally, as she gazed through the window, she saw the backs of Shlomie and Zofia as they were walking away. She kept watching until the two figures became too small to see.

Then heart-wrenching sobs of relief came pouring from Helen's throat.

CHAPTER SIXTY-NINE

Helen forced herself to get up and wash her face with cold water in the kitchen sink. If Ela saw her crying she would want to know what was happening. And Helen did not want to explain. She had been given a gift from God that day, and she was going to give thanks and accept it without any further discussion.

Later, when Ela came upstairs, Helen had composed herself completely.

"Go and get washed up. Dinner is ready."

"What smells so good?" Ela asked.

"I baked an apple pie for us."

"I love apple pie. But it's not either of our birthdays. What are we celebrating, Mommy?"

"We are celebrating being alive and being together."

"And of course, my winning the contest," Ela said.

"Of course, my little winner," Helen said.

Ela ran into Helen's arms and hugged her. Helen felt her whole body melt. For the first time in as long as she could remember, she felt complete relief from fear.

That night, after they had both eaten and bathed, Ela climbed into bed with Helen. The window shades were open because it was a full moon and they both liked to gaze at it. Ela cuddled into her mother as the stars flickered like tiny beacons of light in the inky sky.

Helen pulled the quilt up over Ela. She hadn't really thought much about the quilt until that night. But now she remembered that Zofia had given it to her as a wedding gift. Zofia was so talented with needlework. Helen touched the perfectly embroidered initials at the bottom of the quilt … HDN … for Helen and Nik Dobinski. A sad smile came over Helen's face.

Zofia. My dear friend, Zofia. You have made the ultimate sacrifice for Ela, and I will never forget you. Never.

"What's wrong, Mommy?" Ela asked.

"Nothing, my love."

"You seem to be upset about something all of a sudden. Did I do something wrong?"

"No, no, sweetheart. You did nothing wrong. In fact, I was just thinking about how pretty this quilt is. Don't you think so?"

"It's beautiful, Mommy."

"You know there was a time when I could have traded it for food during the war. We could have used the extra. But I couldn't do it; I loved it too much."

Ela ran her small slender fingers over the fabric of the quilt. "I like it a lot. You know, Mommy, I love it when we cuddle up in bed and pull the quilt over us. The quilt smells like you."

Helen laughed. "How do I smell?"

"Like lilacs."

Helen kissed the top of Ela's hair. "Lilacs? You couldn't know this, but they were my mother's favorite flower."

"They are my favorite, too. I guess I take after my grandmother."

Helen smiled at Ela, but she felt a pang of guilt for lying to her. After all, Helen's mother was not her grandmother. But Helen quickly put the thought out of her mind. This was a happy night. She kissed Ela's hair again.

Then Ela continued, "Whenever the lilac bush on the corner is in bloom, I stop to smell the flowers on my way home from school."

"I noticed that when we were walking home together," Helen said.

"Mommy?"

"Yes, love."

"Who was that woman who came to our home today?"

Helen hesitated for a moment. She felt the breath catch in her throat. "An old friend."

"But she seemed a little bit strange. And it seemed like something happened to her and maybe she is the reason you're acting so sad."

"No. First of all, I am not sad, my love. I am very happy. And as far as the lady today, I was just very touched to see a friend whom I hadn't seen since the war began. You see, so many of my friends didn't live through the war."

"That woman today looked at me very oddly. Did you notice? I was a little scared of her but I don't know why."

"Don't be afraid of her. She was only looking at you because I had written to her and told her all about you."

"But she was staring, looking at me so deeply. Did you see it? I don't know what it all meant but I felt so strange. Her eyes were dark and she hugged me too tightly. I was really afraid of her."

"You have nothing to fear from my friend Zofia." Again, Helen tried to relax Ela but she could feel the child's angst.

"What did you tell her about me that would make her look at me that way?"

"What way? I didn't see her look at you in any strange way," Helen said, but she knew what Ela was talking about. Ela had felt the intensity from Zofia and couldn't understand it.

"She looked at me like she wanted something from me. Sort of like she wanted to hold me and never let go. Maybe I am just talking crazy. I don't know. All I know is that she scared me."

"Again, I will tell you ... don't be afraid. All I told her about you is that I love you and that you are beautiful. She was just looking at you. That's all there is to it. There was no other reason. Sometimes people who were in the war seem to be very intense."

"What does intense mean?"

"I guess it means that they look scary," Helen said.

"You wrote to her about me in letters? But did she know me when I was little?"

Helen trembled. She avoided the complete answer to the question. Instead she stammered, "Yes, I told her about you in letters … I wrote letters to her mentioning you and Lars."

"But why?"

"Because she is my old and dear friend. There is no other reason. What else would a mother have to write about? I just told her about my children. I told her about you because I love you. That's all. Stop asking questions please, I am telling you that you have nothing to fear." Helen was starting to feel on edge from all the questions. She tried to control the sound of annoyance in her voice.

"Does she have any children?"

"I don't know. She never mentioned children in her letters. Enough questions, Ela. Please, I am tired."

There was a long silence. Helen heard Ela sucking her thumb. She had stopped doing that on a regular basis, but when she was scared or confused, she reverted back to the thumb sucking.

"Please my sweet Ela, don't be scared. My friend Zofia wishes us no harm. She is a good lady. A kind lady."

Ela nodded. Again, there was a long silence. Ela cuddled closer to Helen. Helen put her arm around Ela, drawing her near.

"I guess you're too tired to tell me a story tonight, Mommy," Ela said, curling herself against Helen's body.

"No, of course not. I think that a story would be a very good idea. It would help both of us fall asleep," Helen said, running her fingers through Ela's golden curls.

"Which one tonight, Mommy? David and Goliath?"

"No, I don't think so. Not tonight, my love." Helen took a deep breath and thought for a few minutes. Then she asked, "Have I ever told you the story about the wisdom of King Solomon?"

"I don't remember you ever telling me that one."

"All right then. I will tell you that story," Helen said.

It feels appropriate tonight.

"Lay your head on my pillow and I will begin."

"Who was King Solomon?" Ela repeated.

"King Solomon," Helen said, as she looked outside at the twinkling stars. "King Solomon was the son of King David. He was known by his people as the wisest of kings. Whenever two people had an argument, they would go to see King Solomon to help them decide what the outcome of their argument should be. And the great king was always able to find a way to help them."

"No matter what they asked?"

"Oh, yes. People came to see King Solomon with very difficult questions. And often, he had unusual ways of deciding how to solve the problem." In the light of the moon, Helen could see that Ela's hair had fallen into her eyes. Gently, she smoothed Ela's hair behind her ears. "So, let us begin the story. As I said, King Solomon was the son of the powerful King David. His mother was the beautiful Bathsheba. When Solomon became king, he asked God to grant him the wisdom he would need in order to govern his people with kindness and good judgment."

"What does govern mean?"

"It means to rule."

"Like the Russians rule us?"

"Yes. Sort of, but not exactly," Helen said. "He wanted to Rule the people with kindness and intelligence. Not with fear like the way the Russians rule us."

Helen felt Ela nod her head in the darkness.

"So, back to the story," Helen said, cuddling Ela closer and inhaling the child's essence. "Whenever someone had a problem they would travel from far and wide to see King Solomon."

Helen could hear Ela sigh in the darkness.

"One day, as King Solomon was sitting in his garden, two women came to see him. They brought an infant wrapped in a blanket with them. It was a little boy. Each of the women claimed that they were the boy's real mother."

"Didn't anyone know the truth?" Ela asked. "Didn't anyone in the village know who the mother was?"

"No one knew. But the great King Solomon had a plan. He was going to do something to find out who was the real mother. He took the baby from the women and held it up high in the air. Then he requested that his sword be brought to him. The infant began to squeal in fear and the two women watched the great king, wondering what he had planned. Looking first into one woman's eyes and then the other's, the king bellowed, 'I will slice this baby into two halves and give a half to each of you. Since we cannot decide who is the real mother, that will be fair." By now, the baby was crying. One of the women readily agreed to the decision that the great King had made. She said that she thought it was fair that they each get a half of the baby."

"What does 'readily' mean?"

"It means right away."

"She wanted him to cut the baby? Wouldn't the baby die?" Ela asked.

"Yes," Helen said. "But do you want to know what happened?"

"I don't know if I want to know. I thought that King Solomon was wise. But if he was going to kill the baby…" Ela said. Her voice was shaking as she spoke. "That was a terrible thing to decide to do. What about the other woman, did she agree to it too? Did the king kill the infant? Did he cut a little boy into two halves?"

"Listen and I will tell you. King Solomon held the baby by the feet. Then he raised his sword, but before he had the chance to chop the baby into two pieces, one of the women cried out, "Stop! Please, don't hurt the child. Give him to her. Give him to the other woman. I would rather sacrifice my own happiness than ever hurt my baby."

"Was that the woman who didn't agree readily to the King's decision?"

"Yes, exactly. It was the other woman. The one who did not agree to cut the child in two."

"What did King Solomon do?"

"He gave the child to the woman who said not to cut him, because he knew then that she was the real mother. A real mother will sacrifice her own happiness for her child. She will give up everything for her child. You see Ela, King Solomon never really planned to hurt the little boy. But he knew that if he threatened to cut him in half, the real mother would say no. A real mother would rather give her child away than see him hurt. That is why he was known as the wisest king."

God bless you Zofia. God bless you for your sacrifice, Helen thought.

"Mommy?"

"Yes, my love?"

"Would you give up everything for me?"

"Yes, I would if I had to." *And I have made many sacrifices for you my sweet Ela. More than you will ever know.*

"You love me that much?"

"I love you more than you could ever know."

But there is another woman who loves you just as much as I do, my darling child. You have two real mothers. One who gave birth to you and one who raised you. Both love you very much. If I would have had to give you up, I would have sacrificed my own happiness rather than see you hurt. However, it was your other mother, Zofia, who made the ultimate sacrifice.

"It's getting late and you should get some sleep. You have to go to school in the morning," Helen said.

"I can't believe that I really won the rope jumping contest. I am still so excited."

"I know. I have always had confidence in you, my little love."

"Really, Mommy? You watched and you saw the whole thing. And you were proud of me?"

"The whole thing. And you were wonderful."

Ela moved up and kissed Helen on the cheek. Helen could feel that Ela was smiling in the darkness. "You always make me proud, my sweet little girl," Helen said. She was glad that the room was dark because her face was wet with tears.

"I love you, Mommy …"

"I love you too. Now … goodnight, Ela."

"Goodnight, Mommy."

An owl hooted in the distance. Somewhere a car horn beeped.

Within a few minutes, Ela began to breathe slowly and deeply.

She's drifted off in slumber. My precious darling child, Ela. I almost lost you today. Thank you, God. Thank you for Zofia's kindness and generosity.

Helen stayed awake long after Ela had fallen asleep. She couldn't rid her mind of thoughts of Zofia.

Poor Zofia. I know how hard this was for her. But I, too, was ready to give Ela to Zofia rather than see Ela hurt. Dear God, if King Solomon were here on earth today and he was trying to decide which of us Ela really belonged with, I believe he would have a very hard time. Although Zofia gave birth to Eidel, I raised her and I love her too. What a dilemma our case would have been for the great king. Because

Ela is special … Ela has two real mothers.

Helen turned her head to look out the window, then she turned back to see that the pinpoints of light from tiny stars were flickering over the quilt that covered her and Ela. She took a deep breath and imagined that she saw Zofia's eyes watching over them. Zofia was smiling.

Goodnight, my dear friend, wherever you are. Goodnight, Zofia. Rest well, and know that your Eidel, my Ela, will always be taken care of. And take comfort in the knowledge that we did what we did because we both love her.

MORE BOOKS BY THE AUTHOR AVAILABLE ON AMAZON

Michal's Destiny

Book one in the Michal's Destiny series

Siberia, 1919.

In a Jewish settlement a young woman is about to embark upon her destiny. Her father has arranged a marriage for her and she must comply with his wishes. She has never seen her future husband and she knows nothing about him. Michal's destiny lies in the hands of fate. On the night of her wedding she is terrified, but her mother assures her that she will be alright. Her mother explains that it is her duty to be a good wife, to give her husband children and always to obey him. However, although her mother and her mother's mother before her had lived this way, this was not to be Michal's destiny. Terrible circumstances would force Michal to leave her home and travel to the city of Berlin during the Weimar period, where she would see and experience things she could never have imagined. Having been a sheltered religious girl, she found herself lost and afraid, trying to survive in a world filled with contrasts. Weimar Berlin was a time in history when art and culture were exploding, but it was also a period of depravity and perversions. Fourteen tumultuous years passed before the tides began to turn for the young girl who had stood under the canopy and said "I do" to a perfect stranger. Michal was finally beginning to establish her life However, the year was 1933, and Michal was still living in Berlin. Little did she know that Adolf Hitler was about to be appointed Chancellor of Germany, and that would change everything forever.

A Family Shattered

Book two in the Michal's Destiny Series

Taavi Margolis is arrested on Kristallnacht when he races out of his apartment to protect his daughter's fiancée, Benny, who is being attacked and killed by a gang of Nazi thugs as they pillage and destroy the streets of a little Jewish neighborhood in Berlin. Taavi's wife, Michal and their two daughters stare in horror through the window as Benny is savagely murdered. Then, they watch helplessly as the gang turns their attention to Taavi. They beat him with clubs until he is on his knees and bleeding on the pavement. When the police arrive, instead of arresting the perpetrators, they force Taavi into the back of a black automobile and take him away. Michal, pulls her daughters close to her. No one speaks but all three of them have the same unspoken questions. Will they ever see their beloved husband and Papa again? They realize, after tonight, the Anti-Semitism that is growing like a cancer all around them can no longer be ignored. Their future is uncertain. What will become of this family, what will become of the Jews? This is the story of the struggle of one Jewish family, to survive against the unfathomable threat of the Third Reich

Watch Over My Child

Book Three in the Michal's Destiny Series

After her parents are arrested by the Nazi's, twelve-year-old Gilde Margolis is sent away from her home, her sister, and everyone she knows and loves. Alone and afraid, Gilde boards a train through the Kinder-transport bound for Britain where she will stay with strangers, in London. Over the next seven years as Gilde is coming of age, the Nazi's will grow in power and London will be thrust into a brutal war against Hitler. Severe rationing will be imposed upon the British, while air raids will instill terror, and bombs will all but destroy the city. Against all odds, and with no knowledge of what has happened to her family in Germany, Gilde will still keep a tiny flicker of hope buried deep in her heart, that someday she will be reunited with her loved ones.

Another Breath, Another Sunrise

Book Four. The Final Book in the Michal's Destiny Series

1945. The Nazi's surrendered. Hitler was dead. But, the Third Reich had already left a bloody footprint on the soul of the world.

The Margoils family and their friends Lotti and Lev Glassman were torn apart by Hitler's hatred of the Jewish people. Now that the Reich has fallen, the survivors of the Margolis and Glassman family's find themselves searching to reconnect with those they love.

Lotti Strombeck Glassman, was a German woman, living in Berlin. She had been a good friend to the Margolis family. Lotti had been married to Lev, a Jewish man, who was taken away by the Gestapo and never seen again. In 1945 the curtain came down on Hitler. Meanwhile, Stalin was pushing his army towards Germany's capital city. They were an angry mob of Russian soldiers who were on their way to punish the Aryan race. They would take out all of their hatred for the Third Reich on the terrified women left behind in Berlin.

Alina Margolis escaped to America with her lover at the beginning of the war. Although she was not in Germany, she did not have an easy life. Alina struggled to make her way in a foreign land that did not welcome Jews or Jews of German decent.

At ten years old Gilde Margolis , along with a group of other children boarded a train out of Germany. They were headed for Britain on the Kindertransport. Alone and frightened, Gilde left everyone and everything she knew behind. But she was taken in by a family in London. However, London was in the throes of war. Bombs rained down on the city. Food, clothing, even bath water was rationed. As air raid sirens blared and buildings were turned to rubble, Gilde Margolis came of age. She learned to love, to sacrifice, but most of all to survive.

This is a story of ordinary people whose lives were shattered by the terrifying ambitions of Adolf Hitler… a mad man.

All My Love, Detrick

Book One in the All My Love,
Detrick Series

Detrick, a German boy, was born with every quality that the Nazis considered superior.This would ensure his future as a leader of Adolf Hitler's coveted Aryan race. But on his seventh birthday, an unexpected event changed the course of his destiny forever. As the Nazis rose to power, Detrick was swept into a life filled with secrets, enemies, betrayals, alliances, and danger at every turn. However, in spite of the horrors and the terror surrounding him, Detrick would find a single flicker of light. He would discover the greatest gift of all, the gift of everlasting love.

You Are My Sunshine

Book two of the "All My Love, Detrick" series

Munich, Germany, 1941

A golden child is genetically engineered in the Nazi's home for the Lebensborn. She is the daughter of a pure German mother and a member of Hitler's SS elite. With those bloodlines, she is expected to become a perfect specimen of Hitler's master race. But, as Germany begins to lose the war and the Third Reich begins to crumble, the plans for the children of the Lebensborn must drastically change. Alliances will be broken. Love and trust will be destroyed in an instant, secrets will rise to the surface, and people will prove that they are not as they seem. In a time when the dark evil forces of the Third Reich hung like a black umbrella of doom over Europe, a little girl will be forced into a world spiraling out of control, a world where the very people sworn to protect her cannot be trusted.

The Promised Land:

From Nazi Germany to Israel
Book Three in the All My Love, Detrick Series

The Holocaust robbed Zofia Weiss of all she holds dear. The Secret State Police have confiscated her home, killed her friends, and imprisoned the man she loves. After searching through displaced persons camps and finding nothing, Zofia is sure that her lover is dead. With only her life, a dream, and a terrifying secret, Zofia illegally boards The Exodus, bound for Eretz Israel.

Along with a group of emaciated Jewish survivors, Zofia sets out to find the Promised Land. Despite the renewed sense of hope, Zofia lives in constant fear, since the one person who knows her dark secret is a sadistic SS officer with the power to ruin her life and the life of an innocent Lebensborn child.

When the Nuremberg trials convict the SS officer of crimes against humanity, Zofia believes she is finally safe and does her best to raise the beautiful girl entrusted to her care. As the child becomes a woman in her own right, can she find true love and belonging in a post-war society, or will the secrets of her heritage tear apart the only family she's ever known?

To Be an Israeli

Book Four in the All My Love,
Detrick Series

Elan Amsel understands what it means to be an Israeli. He's sacrificed the woman he loved, his marriage, and his life for Israel. When Israel went to war and Elan was summoned in the middle of the night, he did not hesitate to defend his country. Even though his wife had warned him that he would pay a terrible price for his decision. Elan is not a perfect man by any means. He can be cruel. He can be stubborn and self-righteous. But he is brave, and he loves more deeply than he will ever admit. This is his story.

However, it is not only his story; it is also an account of the lives of the women who loved him. Katja, the girl he cherished but could never marry, would haunt him forever. Janice, the spoiled American he wed to fill a void, would keep a secret from him that would one day shatter him. And…Nina, the beautiful Mossad agent Elan longed to protect, but knew that he could not.

To Be an Israeli spans from the beginning of the Six-Day War in 1967 through 1986 when a group of American tourists are on their way to visit their Jewish homeland.

This book is a saga of a people who to this day live under the constant threat of war and terrorism. It is the story of a nation built on the blood of her people, a people who understand that if Israel is to survive they must put Israel first. These are the Israelis.

Forever My Homeland

The Final Book in the All My Love,
Detrick Series

A group of Americans go on a tour of Israel with their synagogue. One of them has a secret.

Meanwhile, a group of radical Islamists plan to use the visitors to bend Israel's policy of never negotiating with terrorists in order to free members of their group who are being held in Israeli prisons.

However, the terrorists must contend with Elan Amsel, a Mossad agent who's devoted his life to the preservation of his beloved Israel. Elan believes that nothing can break him, that is, until the fate of two innocent girls is thrust into his hands.

Forever My Homeland is the story of a country built on blood and determination. It is the tale of a strong and courageous people who don't have the luxury of backing down. They live with the constant memory of the Shoah, and a soft voice that whispers in the desert winds... "Never Again."

THE VOYAGE:

A Historical Novel Set during the Holocaust

Inspired by true events. On May 13, 1939, five strangers boarded the MS *St. Louis*. Promised a future of safety away from Nazi Germany and Hitler's Third Reich, unbeknownst to them they were about to embark upon a voyage built on secrets, lies, and treachery. Sacrifice, love, life, and death hung in the balance as each fought against fate, but the voyage was just the beginning.

A FLICKER OF LIGHT

Hitler's Master Plan

The year is 1943...

The forests of Munich are crawling with danger under the rule of "The Third Reich," but in order to save the life of her unborn child, Petra Jorgenson must escape from the Lebensborn Institute. Alone, seven months pregnant and penniless, avoiding the watchful eyes of the armed guards in the overhead tower, she waits until the dead of night. Then Petra climbs under the flesh-shredding barbed wire surrounding the institute, and at the risk of being captured and murdered, she runs headlong into the terrifying desolate woods. Even during one of the darkest periods in the history of mankind, when horrific acts of cruelty become commonplace and Germany seems to have gone crazy following the direction of a madman, unexpected heroes come to light. And although there are those who would try to destroy it, true love will prevail. Here, in this lost land ruled by human monsters, Petra will learn that even when one faces what appears to be the end of the world, if one looks hard enough one will find that there is always *A Flicker of Light*.

THE HEART OF A GYPSY

If you liked *Inglourious Basterds*, *Pulp Fiction*, and *Django Unchained*, you'll love *The Heart of a Gypsy*!

During the Nazi occupation, bands of freedom fighters roamed the forests of Eastern Europe. They hid, while waging their own private war against Hitler's tyrannical and murderous reign. Among these Resistance Fighters were several groups of Romany people (gypsies).

The Heart of a Gypsy is a spellbinding love story. It is a tale of a man with remarkable courage and the woman who loved him more than life itself. This historical novel is filled with romance and spiced with the beauty of the Gypsy culture.

Within these pages lies a tale of a people who would rather die than surrender their freedom. Come, enter into a little-known world, where only a few have traveled before… The world of the Romany.

If you enjoy romance, secret magical traditions, and riveting action … you will love *The Heart of a Gypsy.*

Please be forewarned that this book contains explicit scenes of a sexual nature.

A NAZI ON TRIAL IN GOD'S COURT

This is a very short story. It is 1,235 words long. Himmler, Hitler's right-hand man, has committed suicide to escape persecution after the fall of the Third Reich. What he doesn't realize is that he must now face a higher court. God's court. In this story he will meet Jesus and be tried in heaven for crimes against humanity, and the final judgment may surprise you.

Made in the USA
Middletown, DE
25 May 2018